FOR ALL INTENTS

AND PURPOSES

SHERRYL D. HANCOCK

Published by Vulpine Press in the United Kingdom in 2018

ISBN 978-1-83919-267-8

Cover by Claire Wood

www.vulpine-press.com

Also in the *MidKnight Blue* series:

PROLOGUE

Captain Midnight Chevalier put down her office phone, looking rather pale. She rose unsteadily to her feet and walked out of her office and down the hall to FORS headquarters. She headed straight for her husband's office, formerly her own. Rick wasn't there, and she turned, looking for the secretary. Breann Lacey sat at her desk typing a memo, but looked up immediately when she saw the captain of vice walking over.

"Good morning, Captain. What can I do for you?" she asked, looking very proper. Midnight grinned, thinking the woman didn't really fit in around this office, but Rick and Joe relied heavily on her.

"Good morning, Breann. Where's my husband—err, Sergeant Debenshire?" Midnight knew it only flustered Breann more if she referred to Rick as her husband rather than by his title.

"The sergeant is down at the BNE office, meeting with SAC Griffin."

"I see," Midnight said, nodding. "Do me a favor, please—call Phil Griffin's office and tell them to tell Rick to come see me as soon as possible. It's very important."

"Yes, ma'am," Breann said, efficient as ever.

Midnight left the FORS offices still in a bit of a daze and walked

1

back to her own. It was still very strange to her that she could go into FORS on a daily basis and not recognize everyone. There were many new members, and a lot of the older ones had gone on to detective spots or were just out in the field more often.

Midnight waited in her office for Rick, feeling a sense of unrealism. He poked his head in her door a half hour after Midnight had spoken to Breann. "What's up?" he asked, his boyish grin ever present.

Midnight motioned for him to come in and close the door. Rick did as she wished and sat down in front of her desk.

An hour later, Lieutenant Joseph Sinclair, Detective Spider Nguyen, Sergeant Tiny Ako, Officer Jessica Ako, Sergeant Kana Sorbinno, and Officer Randy Sinclair were called to Midnight's office. They straggled in, each noting the somber look on Rick's and Midnight's faces; neither was talking. Randy was the last in, having been called from patrol. She closed the door and took a seat in front of Joe, who was sitting on the credenza to the left of Midnight's desk. Randy reached up, taking Joe's hand. Any other time she wouldn't have done so, but she could tell Joe was nervous about what was going on, and she was too. The fact that Midnight and Rick's closest friends were in the room at this moment made everything seem more serious.

"What's goin' on, Night?" Joe asked, his tone belying his anxiety.

Midnight looked over at him, and then at Randy. She looked to each member of what she considered her extended family. Her gold-green eyes were very serious. "I wanted to talk to all of you, as my friends and as officers," she began, her tone all captain. She looked at Rick then, and he nodded to her, his expression still very serious. "It looks as though I may need to take a leave of absence here in the coming months…" She trailed off as she saw the sharp look Joe shot in her and Rick's direction. She held up a hand, looking at her former partner and best friend. "No, Joe, it's not what you're thinking," she said, almost grinning at him. She knew he had thought she was pregnant, and after all they'd all been through the last time she'd been pregnant, it would not be a happy announcement. Part of Midnight still wished she could make that kind of announcement again, but this wasn't the time to think about that.

"Anyway," she said, continuing with a smile at everyone else as it dawned on them what Joe had been thinking. "It seems that I might have to take a leave of absence as captain of vice, because…" She paused, taking a deep breath. "The city council wants to appoint me to chief."

Her words fell in the room, and for a full minute there was total silence as each person digested what she had just said.

"The Chief of Police?" Tiny said, looking rather dumbfounded.

"Duh!" Spider said, breaking into a grin. And everyone started talking and laughing at once.

Midnight glanced over at Joe, who was staring at her with his mouth hanging open. Then he started to smile. He walked over to her, and Midnight stood to meet him, looking up at him with a grin.

"I don't believe it," he said, smiling almost like a proud parent.

"Believe it. They just told me an hour and a half ago. And they have the full backing of the Attorney General and governor. Go figure, huh?"

Joe grabbed her up in a fierce hug, and Midnight laughed. Rick looked on, grinning at the two of them, as did Randy. When Joe released her, everyone else moved in to hug her and congratulate her. It was incredible news. Midnight Chevalier-Debenshire, at the age of thirty-four, would be the youngest Chief of Police of a major city in the country.

Later, after everyone else had gone back to work, Rick sat in Midnight's office.

"So…" she said softly, looking over at him. "I really need to know how you feel about all of this. I know how Sergeant Debenshire feels, but I need to know how my husband feels. Nothing is set in stone yet."

Rick looked at his wife of almost seven years, still amazed sometimes by the woman that she was. Midnight was both soft and sweet, and fiery as hell. She could still drive him absolutely crazy with her headstrong ways, but then she could drive him crazy in other ways too. At thirty-four she still looked as incredible as she had when he'd met her. Their torrid marriage had always been just as exciting and unpredictable as ever. Joe said they had a love/hate relationship, and sometimes it was hard to tell which side was winning.

On the professional side, Rick couldn't help but respect Midnight for her work and determination. As the leader of FORS she had built a unit that had won national acclaim. As the captain of vice she had alleviated a great deal of paperwork for the units, bolstered morale one hundred and fifty percent, and strong-armed the city for better equipment and more training for the officers. She had done a lot in the time that she'd been with the department, and Rick felt that not only did she deserve the chief's job, but it seemed like her right to have it.

"I think," he said finally, "that you damn well better take it."

"Yeah?" She sounded a little unsure of herself, which was a rarity.

"Midnight!" Rick exclaimed, trying to get through to her. "This is it—this is the big time for you. It's what you deserve for all you've done."

"Yeah, but will I be effective in the ivory tower?" she asked, her true concern coming out.

"If I know you, you'll have them move the chief's office to the basement, just so you can feel like one of the guys," Rick chided, knowing there was more than a little truth to his statement. "If you're the chief, love, they have to do what you say, right?"

"Oh sure, it's always that easy," Midnight said caustically.

"You can make the job what you want, just like you did this one. Remember how you hated the idea of leaving FORS?" Midnight nodded. "Okay then, look at all you've done in vice. Now you'll have a chance to do it for the whole department." He shrugged, grinning. "And now maybe half the force won't be knocking down the door with transfer requests for vice."

That part was true enough. In the four years Midnight had been in charge, requests to transfer to the division had tripled. Midnight was a great leader, but she was also a great cop, and that made all the difference.

Midnight looked at Rick again, her smile slow in coming, but eventually she nodded. Rick hugged her to him, not caring if the whole damned department saw them. Right now, she wasn't just his captain, or his soon-to-be chief. She was his wife, and he was very proud of her.

Later that night, Randy and Joe lay in bed.

"You thought she was pregnant, didn't you?" Randy asked, her head resting against the hollow of his shoulder. She felt him nod. "She'd be crazy to get pregnant again." Randy remembered the horrible time when Midnight had lost the last baby she'd been pregnant with, and she subsequently felt that old stab of guilt for her part in the miscarriage. She felt Joe's hand squeeze her shoulder.

"Don't start that," he said, knowing what she was thinking about. "It's the past, it's over, Midnight's forgiven you. Everyone has except you." His English accent was thicker than normal because he was tired.

"I know," Randy said solemnly.

"Randy, Midnight shouldn't have even been pregnant then. Having that baby may well have killed her in the end anyway. Things happen the way they do. You have to admit, seeing Dickerson do what he did to her made you realize what a monster he was..." Joe trailed off, and Randy knew he was reliving some of that awful time too.

"Don't start that," she said, echoing his words, as she reached up to kiss him on the lips. "Besides, I want to talk to you about something important."

He grinned down at her. "And what would that be?"

"Well, I think I want to try something..." She laughed at the look on Joe's face. "Don't get nervous, Sinclair. I meant, I think I want

6

to go back to school."

"Why?" he asked, surprised.

"I think I want to study psychology. Maybe even get a degree…"

Joe looked down at her, turning on his side so he could see her face better. "How're you gonna use that as a cop?"

"Midnight has a degree in psychology," she reminded him. "But I was actually thinking more along the lines of social work. You know, working with abused kids and stuff."

Joe looked at her for a long time, and Randy could almost read his thoughts. After everything she had put them all through, wanting to become a police officer, and now she was changing her mind. But she wasn't really. She enjoyed being a police officer, but what she enjoyed the most was the social aspects of the job. Working with the kids and the abused women, trying to help them, made her feel like she was actually making a difference. And now she had another reason to want the world to be a better place.

"Oh yeah," she said offhandedly. "There is one other thing."

"What would that other thing be?" Joe said with a grin, ever surprised by her.

"I'm pregnant," she said, so matter-of-factly that Joe just stared at her, not sure he had heard her correctly.

"Excuse me," he said, sounding very English. "But did you say 'pregnant'?"

Randy held her lower lip between her teeth and nodded. She was rewarded with the most brilliant smile she'd ever seen.

Joe hugged her so tight she could barely breathe, but she didn't care. She'd known he'd be happy about it, but he was ecstatic. He looked down at her again, as if he were searching for some sort of clue to prove that she was telling the truth, but the smile remained on his face. He shook his head, as if he just couldn't believe his good fortune.

"I love you, you know that?" he said, his voice colored with emotion. And Randy couldn't stop the tears that sprang to her eyes as she nodded. Joe hugged her again, holding her and stroking her hair. He pulled back after a few minutes, looking down at her. "Did you tell anyone else?"

Randy gave him a look that told him he was being stupid. "Of course not."

Joe was grinning widely.

Randy sighed dramatically. "Go ahead, call her."

Joe reached for the phone but stopped mid-dial, his expression unsure. Then he looked down at Randy. "Maybe I shouldn't... I mean, she's still pretty tense about the no more kids thing."

Randy was once again surprised at his sensitivity, but she shook her head. "She'll be happy for you, Joe."

"For us, Randy."

"That's what I meant," she retorted, smiling at him.

Again Joe started to dial Midnight's number. She answered on the third ring.

"'Lo," she said.

"Night, it's me."

Midnight looked at her watch; it was 10:00 p.m. "Who else would it be at this hour?" she said, glancing at Rick as he came down the hall toward her. He stopped just beside her, sliding his hands up her arms to her shoulders, his lips touching her temple softly. Midnight moved to stand in front of him, and his arms encircled her waist as he pulled her back against him. "So what's goin' on, Sinclair?"

"Well, that was a nice little bombshell you dropped today," Joe said chidingly.

Midnight grinned. "Gotta keep you on your toes."

"I guess so. Well, I have some news too."

"Don't tell me," Midnight said, laughing. "You're quitting?"

"Nope."

"You want a raise?"

"Nope."

"You've thrown your wife over and you want me back?"

She laughed as Rick squeezed her tight and said, "He'd have to come through me first."

"Well, what is it, Sinclair?" Midnight asked.

"Well, it looks as though I'm going to be needing a leave of absence here in a few months…" Joe said, echoing her words from earlier that day. "And it is exactly what you're thinking, Debenshire."

It took Midnight a few seconds to catch up, but within moments she was saying, "Oh my God, are you serious?"

"Oh yeah," Joe said, sounding incredibly happy.

Midnight glanced up at Rick. "Randy's pregnant."

"About fucking time!" Rick said, grinning.

"Tell him to shut the hell up," Joe retorted good-naturedly.

"I'll do that," Midnight said very diplomatically. "Well, congratulations, Dad," she said with a wide smile and tears in her eyes.

"Thanks." Joe sounded a little more sober. "Night…" he said, his tone softer now. "You okay?"

Midnight nodded, not thinking about the fact that Joe couldn't see her. Rick hugged her tighter, his lips pressed against her head. "I'm fine, Joe," she said, making her voice sound normal. "And I'm really happy for you two. What's Randy going to do about patrol?" she asked, wanting to move the conversation forward.

"Well, she's talking about going to school. She'll probably take a leave of absence from the department. I figure that shouldn't be a problem, considering her connections and all…"

Midnight laughed. "Knew that chief's job would come in handy somehow."

"Yeah," Joe said, his smile back.

"Well, you better go," Midnight said chidingly. "Randy needs to get her sleep, and I know you. She's lying right there, and you're on the damn phone keeping her awake."

"You caught me," Joe said, sounding guilty.

"Of course I did."

"Goodnight, Chief."

"Goodnight, Lieutenant. Or maybe Captain… Hmmm."

Joe laughed. "Don't even think about it, Night. I'm having a kid—I don't need more work, I need less."

"Yeah, yeah," Midnight said, grinning all the while.

They hung up, and Midnight turned to her husband and buried

her face in his chest. Rick held her for a long time, knowing the torment she was going through. His eyes were narrowed as he cursed the fates that had caused her anguish. He just hoped that seeing Randy have a baby wouldn't cause her too much pain, but he had a feeling it was going to be rough. The next few months were bound to be interesting...

CHAPTER 1

San Diego, California, 1999

Two years later Joe and Randy not only had one child, a year-and-a-half-old girl named Katherine Renee, but they had a nine-month-old son as well. His name had been a matter of argument for a couple of days after his birth, but Randy had been adamant and had called him Joseph, much to Joe's chagrin. His middle name, however, did please Joe. It was Thomas, in respect for Midnight's brother, who had died so many years before. It was, in Randy's way of thinking, because Thomas had died so tragically that Midnight had ended up starting FORS, and that had subsequently brought her and Joe together. Joe didn't like the idea of making his son carry on the Sinclair tradition of being stuck with his name, but Randy reasoned that he would have done that unquestioningly if his parents had been alive. Joe had given in then, knowing that Randy was right. However, he did persist on calling their son JT; it drove Randy crazy for a while, but eventually she caught herself doing the same thing.

It became evident after their second child in two years that they needed assistance with them. Randy was attempting to go to college to obtain her degree in psychology, and Joe was now a captain with all the responsibilities the job entailed. They spent every extra minute with the children and ended up on opposite shifts from each other to keep from putting the kids in day care, which Joe didn't like the idea of. "I like to know who's taking care of my kids," he told Randy when she said they had to look into it. Working opposite shifts had been taking its toll on their marriage, and neither of them liked that in the least. Before long they were fighting a lot, and many nights Joe ended up on the couch in his office because he couldn't face going home to one more night of fighting or silence.

Finally, one night when Randy was off from school, she arranged for Midnight to take care of the kids for the evening. Mikeyla, who was now eight and absolutely adored Kat and JT, was happy to tell Randy that she would take care of the kids; Mom would just help out. Midnight had grinned at Mikeyla's enthusiasm, wishing once again that she could have another child. She and Mikeyla had long since had the discussion about why there would never be a baby brother or sister for her to take care of.

After dropping the kids off at Midnight and Rick's, Randy went back home and finished cooking dinner. When Joe arrived she was sitting on their couch, drinking a glass of wine. Joe was surprised. Usually when he arrived home she was chasing after one or other of the children, trying at the same time to get ready to go to school.

"No school tonight?" he asked mildly as he took off his jacket, his English accent still evident after many years in America. He looked as good as he always had to her. He was dressed especially nicely that day because he'd been meeting with some executives from other departments. He wore black slacks, a royal blue Oxford-style shirt, and black dress shoes. His dirty blond hair was still long; Randy had threatened him with dire consequences if he cut it. To her, his long hair embodied the wild side she had been attracted to from the beginning. Even at thirty-six it seemed to fit him. Randy couldn't even picture him with short hair, and didn't want to. The color of his

13

shirt set off his light blue eyes as he looked over at her.

"Nope," she replied, watching him from her place on the couch.

Joe glanced around, as if searching for the children. "No kids either?" The beginnings of a grin tugged at his lips as he walked over to the couch, looking down at her.

"Nope," she said again, standing and handing him a glass of wine.

Joe took a long, slow drink, recognizing the wine as one of his favorites. His eyes twinkled as he looked at his wife over the rim of the crystal glass. "I think I'm gonna like this," he said, setting the glass down on the coffee table and pulling Randy into his arms. "So what's this about?"

"It's about dinner," she said, her voice quiet but determined. "It's about a conversation not involving ba-bas, Barney, or Muppets. It's about you and me regaining our sanity and getting a little closer to being us again."

Joe gave her a long look, staring down into her eyes. "That bad, huh?" he said regretfully.

"Not bad." Randy shrugged. "Just not what we had before, and I want it back."

Again the grin tugged at Joe's lips. Randy had become more and more forthright over the years, and he liked it. There weren't usually any games with her, needing to ask her what was wrong and all that. If something was wrong she'd tell him. He nodded, then leaned down to kiss her softly, pulling her closer.

After a few minutes, she led him over to the dining room table. She had dinner set out within minutes and they ate in companionable silence. Afterward they moved back to the couch, where they drank wine and talked about inconsequential things. Joe sat with his back against the arm of the sofa, and Randy sat between his legs, leaning back against him.

"This is nice," Joe said, his lips close to her ear.

Randy felt a shiver run through her at the pleasure in his voice. It had been so long since they'd had time like this together. "We really haven't been trying, have we?" she said, not blaming him for the distance between them. She understood his concern for his children's well-being, and his distaste for sending them to day care. But understanding things didn't always make them easier to handle.

"No... I guess I keep thinking that when the kids are older... I don't know," Joe said, trailing off as Randy started to nod.

"I know, Joe. It's just that by the time they are we may have grown so far apart we'll never get back what we had. We almost lost it once..."

"And I swore then that it'd never happen again," Joe said, finishing her thought with irony in his voice.

"But we are, aren't we?" There was no blame in Randy's voice. Joe was silent and she turned around to look at him, seeing a look on his face. "What is it?"

Joe closed his eyes for a moment, shaking his head. "I guess it's just harder to hear that we're not right anymore than to think it." He sounded stricken, and Randy immediately felt sorry.

"Joe, I didn't mean to sound so dire." She touched his cheek, watching his eyes. "I love you, and I want to be with you for the rest of my life. I love our children, and I love you more because you made me a mother. I just want the romance and spark that we had before.

We've been neglecting our relationship, and I know it's because of our concern for the kids."

"Okay…" Joe said, waiting, knowing she was trying to get to an answer.

"I have an idea, and I want to run it by you to see what you think. I think it could be a solution for us."

"Uh-huh," Joe said cautiously. He wasn't ready to get into another argument about the kids and why he didn't want them in day care.

Randy held up her hands. "Now wait, Joe. Hear me out before you veto the idea, okay? I've been thinking about what we could do to take care of the kids and still have some time for us. Basically, we need a nanny." She saw the skeptical look in Joe's eyes immediately, but she gave him a stern look of her own, so he said nothing. "I talked to Midnight. I even tried to talk her out of Marie, but Midnight said that Mikeyla would basically disown her and Rick if they gave Marie up. Anyway, Midnight talked to Rick and Rick came up with an idea…"

"Great…" Joe muttered, looking ever pessimistic.

"Now wait," Randy said, smiling at him. "It would seem that Deborah—you remember Rick's sister?"

"Yes," he replied caustically.

"Well, it seems that her oldest daughter, Susan, has been attending one of the best nanny colleges in London for the past two years."

"That's in England, Randy. We live here," Joe said, his tone informational.

Randy poked him in the ribs. "I know that, Sinclair. Well, she's dying to come to America, and Rick already talked to Deborah, who talked to Susan, and Susan loves the idea of coming here to take care of your babies." She'd emphasized the "your" because she knew the idea of taking care of Joe's children was what appealed to Susan. She knew from Midnight that Susan had had a crush on Joe years before, and Randy suspected that some of that was still left over.

"I see. Got this all figured, do you?" Joe said, looking at her with narrowed eyes.

"Yes, I do, Joseph Michael, and don't give me any crap about it. You know it's the best possible solution. You've known Susan since she was a baby, so you have to trust her. Hell, she's almost family. Of course, there will be the issue of her crush on you, but that's minor."

Joe made a face then. "What crush? You mean what Midnight thought was a crush over six years ago? I think the child will have moved on by now, dear."

"Well, it doesn't matter anyway."

"Why's that?" Joe said, his voice softening as he saw the posses-sive look in her eyes.

"Because we know who you belong to."

"Yeah?" Joe's grin was barely contained. "Maybe you need to re-fresh my memory."

"No problem." Randy leaned in to kiss him. Joe moved his hand to the base of her neck immediately, not allowing her to make the kiss too quick. After a few moments he leaned forward, setting his wine glass on the coffee table and taking Randy's from her and doing the same, their lips never parting. He guided her hands to his chest and then wrapped his other arm around her waist, dragging her closer.

She deftly unbuttoned his shirt and slid her hands inside. Joe's hand tightened on her waist at the feel of her nails on his skin. "I think I vaguely remember this," he whispered against her lips.

Randy grinned. "Or something like it," she said, gasping as his lips trailed down her throat. He unbuttoned her blouse and slid his hands slowly from her waist to her shoulders, caressing her.

Her hands were buried in his hair, inciting him to deeper passion. After a few long minutes of making out on the couch, they made love. Lying there together afterward, they laughed like teenagers, feeling like somehow they were breaking the rules. Then Joe gave her a serious look, staring up into her eyes.

"I don't want us to ever get that far apart again," he said, his voice stern even as his eyes showed the concern in his heart. Randy looked back at him for a long moment, knowing that he was very serious and not wanting to trivialize his distress, but not sure exactly what to say. They'd both allowed the drift that had happened between them, and it had been so easy to do. His obvious concern made her realize that she had managed to convince herself that it wasn't a big deal, that it was a minor issue. She could see now that she had been wrong.

"Joe—" she began, resting her head on his chest.

"Don't, Randy," he said, cutting her off. "Don't say that it won't happen again. And don't tell me that it isn't major." His tone was sharp, but he was still caressing her back, letting her know he wasn't angry at her; he was worried. "We said we'd never be apart again after all that shit with Dickerson, and look where we've gotten to now. It scares me to see how easy it can be to lose something so important. You don't even have to be conscious of it."

"We were conscious of it, Joe, we just didn't want to see it. The kids are important to us—that overrode our concern for us," Randy said logically. She raised her head and looked at him seriously, her eyes searching his. "But never once, Joseph, did I think about leaving you. I love you more than anything. I won't ever give you up again." Joe closed his eyes, and Randy could see relief evident on his face. "Is that what you thought?" she asked. Joe didn't answer, but she could see the affirmation in his light blue eyes when he opened them again. "Jesus, Joe... Why didn't you say something? Why didn't you ask me about it?"

Joe shook his head, giving her a wry grin. "This is the first time in months I've seen you alone and awake, Randy. When was I gonna say something?"

"So you've been thinking that for that long?" Randy said, surprised.

Joe shrugged. "It's been sitting there in the back of my mind, that and a nice little knot in my stomach. I didn't think about it unless I was really tired, and that's usually when it would get to me."

"And those are the times when you curled up behind me and held me so tight I could barely move," Randy said, knowing him well enough to know how he reacted to things and remembering those nights well. Contrary to her words, she had enjoyed feeling him that close to her, even if they were both usually asleep for the most part. There had been a few occasions when he had begun to kiss her neck, caressing her skin, and they'd ended up making love, but even then things had seemed different and it had been cause for more concern, not less. But they'd never had time to discuss the change. Joe nodded, affirming her thoughts.

19

"Okay," Randy said, moving to sit up and looking down at him. "From now on, Joseph Michael Sinclair the Fourth, if you have any doubts about how much I love you, you ask me and I'll be very happy to show you."

Joe grinned, his eyes traveling suggestively down her naked body. "Why don't you show me again now, just so I know for sure," he said, his accent thick with desire.

Randy was all too happy to do just that. Later that night, once they'd made it to their bedroom, they slept as close as ever. Randy lay on her back and Joe on his side, facing her, with one arm under her neck and the other wrapped tightly around her waist, holding her close to him. During the course of the night he would wake and kiss her lightly on the temple, the forehead, or on her cheek, and then fall back asleep.

Things between them had gotten much better in that one evening. Joe spent the next month waiting impatiently for the time when Susan would arrive and Randy would go back to college during the days.

When he picked Susan up at the airport a month later, he hugged her extra tight, having come to think of her as the tool with which to fix his ailing marriage. Things had been better between him and Randy since the night they decided to bring Susan over, but they still never had real time for each other.

Joe led Susan to the black Boxster he had bought the year before, having finally given up his older Porsche for the sportier model.

"New Porsche?" Susan asked, knowing Joe wasn't given to throwing his money around.

Joe grinned. "I thought it was time for a change."

Susan looked back at him as he started the engine and drove out of the parking lot. Randy had been correct in assuming that Susan still had a crush on her husband. To Susan, Joe was the ultimate man to which she compared all other men. The young men she'd dated had paled miserably by comparison. She'd never even gone on a second date with most of them. Now, seeing Joe again, she realized he was just as handsome as she'd always remembered. She'd come to wonder over the years if she was just remembering him more fondly than she really should, but seeing him standing at the end of the gangway when she got off the plane had put the kibosh on that thought. He looked gorgeous, even in the faded jeans, black cotton shirt, and black leather FORS jacket he wore. His light blue eyes had been warm as she'd approached, and when he'd hugged her, she'd inhaled the mingling of leather and cologne that she'd always associated with him. Now, watching him as he drove, she couldn't help but be impressed by him again.

Joe glanced over at Susan and caught her watching him. He narrowed his eyes just slightly, wondering if Randy had been right, but dismissed the idea just as quickly. "I hope you don't mind, but I gotta make a quick stop back by the office. I meant to have all this stuff wrapped up before I came to pick you up, but it just didn't work out that way."

"No problem," Susan said, her accent very proper. She sounded very much like the debutantes Joe remembered in England. Susan had indeed grown into a young woman with a lot of potential, although she seemed to take pains to hide her looks. She looked a lot like her mother, Deborah, Rick's sister. She had been fortunate to get nothing in terms of her appearance from her father. She had a very

21

elegant look about her, with delicate features. She had Rick and Deborah's deep blue eyes and Deborah's beautiful golden-blond hair, which she wore pulled back in a severe-looking bun. She did, however, dress in very plain clothes. "Nanny clothes" would be Joe's way of classifying them. In a way, she reminded Joe of Randy years before, but he figured she had her reasons for making herself dowdy.

A few minutes later Joe's phone rang. He hit the hands-free, glancing over at Susan apologetically. She smiled and watched him as he answered the call, fascinated by everything he did.

"Sinclair," he said.

"Yeah, hi, Cap," a man's voice said. "I, uh, wanted to run this warrant by you before we ran with it. It's the one that got kicked back by Judge Parsons."

"That guy," Joe said with absolute distaste, his eyes narrowing.

"Yes, sir," the other man said placatingly. "Thing is, sir, I want you to check it before we forward it again."

"Well, I'm not exactly there to read it at this point, am I?" Joe snapped, his eyes flashing.

"No, sir, but I was wondering if you were coming back in…" The man trailed off, as if he was worried about Joe's reaction.

"Yeah, I'm on my way now," Joe said, sounding irritated.

"Thanks, Cap." The man sounded relieved, but cautious too. He knew Joe had been on edge for the last few months, and he didn't want to be the one to set him off; he'd heard what had happened to the last sergeant who had gotten on Joe Sinclair's bad side, and he wasn't ready to end his career that quickly.

Joe hung up, looking annoyed.

"Problems?" Susan asked meekly, never having seen Joe so angry before.

Joe looked over at her, his face still drawn and angry, then blew his breath out, shaking his head. "Just more of the usual. I'm just not in the mood for it lately."

His phone rang again, and he hit the hands-free button angrily. "What!"

There was a momentary silence, then Randy's voice came over the line. "Hello to you too," she said mildly, and even Susan could hear the smile in her voice.

Joe's expression softened immediately. "Sorry," he said, the beginnings of a smile on his face.

"Bad day?"

"Yeah… I'm headed back into the office right now—I'll try to make it home early," Joe said, his tone reflecting his regret.

"Don't worry about it. Do you want me to drive down and pick up Susan?"

"No, I won't be that long," Joe said determinedly. "She can visit with Night and Rick for a while." He glanced at Susan for confirmation. She nodded.

"So what's goin' on, anyway?" Randy asked.

"Well, it's not like I don't have enough to worry about lately with all this IA shit goin' on, but now Judge Parsons is kickin' back my warrants," Joe said, his tone taking on an edge again.

"That liberal jerk." Randy remembered what Joe had told her about the judge, who had a beef with the narcotics division of the department as of late. Judge Roger Parsons was liberal to the nth degree and felt that narcotics were something that should be legalized, hence he was more difficult when it came to search warrants for drugs.

"Yeah," Joe said, looking for all intents and purposes like a stubborn little boy. "Anyway, he's kicked one back again, and I gotta go see what I can do to resurrect it."

"Well, good luck."

"Yeah, thanks…" Joe sounded depressed.

"Hey," Randy said, her voice softer now.

"What?" Joe replied just as softly.

"I love you."

Joe's smile was private, and Susan felt like she shouldn't be hearing the conversation at that point, but she also felt a small stab of envy that he would react that way to her words.

"Thanks," he said. "I needed that right now."

"Thought so," Randy replied, her voice still serious. "I'll see you when you get home."

"You got it, love." Joe was still smiling as he hung up.

Hours later, Susan had yet another insight into Joseph Sinclair. She had just returned from visiting with Midnight and had taken up a seat in the corner of Joe's office, determined to be no trouble for him, when a man in uniform stormed in. It was very obvious that he was angry, and he directed that anger at Joe.

"I'm puttin' that sonofabitch McCauley on report, and I expect your full support," he said, glancing at Susan but dismissing her presence just as quickly.

Joe had glanced up, and the look in his eyes could have frozen the sun, but the other man didn't notice.

"Now I know you like the guy, Sinclair, but I've had it with him," the lieutenant raged. "He's insubordinate as hell, and now he wants to be transferred to vice. Well, it's not gonna happen, I'm tellin' you that right now…" The lieutenant trailed off as he realized Joe hadn't said a word. "Sinclair? Are you listening to me?" he said, making the mistake of taking a superior tone with Joe.

There had been plenty of people who didn't like the fact that Joseph Sinclair had moved up the ranks so quickly. All of those people credited that move to the fact that Midnight and he had been a thing once. Some people still thought they were, and this lieutenant was one of them. Lieutenant John Singleton had been with the department for twenty-five years and had never moved past the rank of lieutenant for one simple reason: he was a royal pain in the ass to every captain he worked for. He'd tried one too many things on Midnight when she'd been the captain of the unit, so when she was promoted to chief, his promotional opportunities ceased to exist. Singleton frequently referred to Midnight as the "broad," and Joe, in Singleton's opinion, was her lackey. For that reason he assumed he didn't need to show Joe any respect whatsoever.

Joe was silent for a full minute longer, his ice-blue eyes narrowed just slightly as he regarded the lieutenant. It was long enough to make the man start to squirm. Singleton moved to sit in the chair in front of Joe's desk, looking very uncomfortable all of a sudden. Susan watched it all in fascination.

"First of all," Joe said, his tone as icy as the look in his eyes, "I approved that transfer personally—I think he'd do well there. Secondly, I don't think you want to get into a pissing match over insubordination, Singleton, since you seem to have written the book." Joe's voice took on an edge. "And if you ever storm into my office again, telling me what I will and will not be doin', you'll find yourself on report so fast it'll make your head spin. You got that?"

Singleton was silent for a long moment, blinking back his disbelief. But then it became evident that the man had once again located his backbone as the look on his face changed to suffused anger. "Don't you presume to override my decisions about my people, Sinclair. I know you think you're hot shit because you made captain here, but everyone knows you did because you're fucking that bitch Chevalier—"

The man's next words were cut off when Joe came out of his chair and all but leapt over the desk, leaning far enough over it to snatch Singleton out of his chair. He dragged him face to face, his eyes burning with fury.

"You just made the biggest mistake of your career," Joe said, his voice deadly low. "You are so out of here that people won't remember your name tomorrow." He tightened his hold on the fistful of the man's shirt. "And on a personal note, if you ever refer to Midnight Chevalier in anything but the most respectful tone in my presence again, I will personally beat the shit out of you." His voice was all gang member now, and Singleton heard it. It made him realize he had indeed made a fatal mistake. He swallowed convulsively as he stared back at Joe. "Now," Joe said, shoving the man back and making him stumble. "Get the fuck out of my office, and do yourself a favor— leave quietly."

Singleton did just that, almost running out of the room.

Midnight was in Joe's office ten minutes later, having heard about the argument from Rick, who had been walking by at the time and had called her immediately.

"So what happened?" she asked, walking in and sitting down, her eyes on Joe, noting that he still looked furious. Her tone was purposely calm, in an attempt to influence Joe's own mood.

"He fucked up, it's that simple," Joe said, not ready to talk just yet, his adrenaline still up from the confrontation.

"Okay…" Midnight said, nodding. She was used to dealing with Joe when he was mad. "Let's try this a different way. What did he say?" Her tone held a touch of humor and her grin was knowing. She knew there were very few things that would make Joe get physical with a subordinate, and most of the time those things were related to people close to him.

"I don't want to talk about it, Night," he said, his tone forbidding. They were friends at that point, not chief and captain. It was interesting to Susan that they seemed to be able to work on both levels. She knew about Midnight and Joe's relationship from years of overhearing conversations and retellings of stories by her family. She thought it incredible that they could be so close and yet married to other people.

"Okay," Midnight said, her look changing again, as if he had just explained a lot. "So it was about me." She shook her head, rolling her eyes. "When are you going to face the fact that not everyone is going to love me? I'm a woman, I'm young for a chief, relatively speaking, and everyone still thinks I screwed my way to the top." She sighed.

27

"It's life, Joe. Get used to it."

"Bullshit," Joe said, his eyes flashing. "Why the hell can't they see everything you've done for this place? Why can't they remember how much progress has been made in the two years you've been the chief? And why the bloody hell do they still think we're sleeping together?"

"Ah," Midnight said, realizing she'd finally gotten to the root of the problem. "Now we have it. He accused you of sleeping with me, and you just about took his head off for him, didn't you?"

"He accused me of fucking 'that bitch Chevalier,' and yes, I did," Joe said, his tone matter-of-fact even as his eyes flashed at the memory of the man's words.

Midnight looked back at him for a long moment, then blew her breath out in a rush. "You can't fire him for that."

"Like hell I can't," Joe snapped, surprised.

Midnight was unaffected by his anger. She canted her head to the side, her lips pursed in a "you know better" expression.

"The sonofabitch was insubordinate to a ranking officer," Joe said, still determined.

"So write him up," Midnight replied calmly.

Joe narrowed his eyes at her, not liking what he was hearing. He measured his words for emphasis. "I don't want him here."

"Joe…" Midnight sighed. "I don't want a lot of people here, but there's nothing I can do about it without breaking a lot of labor laws. We are the law, Sinclair. That doesn't give us the right to break it."

"Damn it, Night," Joe began, but Midnight shook her head.

"Babe, if we fired everyone here that didn't like me, you and I'd be drivin' patrol again," she said caustically. "Face it, you love me, and not everyone is as smart as you are." Now her voice held humor that made Joe smile in spite of his anger.

"Fine," he said finally, his teeth clenched.

"Hey." Midnight caught his gaze. "If it makes you feel any better, it's still nice to know I have my back covered." Her voice was soft, and Susan saw them exchange a look that she knew said everything about how much they cared about each other and how much they'd been through together.

"It always will be," Joe said simply, and Midnight smiled as she stood up.

"Everything okay in here?" Rick asked from the door. His deep blue eyes watched his wife closely.

Midnight looked over at her husband and smiled. "Yeah, Sinclair's just doin' that knight in shining armor thing again."

"Good," Rick said, glancing over at his best friend. "Always in my stead." His voice held no jealousy whatsoever; they'd gotten over all that years before. Rick had come to understand that Joe and Midnight were bound together by a friendship that had been forged in stone. He knew Joe would always be there for Midnight, even against him if necessary, and in a way Rick had come to take comfort from that fact.

Dinner at the Sinclair home that evening was interesting. JT and Kat were in bed by the time the food was ready. Randy had planned it that way. Susan had spent a good two hours with the children, getting to know them. JT had taken to Susan right away, throwing his little arms around her neck when she'd sat down on the floor with them.

Joe and Randy had watched from the doorway. Susan's manner with the children was gentle and warm. She talked with Kat about her new dolly and even showed the girl how to change the baby's diaper. Kat was shy at first, but by the time it was time for her to go to bed she was asking Susan to read her a book. Randy felt a tug at her heart when her daughter looked up to the younger woman with adoring blue eyes as Susan read to her. She felt Joe's lips in her hair then as he pulled her a little closer. He had seen the look in her eyes, and knew what she was feeling.

"She'll always be your baby, Randy," he whispered next to her ear. And Randy nodded, trying to push down the sudden knot in her throat. To avoid saying anything, she turned in his arms and put her head against his shoulder. He held her tight as he nuzzled her hair, kissing the top of her head softly.

At dinner, Susan and Randy had a long conversation about the children's likes and dislikes. Joe put in his two cents every so often, but recognized that he was the third party. He watched as his wife talked about their children and felt his heart warmed. He began to think about his own parents, feeling melancholy for the first time in almost two years. He wondered what they would have said about his choice. Joe had long since accepted that he would never know if his parents would have approved of his marrying Randy, but now he wished they could be there to be grandparents to Kat and JT. Since Randy's parents were gone too, the children didn't have grandparents, although he knew Robert and Anabelle Debenshire considered his children their grandchildren, since they looked on Joe as their son.

Randy had noticed the look in Joe's eyes during dinner, and talked to him about what she was sure she'd seen as they lay in bed together that night.

"You were thinking of your parents earlier, weren't you?" she said softly, her lips touching his bare chest as she lay with her head in the hollow of his shoulder.

Joe smiled in the darkness of the room. She did know him well. "Yeah," he said quietly.

"Is it because of the kids? Are you still worried about that?"

"No." Joe kissed her forehead. "No, you were right about Susan. She's gonna be great with them. I think that was the best thing for us too—it'll take a lot of the pressure off both of us. And less stress right now can only help."

"Then why did you look sad?"

Joe took a deep breath, blowing it out slowly. "I guess I was just wishin' they could be here."

Randy glanced up at him. "They'd love the kids, Joe, you know that… but I know what you mean. It would be nice to see them with them. I wish I'd met them."

"That's kinda what I was thinking. I think they would have loved you. You would have been the daughter my mum always wanted…" He trailed off as he felt his throat tighten.

Randy heard it in his voice. Propping herself up on her elbow, she looked down at him. "This is all hard for you, isn't it?" Joe nodded, not trusting his voice at this point. "Having the kids, moving on with your life…" Randy continued as she realized for the first time that no matter how many years there were since the tragedy in her husband's life, there was always going to be an impact.

Joe didn't answer, and Randy could feel the turmoil in him.

31

"What can I do?" she asked, wanting to ease his pain but knowing there was really nothing she could do. She couldn't change the past.

Joe reached up, pulling her back down to him, bringing her face to within inches of his. "Just keep loving me like you do. It makes everything else easier to take." He kissed her, and a little while later they both forgot their worries for the time being, escaping into their lovemaking. Later that night Randy found herself watching her husband as he slept, and wondered again, as she had many times before, how she'd been lucky enough to be chosen by him.

****

As Donovan Curtis walked down the hall toward the chief's office, many women noticed him. His good looks and open, easygoing personality tended to draw women's attention wherever he went; he never seemed to notice. When he stepped inside the door to Midnight Chevalier's office, he saw a young woman sitting at the desk that had previously been empty. Her head rested on her arms. When Donovan walked in, she looked up. Donovan was taken aback by her. She was beautiful, with long dark hair, golden-brown skin, and the most beautiful dark eyes he'd ever seen.

When Jeanie Franco heard someone walk into the outer office she lifted her head to see who would be coming into the chief's office at lunchtime. Probably someone who knew that Chief Chevalier rarely, if ever, took lunch. The face she looked up into made her catch her breath. The man stood over six feet tall, and he had sandy-brown hair worn in one of the more popular styles of the time, clean-cut sides and longer on top—it looked good on him. His eyes were the most incredible color she'd ever seen, a blue-green. His jawline was strong, but his face seemed open and friendly. He was very handsome, and Jeanie found herself tongue-tied for the first time in a long time.

"What can—I mean, can I help you?" she said, smiling self-consciously.

Donovan smiled at her, nodding. "Yeah, is Midnight in?"

Jeanie looked him for a long moment. He must really know the chief if he referred to her by her first name. He didn't look old enough to be an executive; besides, he was dressed casually, not in a three-piece suit. "Do you have an appointment?"

"Donovan doesn't need an appointment," Midnight said from the doorway. "How are ya, Pony?" She walked over to Donovan and reached up to hug him.

Donovan put his arms around her and hugged her, lifting off her feet momentarily. "I'm good, and what kind of evil are you repelling now?" he asked, setting her back on her feet and stepping back to look at her.

"Oh, the usual," Midnight replied, smiling. She looked at Jeanie. "Have you two met?"

Donovan looked at Jeanie as well, and with a wide smile shook his head. "Can't say I've had the pleasure."

Midnight raised an eyebrow at Donovan's apparent interest. "I see. Well, Donovan Curtis, this is Jeanie Franco. She's going to be working with us on our little project."

Donovan nodded, looking seriously at Midnight, but found he

had a new respect for Jeanie. If she was working with them, then she must have something going on other than just her looks.

"Okay…" he said as he glanced over to Jeanie again, his eyes locking with hers.

"She's been working with Joe, so she's cleared," Midnight said, already getting the feeling that she was talking to hear herself talk.

"Great," Donovan said, finally looking back at Midnight when he noted that she had trailed off. "It's nice to meet you, Jeanie." He extended his hand to her.

Jeanie stood and took his hand. Donovan was further pleased to note that not only did she have a beautiful face, but a pretty fantastic body as well. The scenery around the office was definitely improved. Her handshake was surprisingly firm, and Donovan grinned at her as he noted it. Jeanie returned the grin, knowing what he was thinking.

"Jeanie's going through the process right now," Midnight said, which served to explain her firm handshake. She was working to become a police officer.

"That's cool," Donovan said, nodding again.

"Hey." Midnight gave Donovan a little shove. "I got a great idea."

"What's that?"

"Jeanie has just been drilling me about her psychological, which she just finished up not an hour ago, and she's basically getting on my last nerve at this point. Why don't you take her to lunch, and that way she can drive you crazy instead. Whaddya say?" She gave him a brilliant smile.

Donovan hesitated, giving Midnight a look Jeanie didn't under-stand.

"I'll tell her you'll be back," Midnight said, her tone changing just slightly. She didn't approve of the relationship she thought was going on between her secretary, Cassandra Devereaux, and Donovan.

Donovan nodded then, and looked at Jeanie. "Should we do as we're told?"

Now it was Jeanie's turn to hesitate—she didn't want to go to lunch with him if he wanted to be somewhere else. But Midnight was giving her a look that said "Do it," and Jeanie didn't know the chief well enough yet to counter her. Finally she nodded, reaching over to pick up her purse.

Donovan and Jeanie headed out to the parking lot, and Jeanie was mildly surprised when he walked over to a black 1996 Mustang. "This is yours?" she said appreciatively.

Donovan grinned. "Yeah. It's my major expense in life right now."

"It's great."

She was pleasantly surprised when he opened her door for her and closed it gently behind her. She had noticed walking up to the car that the license plate said "PONYBOY."

"So what's Pony Boy?" she asked when he got in on the driver's side.

Donovan looked surprised; he hadn't realized she'd taken note of his plate. Then he smiled almost self-consciously. "It's my nick-name. It's from the movie The Outsiders..." He trailed off as he looked over at her, his lip curling sardonically. "Are you old enough to know that movie?" He turned the key and started the engine, shift-ing the car into gear and backing out of the space.

Jeanie gave him a sideways glance. "How young do you think I am?"

"Too young," Donovan replied with a smile, and suddenly Jeanie knew he was baiting her—and she was falling for it.

"Shut up. How old can you be?" she said, looking at him as if sizing him up. "Twenty-two, twenty-three maybe…" She allowed her voice to trail off as if in distaste.

Donovan laughed. "Yeah, maybe about four or five years ago."

Jeanie laughed too. "Okay… so they call you Pony Boy because of… your last name?"

"Yeah, that and the fact that I'm a major Mustang fanatic—you know, the pony on the front."

"Ah," Jeanie said, nodding. "And you're an officer for the de-partment?"

"Actually, I made sergeant six months ago."

Jeanie could detect no ego in his tone. "That's cool. I'm just praying I passed the psych."

"Major brain drain, huh?" Donovan said, grinning.

"No, why do you ask?" Jeanie said, with a devilish grin of her own.

Donovan shrugged. "Only the real nutballs think it's easy."

"Well, count me in the nutball collection then," Jeanie said, but then laughed a moment later. "Okay, so I have very few brain cells left—I'm human."

"Don't worry about it. If you were honest, you should be okay."

"Yeah, just so long as they don't find out that I hate my mother and wish my father was a throw rug," Jeanie said sarcastically.

"You too, huh?" Donovan was smiling, but Jeanie detected the merest hint of truth to his tone. She looked over at him for a long, measured moment.

"Do I detect a little honesty there?" she asked finally, not sure where the nerve to ask the question had come from.

Donovan looked back at her, his eyes showing surprise at her intuition. And to Jeanie's surprise, he nodded slowly.

"Wow… What happened?" she asked softly.

Donovan hesitated for a moment—he hardly knew this girl—then shrugged. "They just left one day."

Jeanie looked stunned, her brown eyes widening. "Are you serious? How old were you?"

"'Bout eleven," Donovan said casually, but his eyes showed a lot more. "My brother Darrell raised me and my sister Randy the rest of the way."

"How old was your brother at the time?"

"He was eighteen, Randy was fourteen."

"That must have been really rough," Jeanie said, having been raised in an all-family environment. Her parents had been married for thirty-five years, and she was the youngest of six kids.

"It was no picnic," Donovan said. It was obvious to Jeanie that he was uncomfortable, so she changed the subject as they arrived at a local restaurant. Jeanie noted that he had obvious good taste in restaurants; the one they'd pulled up to was one of the best in town for

37

lunch.

"So what made you become a police officer?" she asked as they walked up to the front door. She was pleasantly surprised when he opened it for her.

Once inside he told the woman at the maître d's podium that it would be two for lunch. Then he turned back to Jeanie. "Probably because everyone I know seems to be a cop."

"At our department?"

"Yeah, I mean, not including Midnight, my sister's an officer, her husband's a captain, I know Midnight's husband, Rick, plus most of the original members of FORS. I'd say I was destined to be a cop."

"I guess. Who's your brother-in-law?" There weren't a large number of captains in the department.

"Joe Sinclair," Donovan said, and saw the smile on Jeanie's face. "Either you've worked for him or you're like half the women in the department and have a crush on the guy."

"It's the former. However, I can't deny that I have had my fantasies..." Jeanie replied, grinning.

"I haven't run into a woman at the office yet that hasn't," Donovan said, his tone easy. Jeanie could detect no jealousy, but there was another emotion there.

She smiled. "Is that respect I hear?"

"Respect, awe, hero worship," Donovan rattled off. "Any of those words would describe my feelings toward my brother-in-law."

Jeanie was taken aback by his honesty. Most men she knew wouldn't admit to admiring another man that easily. "Wow."

"Tell me about it," Donovan said, grinning almost self-consciously. "At least I don't bow to him anymore."

Jeanie stared back at him openmouthed for a full minute before Donovan started to laugh.

"It was a joke," he said, with a wide grin on his face.

Lunch proceeded comfortably. Jeanie told him about her family; he was surprised to find out that she had four older brothers.

"Rough gig," Donovan said, shaking his head. "Bet you don't date much."

Jeanie grinned. "Why do you say that? Just because my brothers are all over six foot tall and carry guns or bats on a constant basis…"

Donovan laughed, nodding. "That might have something to do with it. Seriously, though, I'll bet they're real protective of you."

"They are."

"Yeah, Darrell hated Joe's guts the minute he laid eyes on him the first time. He was majorly protective of Randy."

"He didn't like Joe?" Jeanie was surprised; she couldn't imagine anyone not liking Joseph Sinclair. She'd worked for him for over two years now, and she thought he was the greatest.

"Nope, hated him with a passion. He figured Joe for a cop on the make, and Randy was so shy in those days, Darrell thought Joe saw her as an easy target." Donovan lifted his water glass to his lips. Jeanie had been pleasantly surprised to find out that he was far from the average beer-drinking, hamburger-eating cop. He had taste in food, and knew wines pretty well as well; he'd picked a perfect light one for lunch. She had been surprised when he hadn't had a glass, but he'd reminded her that he was on duty. The wine was excellent all the same.

"But Joe was really in love with her, right?" Jeanie said, not knowing the story of Randy's love affair but imagining it was very romantic, considering how in love they seemed to be now. She'd met Randy and talked to her more than a few times over the last two years, and it was very obvious to her that Randy and Joe shared a very deep love.

"Not really. In fact, when Randy became his secretary, Joe was engaged to someone else."

"No way."

"Oh yeah, and she was pregnant with his kid," Donovan said, realizing belatedly that he probably shouldn't be telling her this. But then he shrugged mentally; most of the department knew the story behind Joe and Tasha Wood.

Jeanie stared at him, stunned. "Wow, I guess I just figured it had been love at first sight with them. I mean, they seem so in love now…" She trailed off as she realized that maybe she'd been wrong.

"Oh, they are, believe me," Donovan said, his voice very sure. "They've been through so much together now I don't think they would ever break up. And actually, I do think that Joe loved Randy long before they actually got together, but there was a lot of stuff going on in those days."

"I heard about all that, the Scorpions and everything, that he almost died, and about Midnight's abduction and all that. But I guess I just figured they were together through it all. I guess you kinda think what you want about people like them."

"Like them?"

"You know…" Jeanie sounded chagrined. "Joe's so much larger than life… I guess I sound like a lovesick teenager, huh?"

"No, you sound like a lot of women. And you're right—my brother-in-law is something else. He's been shot, stabbed, you name it, and he's come through it all."

They talked about other things, and Jeanie got the distinct impression that this man was different from most of the guys she knew.

When he dropped her off back at the office, she thanked him for lunch and he told her that he'd be getting together with her about "the project" later in the week. Jeanie found out later that not only was Donovan in on this project with Midnight, but he was the team leader for the case. It gave her more respect for him, knowing that he was willing to take on such a daunting challenge.

****

Two years into her time as chief, Midnight had come across a number of discrepancies pertaining to property and accounting within the department. Within weeks she'd become obsessed with the idea of getting rid of the "bad apples." Rick had been concerned at first.

"I thought you finally were in a position where I wouldn't have to worry about you," he'd said, shaking his head with a frustrated look in his deep blue eyes. "And now you're starting all this up?"

"Rick," Midnight had said, glancing up at him—they were in bed at the time, and the light from the hallway showed her that he was indeed concerned. "I think Dickerson was the tip of the iceberg, and if I've got dirty cops, I want them out of my department." She had said it with the vehemence that Rick had come to know well over the last ten years.

"Okay, but you don't have to be the one to do it," he said, his voice still holding the protective tone that had irritated her years before; she'd gotten used to it at this point in their lives. "You got a whole fucking staff of people workin' for you, Night. Use 'em." It sounded more like an order than a request, but Midnight knew where he was coming from. They had been through a lot in their years together, and things were finally calm in terms of threats to their safety. Even Rick was in a lot less danger now, since he was a lieutenant in charge of FORS.

"I can't, Rick. I don't know who to trust…" Midnight said, trailing off as she realized what she was saying. "I can't even trust my IA guys at this point."

"You trust me, don't you?" Rick asked, his question rhetorical. "You trust Joe, Tiny, Spider, Dibbs, Jess… Use us."

"I need you at FORS, I need Joe running vice—I need everyone where they are, Rick. I gotta keep hold where I have it. Why do you think everyone is where they are? Because I trust you, because I need you guys to hold it together for me."

"Fine," Rick said, thinking quickly. "Then use Donovan. You trust him, don't you?"

Midnight looked back at him, her eyes narrowed in thought. She had chewed on the idea for a week before talking to Joe. Finally she had requested Donovan's assistance on the case, and Joe had supplied Jeanie for the project. Midnight had decided to keep it all on a small scale, figuring the fewer people that knew, the better. She eventually added her secretary and put Donovan in charge of the whole

42

thing, although she frequently worked directly with them, acquiring files and looking up information.

CHAPTER 2

Christian Collins drove down the wet streets of London in a black Jaguar KX8. His handsome face was set in a constant scowl, his light blue eyes narrowed behind his Ray-Ban Predator sunglasses. At first glance he could pass for a rich playboy, but he was far from rich—the playboy part was true enough, though. He could feel the cold steel of the gun pressed against the small of his back, and drew strength from it.

Christian was the illegitimate son of the Lord of Glenenshire. He had been conceived the night the lord of the manor finally seduced the beautiful maid of Spanish descent on his staff. Christian had, as far as he was concerned, been conceived in sin and was, therefore, the culmination of that sin. He liked to say he was the devil himself. Many of the women he'd been with had been sure of it as well.

Christian, or Blue, as most people knew him, was as cold as his ice-blue eyes seemed to imply. He didn't get involved, he didn't get emotional. He was cool and clearheaded, his judgement never clouded by feelings. The only person he loved was his mother, who had literally given up everything to have him. Christian had her coloring. His hair was jet black, worn all the same length, just an inch above his collar, and his eyelashes and eyebrows were the same color, which set off his light blue eyes very dramatically. The contrast of his dark coloring and pale eyes combined with sharp good looks always caught people's attention. Ever since childhood, people had always stopped and stared at him, a reaction Christian used to his advantage whenever necessary.

On this particular day, he was running for a local high-level drug dealer. He'd been told to pick up a woman in front of Harrod's. The dealer, Willie Charmè, liked to use Christian for this type of assignment because he knew his customers would be impressed with his "employee."

Geneva Glasstone was duly impressed. When the black Jag pulled up in front of Harrod's, the vehicle caught her attention. She was taken aback when the young man wearing all black got out and, pulling off his sunglasses, looked directly at her. "You Glasstone?" he said, his accent crisp.

Geneva had to take a moment to find her wits; she had never seen such an incredible-looking man before. He was stunning. "I— Yes, I am," she said, her own accent very cultured.

Christian curled his lips just slightly, knowing the impact he'd just made on her and as usual taking remote satisfaction from it. "Get in," he said curtly, his blue eyes staring directly into hers.

Geneva was taken aback by his direct manner, but she was the type to appreciate a candid individual. Geneva had come a long way by being direct, so she understood the power of saying what you meant.

She looked over at the young man as he drove and couldn't find a single flaw on him. His face was perfect, even in profile. From what she could detect of his physique, he had a nice body as well. And she realized suddenly that she really wanted to find out.

"So," she said, her tone purposely bored, "what is your name?"

Christian waited a full minute to look at her, and when he did, his expression was veiled. "Blue," he said finally.

"That's unique," she said, surprised. "Is it your given name?" she asked, feeling compelled to talk to him.

Christian pulled up at a light and turned his head, his look telling her he knew what she was doing and that it was amusing to him. She was once again taken aback.

At forty-five, Geneva Glasstone was still considered beautiful. She was well kept, her hair, nails, and makeup all flawless. Her body was in perfect physical condition from hours with a personal trainer. Her skin was as tight and youthful as it had always been. She had blond hair and blue eyes and was well known for her propensity for young men. This young man with the dark looks and light eyes made her want to do anything to get to him.

"I have to tell you," she said finally, her tone matter-of-fact, "you have got to be the most amazing-looking man I have ever seen." Christian didn't react the way she'd expected; he simply curled his lip sardonically and nodded. Geneva looked back at him, surprised. "And you obviously already know that?"

Again Christian nodded, his eyes still on the road ahead of him, but the look on his face indicated his confidence.

"How about this." Geneva put her hand suggestively on his leg, watching him for a response. "What does it take to get a man like you into bed?"

Again, he didn't react the way she'd expected, only giving her a long, measured look. "Is that what you're looking for?" he asked mildly, as if he believed anything but that. "Or are you just looking for a show piece?" His tone was cold, his eyes narrowed.

"Does it matter?" Geneva asked evenly.

She was shocked when he turned his eyes on her; she could almost feel shards of ice hitting her. "Nobody owns me," Christian said, his voice low.

Geneva didn't speak for a long moment. A thrill had gone up her spine at the timbre in his voice. "I don't want to own you," she said. "I just want you."

Christian actually grinned at her statement, shaking his head with bemusement. A few minutes later, they arrived at Charmè's opulent townhouse in the heart of London.

Christian left after escorting her inside, but Geneva couldn't think straight the rest of the day. She made her connection with Charmè and asked endless questions of the flamboyant drug dealer. Questions Charmè couldn't answer.

No one really knew much about Christian Collins. They knew exactly what he wanted them to and nothing more. He basically had no friends, no one he confided in, and that was the way he liked it. Over the years he had discovered that people wanted to use him for whatever reason. He'd gotten used to that, and had come to accept that it was the way people were. He knew they latched on to his looks and couldn't get past them. He allowed himself to be the dark iceman everyone thought he was; it had become his personality.

The only person that saw a softer side of Christian was his mother. The Lord of Glenenshire had fired her right after she told him she was pregnant with his child, and now, at forty-five, she had many health problems. Christian cursed his sire for his lack of backbone or common decency. His mother had been a pawn in the Lord of Glenenshire's sexual games.

Josephine Collins had, at twenty, foolishly believed that the lord had actually been in love with her. After all, he had told her he was. The other servants had tried to tell her he was a randy old lush, but she never listened. She had chosen to see him the way she wanted to. He was a lord, a powerful man in her eyes. He had turned his beautiful light blue eyes on her and she had fallen under his spell. When after two encounters she discovered she was pregnant, she fantasized about telling the Lord of Glenenshire, imagining he'd be overjoyed. Since his wife, Lady Sarah, hadn't been able to bear him a son as yet, Josephine felt sure that her son would one day be the Lord of Glenenshire.

That dream had been dashed the moment she told the lord. Lord Glenenshire had slapped her, telling her she was a halfwit for not using some sort of protection to keep it from happening. The following day he had had her removed from the house, and refused to give her either a penny or a recommendation so she could obtain work in another home. She had ended up a maid for a lower-priced hotel, making a pittance.

She had attempted to contact her family in Spain, but they had disowned her for disgracing the family. In truth, her family came from royal bloodlines stemming back to the Elizabethan age, but Josephine's family was on the poorer side of that line. Her family roots were rumored to have ties with the prince that had won Mary, Queen of Scots' heart hundreds of years before, and it was for that reason that Josephine had been thrilled to be raised in London, England.

Her parents had retired to Spain a year after she started working for the house of Glenenshire. She had been seventeen at the time. When she contacted them after being fired, she tearfully explained what had happened. They had berated her for being so stupid and had refused to help her. That left her alone and penniless, but she was determined to have her baby. When Christian was born, she had taken one look at his perfect face and full head of black hair and cried. She loved him on sight.

As Christian grew, Josephine had begun to see his father's features. His light blue eyes, his broad shoulders, and slim waist. By the time Christian was sixteen he had grown to his father's full height of six feet, and he added two inches to that the following year.

Josephine knew her son was handsome, and she knew that he received a lot of attention for his striking looks. She also knew the kind of trouble he was in. She didn't like it. But she was aware that it was how her son helped with the bills and the rent on her flat, so it was hard to criticize him. She knew Christian felt it was his responsibility to take care of her, since she had given up a lot to have him, but Josephine didn't like the direction her son's life was taking and she intended to stop him.

That evening, after dropping Geneva Glasstone off at Charmè's, Christian went to his mother's apartment to check on her. He stopped in on her frequently during the week, even though he'd had a flat of his own for years now.

"Mum?" he said as he walked in.

"In here," Josephine called from the kitchen.

Christian went into the kitchen and, showing a contrast to his somber clothing and dark looks, stood right behind his mother and leaned down to kiss her on the top of her head. "Smells good," he said, moving to sit at the small table.

"Stay for dinner, then," Josephine said mildly.

Christian narrowed his eyes suspiciously. "Why?"

49

"No reason." Josephine glanced back at her son. "Good lord, Christian, not everybody has an ulterior motive, you know."

"Yeah," Christian said, grinning. "But you do."

Josephine turned around, crossing her arms and looking at him. "And what would that be?"

Christian sat back in his chair, folding his arms in front of him. He looked at her for a long moment, his eyes narrowed as if he were trying to detect her motive by sight. He pursed his lips then, and shook his head. "Don't know. But I suspect I'll find out before the evening's over."

Josephine made a face and wagged her stirring spoon at him. "You are an evil child, Christian Joseph Collins, and I should take you over my knee for such blatant disrespect of your dear sick mother. To think that I labored for thirty-six hours to bring you into the world, and to have you talk to me like this. I could have died, you know? Right there, on the table, died, and then you would have been without the benefit of my experience to guide you through the treacheries of life…"

By the time she was halfway into her speech, Christian was laughing. Josephine was trying to keep a straight face as she recited the speech he had heard so many times in his twenty-five years of life that he could recite it with her, and often did.

"I know," he said, nodding, with a look of resignation in his light blue eyes as he looked down at the floor, the grin still on his face. "I am a sacrilegious youth, and I'm just lucky you've allowed me to grow to the ripe old age that I have…"

"Shut up, you," Josephine said, laughing as well. "Are you staying for dinner or not?"

"I am. Want me to do anything?"

"Sit there and tell me about your day," Josephine said, turning back to her stove.

Christian scratched a jet black eyebrow with his index finger, his expression troubled. "Well, there's not much to tell, really. Just did some running around and all that," he said, his voice non-committal.

Josephine suspected he was telling her a half-truth; when she turned to look at him and noted his index finger at his brow, she knew it.

"Are you still working for that drug dealer?" she asked point blank.

Christian was taken aback. He hadn't known that she knew about that in the first place; he certainly hadn't expected her to ask him about it directly. "I, uh…" he stammered, not sure how to answer.

"It was a yes or no question, young man."

Christian looked back at his mother, surprised. She wasn't usually this forthright. Finally, he lowered his eyes from hers, something no one else had ever seen Christian Collins do and probably never would. He nodded, staring at the floor.

Josephine didn't reply, merely nodded in acknowledgment and turned back to the stove. She didn't speak again until they were seated at the table. Christian had poured himself a stiff shot of brandy and followed it with a couple more, and now he waited for his mother's tirade. They ate in silence for a few minutes, then Josephine gave him a long, hard look.

"I want you to stop," she said simply.

Christian looked up at her, his eyes showing his surprise. "It's not that easy."

"It is, and you will."

"Mum—"

"Don't 'Mum' me, Christian. I did not bring you into this world to have you killed by some lowlife junky," Josephine raged. It was obvious she'd been chewing on this for a while.

Christian sighed. "I'm not gonna get killed. I gotta do this, Mum. It's the only way I can make ends meet."

"Yes, and I suppose you have to drive a brand new Jaguar too, right?" Josephine said, not willing to be placated.

"That car isn't mine, it's Charmè's," Christian said, feeling a stab of anger at the thought.

Josephine looked taken aback for a moment, but then the fight came back to her. "I don't care. You can do something else. I don't want you working for a drug dealer, Christian."

"What else can I do?" Christian said, his anger starting now. "What, be a checkout boy at the local grocer? A waiter? A bellman? You tell me."

"Don't snap at me, Christian Joseph Collins. I don't care what you do, I just want it to be legal. Do you understand?" Her tone was no-nonsense, and Christian could almost feel her digging her heels in. He knew if he wanted to keep his mother happy, which was basically what he strove for most of the time, he'd have to break with Charmè. The thought did not sit well with him, because he didn't know what else he was going to do.

The solution presented itself later that night.

Christian was asleep in bed when the bell on the security gate rang. Groaning, he turned over and listened for it to sound again. When it did, he dragged himself from the bed and padded into the living room, over to the front door. He depressed the button for the intercom system at the front gate and spoke into the monitor.

"Yeah?" he said, his irritation at having been awoken clear.

"Blue, it's me," came a cultured voice. Geneva Glasstone.

"What do you want?"

There was silence on the other end of the intercom for a moment, then, "First of all, I want you to open this bloody gate. Then I want to talk to you." She sounded irritated now as well.

Christian grinned at having affected her mood so easily. He enjoyed making people react, either to his words or to himself. So far Geneva Glasstone was pretty easy. After a long pause he finally pressed the button that would release the lock on the gate, then reached over to open his front door. Leaving it ajar, he walked over to his couch and sat down, lounging almost indolently when she came in.

Geneva caught her breath when she walked into Christian's apartment. To begin with, the apartment itself was a striking combination of white walls and black and charcoal-gray furniture. The carpet was a deep sapphire blue. Secondly, the young man she'd come to see lounged before her wearing black sweatpants and no shirt. He looked incredible. Geneva couldn't believe she'd temporarily forgotten how good-looking his was. His light blue eyes watched her with interest, even as the rest of his body screamed indifference.

Christian watched Geneva's expression and gave her a knowing look. He could see she was deeply affected by him—not that it was unusual, but it gave him the upper hand, and he liked that. She was wearing a fur coat, a sable that fell to her mid-calf, and black stiletto heels. He noted that she made no move to take the coat off, and he didn't offer to help her, something he was sure would bug the hell out of her, but she didn't seem to mind at all. She walked over and looked down at him. Normally, when a person stands above another person and looks down at them it creates an air of superiority in the individual standing. Geneva didn't feel in any way superior in this instance. Perhaps it was the way he was staring up at her with naked truculence in his eyes. She had hoped that he'd be pleased, or at least flattered that she'd obviously gone out of her way to find out where he lived and to come there at this hour. That hope had already been dismissed.

But Geneva Glasstone was not one to allow disappointment to hinder her intentions in the least. She wanted this young man in the worst way possible, and she was going to get him, one way or the other. She knew she just needed to figure out what made him tick. Find out what he wanted most and give it to him, then he'd be hers. She knew; she'd done it before with other young men. Geneva had actually made a few millionaires that way. The smarter young men took what she offered and built on it. The foolish ones took everything for granted and found themselves on the outside looking in when Geneva tired of them. Right now she had her sights set on one Christian "Blue" Collins, and she had no intention of stopping until she got him. Her first priority once she had him, however, would be to break him of this defiance that seemed ingrained in his very nature. While exciting in the beginning, she knew that a "rebellious youth" was more trouble than he was worth.

"Charmè told me where to find you," she said finally, her tone conversational. "Rest assured that I paid handsomely for the information." She moved to sit down next to him.

Christian didn't move, which she had half expected him to do. Instead he gave a short, derogatory laugh and shook his head. "You should have asked me," he said depreciatively. "It would have cost you a lot less."

Geneva didn't reply, surprised. She had figured him for difficult, considering his comment about no one owning him and his condescending attitude. Maybe she'd been wrong. Even after her extended interrogation of Charmè she knew almost nothing about Blue; all she knew was where he lived, that he'd worked for Charmè for a year, and that he usually did what he was told.

Charmè hadn't told her about the time he'd asked Christian to carry out a hit on a customer and Christian had refused. Charmè had attempted to strong-arm the younger man with two of his bodyguards. Christian had taken the bodyguards out instead and had, in no uncertain terms, told Charmè that if he ever sent his goons after him again, it would be Charmè that would end up in a body bag. Charmè had never asked Christian to do a hit on anyone again, for fear that he would carry out his threat. Charmè didn't tell anyone about the incident, not wanting anyone to know that he was literally terrified of Christian Collins. Except for that, Charmè adored him, thinking he'd love nothing more than to see if the young man swung both ways but afraid to chance asking him. He was just waiting to see any signs of bisexuality in the young man.

The flamboyant drug dealer had told Geneva that little tidbit of information, and looking at Christian now, Geneva seriously doubted Charmè would ever glimpse anything hopeful in Christian Collins' mannerisms.

"Well," she said, breaking the silence, "it doesn't really matter now, does it?"

Christian didn't answer; he just shrugged slightly and shook his head.

"I wanted to see you again." Geneva reached out to touch his arm. Christian turned his head to look down at her hand, then his light blue eyes trailed up to hers, but he said nothing. "I wanted to offer you a proposition." This time Christian grinned knowingly, the look in his eyes wintery. "Hear me out before you say anything," Geneva said, her tone cajoling. Christian nodded, but the look in his eyes didn't change.

Geneva took a deep breath and began again, trying desperately not to be affected by how close he sat to her and the smell of his cologne, still evident even after he'd been in bed. Good Lord, Geneva, don't think of him in bed—you'll never get through this!

"I want to offer you a job, of sorts. You see, my husband died many years ago, and since then I have attended parties in the homes of the people in the same society set. Well, it seems these people are forever setting me up with eligible men my age, to try and get me married off again. The men they set me up with are, to say the least, detestable." She made a face, showing her distaste, and Christian couldn't hold back a grin. "Well, as you can imagine, since I was only twenty-eight when my husband died, I was far from ready to settle down with some old codger and grow old like him. My husband left me all of his vast fortune, and I don't feel the need to get married again. And so, since if I go to these parties alone I get stuck with old men, I have ceased going to them by myself. Now I take handsome young men who end up being the envy of every woman at the party, young or old. I've developed quite the reputation for discovering the most handsome young men in England and abroad. In any case, I think you would probably cause a huge uproar anywhere you go, and that is very appealing to me."

"Okay," Christian said, not bothering to deny her last statement; he knew she was right.

"What I want is for you to be my escort, and I'll pay you."

"That's it?" Christian said, the look in his eyes belying his guileless question.

"It can be, if that's what you want," Geneva said, gazing up at him.

"But it's not what you want."

"No," Geneva said, feeling herself being drawn in by him.

"And what is it you want?" His tone was cool, but he was staring straight into her eyes.

"Everything," she said breathlessly.

"But can you handle it?" he asked then, his look heating up a few more degrees.

"I can handle you better than you know," Geneva said, her own confidence finally showing.

"How much better?"

Without a word Geneva stood up and unfastened her coat, dropping it to the floor. She wore nothing underneath. Christian stared up at her with a look that was a combination of amusement and surprise. "You are rather daring, aren't you?" he said finally, his tone indicating a new respect for her.

"I can be," Geneva said proudly.

"Where did you park when you came here?" There was no parking near his building.

"Two streets down."

Christian grinned, inclining his head just slightly.

"Why?" she asked, feeling the warmth of sexual tension start in her.

Without warning Christian reached up, taking her hand and pulling her down. She straddled his lap, staring down at him. "Because it excites me to think of you walking up the London streets dressed like that."

Geneva felt a shock of electricity light up her whole body as he pulled her head down to him and kissed her. They spent the next three hours having sex. In the end, Geneva was happy to realize that there were indeed things she could teach him. Christian had all the makings of an incredible lover, with the looks and the body to back them up, but there were nuances, touches, and other things that could make him a legendary lover, and Geneva intended to teach him them all.

Later they discussed their business arrangement. She would make the payments on his flat as well as buy the Jaguar from Charmè and sign over the title to Christian. She would pay him a fair amount for escorting her to parties and there would be the added bonus of sex, for which Christian refused to actually take money. To his way of thinking, if he didn't take money for that part, he was still within an acceptable realm of employment. That way he wasn't really a whore. Well, not totally.

****

After their first meeting, Donovan and Jeanie worked together often. Jeanie found that she enjoyed spending time with him. His laugh was contagious, and he'd often have her laughing over something really dumb till her sides hurt. They talked about inconsequential things, but in no time, Jeanie counted him among her friends. One day, about three weeks after they met, Jeanie and Donovan were working out at the department warehouse for the day. They'd taken a radio and had spent the day debating what songs were good or not. They found that they had a lot in common when it came to music.

Jeanie sat on a stack of boxes, watching as Donovan opened yet another box and started examining the contents. He was wearing jeans, dark brown Dr. Martens boots, and a teal shirt that just about matched the color of his eyes. Jeanie found him terribly handsome, and his personality went a long way to making him perfect. He had an even temper, and such an easygoing way about him that she couldn't help but like him.

"Okay, Jay," he said, using the nickname he'd coined for her almost right from the beginning. "This one's got four Motorola Saber radios and one Motorola Midland radio." He glanced up at her, his sandy-brown hair falling over his forehead and making his teal eyes seem more blue-green than ever.

"Got it," she replied, writing it down on the list they were making. Midnight had decided to inventory the equipment in the warehouse, in the event that any of it started to disappear—if it hadn't been taken already. "You know, if you'd let me help, you could sit down for a while…" she said as she saw him reach for another box.

He looked over at her as he hefted the box down from the shelf and put it on top of the other one. "Didn't we have this discussion already?" he asked, a half-smile on his face.

"Yes, we did," Jeanie said, rolling her eyes. "And you're being a male chauvinist pig about it."

Donovan nodded, twisting his lips in a grin. "I think the term you were looking for was 'gentleman.'"

Jeanie laughed, shaking her head. "No, I had the right term, you're just in the wrong century."

"Yeah, yeah," Donovan said, nodding. "You can call me anything you want, but you're not lifting heavy boxes and getting hurt, okay?"

"Aye, aye, aye," she said, rolling her eyes heavenward. "How am I ever going to pass the physical agility if I'm not allowed to do anything physical?"

"You'll pass," Donovan said confidently.

"I will, huh?" Jeanie said with a lot less confidence.

"I told you I'd help you, didn't I?" Donovan opened the box and surveyed the items inside it. "Three Motorola Sabers, two Midlands."

"Got it. Yes, you told me you'd help me, but what if I don't have the actual physical strength to handle it?"

Donovan looked up at her contemplatively. "Okay…" he said, walking over to some shelves. He pulled boxes out and lifted them away, eventually finding what he wanted. "Come here," he said, and moved over a couple of aisles away.

Jeanie stood up and followed him. He set the box down on the floor and stepped back. "Okay. Bend down, and using your legs to lift, drag that box from here to that next row." He gestured down the aisle. Jeanie looked at him for a long moment, not sure if he was joking, but he looked serious so she did as he'd said.

When she got to the next row she was out of breath. She set the box down on the floor and straightened up. She looked at Donovan as he walked up to her; he was nodding.

"Okay," he said, extending his arms out toward her. "Take my wrists. I'm going to apply some resistance—you just hold them this distance apart if you can."

Jeanie took his wrists in her hands, feeling the warmth of his skin and making a point of ignoring it.

"Ready?" he asked, and she nodded.

He began applying pressure to move his arms apart, and Jeanie tightened her hold on his wrists, using all her strength to hold them together. Before she knew it, he'd lightened the pressure. Jeanie blew out her pent-up breath, nodding to him and belatedly releasing his wrists.

"You'll pass," Donovan said, nodding confidently.

"Because I could do that?" Jeanie said disbelievingly.

"That," he said, pointing to the box on the floor, "was fairly equal to the fifty-pound body drag, and this," he said, pointing to his wrists, which were still colored from the test, "was equivalent or more than the cuffing exercise. You'll do fine—those are the hardest ones."

Without thinking, Jeanie reached out and took his wrists in her hands, rubbing them, because they were red and looked like they hurt. But she looked up at him with surprise at what he had said. "Really, that's like what the tests will be?" Then her expression changed. "But what about the six-foot wall?"

Donovan glanced down at her hands rubbing gently at his wrists and smiled, then looked back at her. "I told you there's a trick to the wall, and I will teach you that trick, okay? Trust me!"

"Oh, sure, that's what they all say," Jeanie said, smiling back at him. She stopped her ministrations but didn't let go of his wrists. "So do you think I could cuff somebody like you?" Her look was challenging.

Donovan grinned, then shook his head. "I don't roughhouse with women either."

"Who was talking roughhousing? I'm talking serious police work here, Sergeant Curtis."

"Okay." Donovan nodded and moved toward one of the shelving units. Standing with his feet just over shoulder-width apart, he put his hands out on either side of him, placing them on the shelves in a search stance. "You're arresting me," he said, his tone instructional now. "Take my left wrist and start to bring it around to my back."

Jeanie had to stand on tiptoe to reach his wrist, but she took it and did as he said.

"Okay, now I'm going to start resisting. What I want you to do is to grab my hand around the thumb area, putting your thumb into the palm of my hand," Jeanie did as he said. "Now as I resist, put pressure on the palm of my hand and twist my wrist outward toward you. At the same time, put your other hand just above my elbow and guide me to the floor."

Donovan started to move his arm as if he were a suspect trying to resist, and Jeanie did as she'd been instructed. She was surprised when within moments Donovan was down on his knees. She let go of him immediately for fear she'd actually hurt him.

"My God, it worked," she said excitedly.

Donovan nodded, glancing up at her and moving his head as if to stretch his neck. "Yes, it works, and you learn too damn fast!" His tone held mock disgruntlement.

"Did I hurt you?" She extended her hand to help him up.

"No, you did exactly right, except if I was really a bad guy, you shouldn't let go right away."

"Well, I know that, but I didn't want to hurt you."

"Well, thank you, Ms. Franco," Donovan said, grinning. "You did good though."

"You're a good teacher," she replied, patting him on the back.

Donovan sighed dramatically. "Just one of my many talents."

"I'll just bet."

They went back to work then, and the rest of the day passed quickly. At four o'clock, Donovan escorted her back out to his car; he had driven over to the warehouse. Jeanie found herself sorry that the day was over. She had enjoyed the time alone with him. In the office there was always some feeling of not being able to joke around too much, or seem too friendly, but today they seemed to have been able to goof off a little bit. She wished in a way that they didn't have to leave. She was happy to note that they hadn't finished, so they'd probably have to come back.

In the car, Donovan called Midnight to tell her they were on their way back to the office. His cell phone was set up for hands-free, so Jeanie could hear the whole conversation.

"You guys get even close to finishing?" Midnight asked, knowing that the warehouse was really loaded with equipment.

"We're probably more than halfway," Donovan said, looking

over at Jeanie for confirmation. She nodded.

"Well, you guys want some overtime?"

Donovan glanced back at Jeanie, and she nodded again. "Sounds good, Night, but personally I'm dusted today."

"I didn't mean today, Donovan," Midnight said. "I know you have lives. I just thought if you wanted to work this weekend maybe you could finish up."

"I can. What about you, Jay?"

"I have no life—I'll be here," Jeanie said, grinning.

"Great, then that'll be done and we can move on. I'll see you two when you get back in here," Midnight said, and they hung up.

A few moments later Donovan's phone rang. He hit the hands-free button again. "Hello?"

"Pony," said a man's voice.

Donovan grinned. "Gregory."

"So… did you totally forget about tonight or what?"

Donovan winced. "Shit, man. Yeah, I did. What time am I supposed to meet you guys?"

"Seven thirty," Gregory said, as if he'd said it a million times already.

Donovan looked contemplative for a minute, glancing at his watch. Then he nodded. "I can make it. I'll be there."

"Hey, man, it's your party," Gregory said chidingly.

"Hey, man, I was promoted six months ago," Donovan replied, his tone equally upbraiding.

"Yeah, yeah. Well, be there, man. Seven thirty at 10-7, got it?"

Donovan grinned. "Ten four." He hung up and glanced over at Jeanie, who had watched the proceedings with amusement.

"Some friends of mine," he said by way of explanation. "They've been trying to take me out to celebrate my promotion for months now."

"Uh-huh, and you forgot about it."

He laughed. "Well, they've changed the date so many times now, I can't keep track anymore. Hey," he said then, as if a thought had just occurred to him. "You want to come?"

Jeanie raised an eyebrow at him. "To your promotional party?"

"Bad idea? I mean, I just thought you might like to go out with me and my friends for a drink. No big deal."

"Sounds fun," Jeanie said. "Are you guys heavy drinkers?"

Donovan gave her a measured look, as if not sure how much to tell her. "Sometimes, but I'm driving tonight so I won't get drunk. I need to run home and shower and change, but I could pick you up if you want to ride with me."

"What if I follow you to your house and ride with you from there?" Jeanie said, surprising him.

"Sounds good to me."

Back at the office, Jeanie told Midnight that Donovan was taking her out drinking. Donovan shook his head, rolling his eyes.

"You aren't supposed to tell her," Donovan told Jeanie.

"Why not?" Jeanie and Midnight asked at the same time.

Donovan blinked, as if surprised by the question. "Because

you're the chief, and…" he started, not sure how to put it.

"It's not a date, right?" Midnight said humorously.

"No," Donovan and Jeanie said together.

Midnight laughed at the denial in their voices. "Knock it off, guys. I wouldn't care if it was. Even if I did, Jeanie, you're not a cop yet. And I'm hardly the chief to worry about fraternization. Hello? My husband's a cop, Donovan, your sister and brother-in-law are cops… We're a family, literally and figuratively." Midnight was smiling by the end of her lecture. "Just be careful, and Jeanie…"

"Yeah?" Jeanie said, her face very serious.

Midnight laughed. "Just keep moving."

Jeanie laughed too, knowing that Midnight was referring to how fast cops could be with their hands. She and Midnight had discussed it often enough.

"Hey!" Donovan said, doing his best to look offended but grinning all the while.

They left a little while later, with Jeanie following Donovan. She drove a newer-model 200SX that she had managed to buy on her student wages. On the drive to Mission Beach, where Donovan rented the house Midnight had lived in before her marriage to Rick, Jeanie reflected on what she was doing. She'd never gone to this particular bar. She and her friends usually went to dance clubs, not bars per se. This was going to be different. It would be interesting to see the social side of Donovan. Jeanie wondered if he'd be any different. Part of her wondered what he'd be like if he did get drunk, but the other part didn't really want to know. What if he was a real jerk? Would she still be his friend? Of course, there was always the concern that he'd be the grabby type, and that he'd try something he shouldn't. She dealt with that all the time.

Guys that took her out always wanted something by the end of the night, and she wasn't really willing to give much on a first date. The fact of the matter was, she was a virgin and she figured she would probably stay that way for a while yet. Every time she got involved with a man, she knew there would come the time when he'd want to have sex, and she'd have to tell him. A lot of times the guy would say it didn't matter, that he respected her for it, but in the end it came down to "give it to me or else." When she didn't give in, they walked. Lately, she'd stayed away from relationships because she wasn't ready to get her heart trampled again. She was very cautious with guys, and she never trusted their motives, figuring they were always angling to get into her pants.

Donovan was the first guy she'd met that had been totally proper with her the whole time they'd known each other. He had never made comments about her looks; he never made sexual comments or jokes about sex. What he had said earlier in the day about being a gentleman seemed to be very true. He treated her with respect and she liked it, a lot. She was amused to realize that she was actually a little upset that he hadn't really made any sort of move to get to know her on a personal level up until this evening. Now the thought of going out with him, even if it wasn't really a date, excited her just a little bit. It was a chance to get to know him away from the office. She found that she wanted to know a lot about him. The most personal thing she knew at this point was that his parents had deserted him and his siblings when he was eleven. But she would have learned that anyway, since Midnight told her about it the day after she first met Donovan. It was obviously not a big secret.

Wanting to know more about him was what had prompted her to suggest that she follow him to his house. She wanted to see where he lived, and how he lived. When they pulled up, she got out of the car and looked at the modest house on the hills above the beach.

"Come on in," Donovan said, his tone holding only a friendly note as he held the door open for her. She was waiting for some comment that would ruin her whole picture of him as a gentleman, but it didn't come. Once inside she looked around. The furnishings were surprisingly nice for a man's house. She had expected at least messiness, but she was far from right. It was clean and nice. The living room held a comfortable-looking sofa and an antique-looking armchair, and an incredible entertainment center with a huge television and a nice stereo setup. His dining room held a fair-sized antique table with four lyre back chairs. Jeanie was further astounded to note that his kitchen was clean. The room was long and narrow with a low island on one side. Everything was clean, and Jeanie couldn't get over it. As she turned around, she noticed that Donovan was watching her.

"This is really nice," she said, sitting down on the low island.

"Thanks." He canted his head back down the hall. "I'm going to take a shower. Make yourself at home. I won't be long."

"Okay," Jeanie said, still trying to absorb this new dimension to him. Donovan disappeared down the hallway. Eventually Jeanie stood up and walked over to the refrigerator, curious what a guy like him would have in his fridge. She opened it to find that not only was it clean, but stocked well. She noticed two bottles of wine and a six-pack of Rolling Rock beer, but that was it for alcohol. She saw vegetables and bottled water, bread and real butter; there was no marga-rine. Everything looked very organized, and she wondered at the va-riety of things in the refrigerator, including fresh herbs. Feeling like a thief in the night, she looked in his cupboards next. She found spices, oils, seasonings, and staples such as rice, flour, and sugar stored neatly in clear containers. She was surprised to note very few canned foods, nor boxed foods either. He had the kitchen of a cook, and now she was curious if he cooked too.

Eventually, she ceased her investigation, after noting that he did indeed have a fairly nice-looking set of copper-bottomed pans that had all the marks of frequent use. She sat down on the couch and found the remote for the television. She clicked it on and was sur-prised when the speakers came on as well. This was obviously a seri-ous man's television. Experimenting with the sound, she found that it was indeed a powerful home theater system.

Well, he has good taste, she thought. She had to tamp down on the urge to investigate the rest of the house, for fear he'd catch her spying on him. She found that she was very curious now about his bedroom. What kind of room would a man like him have? What style of bed? What colors would he use? As it was, the living room and dining room were predominantly navy and cream.

Twenty minutes later, when Donovan came out of his bedroom he was wearing tan slacks and a hunter green polo shirt. He looked good. His hair was still a little damp, but he was clean-shaven and he smelled of Tommy cologne. He was pulling on a brown leather bomber-style jacket. When he walked around the couch, she noted that he still wore the brown Dr. Martens boots, but they looked good with the outfit.

"Acceptable?" Donovan asked, noting her assessing look.

"Oops," Jeanie said, grinning as her cheeks reddened. "You caught me checking you out, huh?"

Donovan smiled good-naturedly. "Well, I figure you want to make sure I'm not going to embarrass you or anything."

"Donovan, appearance-wise, I don't think you could embarrass me if you tried."

"Well, thanks… I think," Donovan said, smiling again.

Jeanie smiled back. "It was a compliment." To her surprise, he extended his hand to her gallantly. She took it and allowed him to tug her to her feet. "Such a gentleman too," she chided gently.

"See, I told you," Donovan said, his voice just a little bit softer this time. Jeanie felt herself shiver at the slight change in it. She wondered if he realized she was leery of men, and that this whole thing had been more or less a test of his personality. Looking up at him, she couldn't tell what he was thinking. She realized then, though, that she was standing very close to him, and she sensed that he was as hesitant to move away as she was. In the end it was Donovan that ended the moment. "Should we go?" he asked surreptitiously.

"Yeah," Jeanie said, feeling a stab of disappointment that he hadn't tried to touch her or anything. The thought surprised her; here she was testing him to see if he would remain a gentleman in his own home, and yet she wanted him to try something with her at that moment.

Once in the car, Jeanie inhaled the combination of scents—his leather jacket, the leather interior of the car, and the Tommy cologne. She wondered belatedly if she looked okay. She glanced down at herself. She was wearing black slacks with black ankle boots, and a lavender silk blouse that actually clung attractively to her. She remembered that she had dressed that morning thinking about the fact that she and Donovan would be alone together. It had never occurred to her that she'd be going out with him that evening as well. She glanced over at him as he drove. "Would it be really too female-like to use the vanity mirror and check my makeup?" she asked with an embarrassed grin.

Donovan laughed, glancing back over at her. "You look great, but if you want to see for yourself, no, I don't think that would be over the top."

Jeanie pulled down the visor and checked her makeup. He was right; it was fine. But he didn't say my makeup was fine, he said I look great, she thought. Did he mean it that way? She clamped down on the thoughts. Here she was acting like a schoolgirl with a crush. And suddenly she realized that that was exactly what it was—she had a crush on Donovan Curtis. Would wonders never cease?

When they reached the bar called 10-7, which was the police code for off duty, Jeanie was impressed. She knew that 10-7 was a "cop bar," so she'd expected it to be some dive. But it was actually nice inside, with a long oak bar and tables off to the side. The lighting was generally dim, like it often was in bars, but even that didn't seem as harsh as it was in ones she'd been in before.

Jeanie was secretly thrilled when Donovan took her hand to lead her over to his friends, who were already stationed at one of the tables in the center of the room. He introduced her to them, and they all seemed nice enough.

There was Gregory Mires, who looked like the classic cop type, with short dark hair in a marine-style cut and brown eyes. He smiled at her as she shook his hand; his shake too was warm like his smile. Next was John Mallory, who looked like an all-star linebacker, with blond hair and blue eyes and a very stout frame. Jeanie could see that his size was due in no way to fat, however; he looked like a little powerhouse, standing only a couple of inches taller than her. Next was David Jones, whose Latino looks belied his last name. He looked Jeanie up and down, and then held her hand a little bit too long when he shook it. Jeanie decided right away that she didn't like him. There were a couple of other people there, but Donovan told her they were friends of friends and he couldn't introduce her because he didn't know them. The rest of the people in the party introduced themselves and then they all sat down.

David Jones leaned over to ask if Jeanie was Donovan's date, and she said they were just friends. David's response was a quiet "good" in her ear. She looked back at him to see if he was joking, but he didn't look like he was. She made a point of sitting next to Donovan to hopefully stave off any passes by David. Donovan asked her what she wanted to drink and headed to the bar. Jeanie watched him go, wanting to follow him.

"Don't worry," said Gregory, one of Donovan's oldest friends, moving to sit next to her. "I'll keep an eye on you till he gets back."

Jeanie looked over at him, expecting to see the same kind of leering look she'd seen in David's eyes, but she was happily surprised that he was smiling a genuine smile. She smiled in return. When Donovan returned, Gregory moved to let his friend sit next to her. Donovan handed her a glass of wine, then sat down with a shot and a bottle of Rolling Rock. He looked at his friends and said, with a sly grin, "So what are we here for again?"

Gregory laughed. "Oh, shut the hell up!"

"Yeah, rub our noses in it, Curtis. Go ahead," John Mallory said.

"Yeah, shut the hell up and drink!" Jones put in, narrowing his eyes but grinning all the while.

Donovan laughed, shrugging. "Can I help it if I made sergeant first?"

"Shut up, Curtis, and drink!" the other three men said, everyone laughing now.

Donovan nodded and downed the shot, then the others drank as well. Jeanie watched in fascination. This was obviously something they did often. She sipped at her wine and was surprised at the taste. She looked over at Donovan and saw that he was watching her.

"Is that okay?" he asked. "You just said wine…"

"It's great," she said, smiling. "Thanks. What is it you just drank?" She'd noticed that the liquid in the shot glass was a caramel color.

"This?" he said, picking up the glass. "This is called Stars at Night. It's a combination of Goldschläger and Jägermeister."

Jeanie stared at him blankly. "And what does that taste like?"

He grinned. "You want to try one?"

"No." She shook her head, smiling widely. "I just wanted to know what it tasted like."

Donovan looked at her for a long moment, and she could see he was debating something. Finally, he stopped a waitress walking by and ordered one.

"I said I didn't want one," Jeanie said, giving him a mockingly reproachful look.

"So I'll drink it, but you can taste it first," Donovan said, giving her a reproachful look of his own. He leaned down close to her, his lips next to her ear. "I'm not trying to get you drunk, okay?"

Jeanie couldn't tamp down on the shiver that went through her at the sound of his voice that close to her. She looked at him as he moved to sit back, and all she could manage was a nod. When the shot arrived a few minutes later, he paid the waitress and handed her the drink.

"Try it," he said, watching her. She sipped it and was surprised that she liked it. It tasted like the candy Red Hots she'd always liked as a kid.

"It's good," she said, handing him the glass.

"You sure you don't want it?" Donovan saw the look of adventure sparkle in her eyes even as he asked.

Jeanie considered the question for a minute. "I shouldn't…"

Again Donovan leaned down to her ear. "Are you worried about getting buzzed around people from work?"

"No, just around men in general," she replied without thinking. Then she realized how it must have sounded when he looked down at her, surprised. "I mean…" she stammered, trying to think of an easy way to explain, but Donovan nodded.

"Do you trust me?" he asked.

"Yes," she said, without hesitation.

"Okay." Donovan looked pleased with her answer. "I promise you, I will make sure you are well protected, and that you get home safe and sound even if you have a little too much to drink."

Jeanie looked back at him, and he moved to look down at her.

Her eyes met his in an almost probing way, as if she were searching for any sign of deception. Finally she nodded and, taking a deep breath, drank the shot down. Donovan blinked in surprise that she'd actually drunk the whole thing in one. Jeanie gave him a rakish grin, then started to cough as the alcohol actually hit her stomach. Donovan laughed, as did the rest of the table.

Things after that were rowdy, and Jeanie was having a good time up until she noticed that David was getting overly touchy. It started with him putting his arm around her shoulder to talk to her. Then his hands seemed to be on her constantly. At one point Donovan had gone off to talk to someone that had come into the bar who he hadn't seen in a while. Jeanie turned to David and told him to stop, hoping he'd get the message without her having to spell it out to him. He didn't. Donovan hadn't noticed all the touching going on because he had been talking with Gregory, and David seemed to be careful not to touch her when Donovan was paying attention. Jeanie wasn't sure what to do. At one point she really just wanted to leave, but she was there without her car and she felt helpless.

Donovan was on his way back to the table when he caught a glimpse of David's hand on Jeanie's leg and her subsequent movement to get away from him. She stood up as if to go to the bathroom, and David stood too. Donovan saw David lean over and say something to her, and Jeanie shook her head and started to walk away. Donovan was stunned when he saw his high school chum reach out and grab her rear end. His anger brought him face to face with David in a fraction of a second. Jeanie stood just behind Donovan, watching in shock as he snatched David up by a handful of his shirt.

"What the hell are you doin'?" Donovan grated angrily.

David stared back at Donovan wide-eyed for a moment, then he started to grin. He was very clearly drunk. "I was jus' bein' friendly, Pony," he slurred.

Donovan narrowed his eyes at him, then shook his head. "You touch her like that again, and you'll be gettin' friendly with the floor." His tone was pure ice, his teal eyes blazing at the other man.

"Hey!" David said, finally regaining some of his wits and starting to realize that he was being berated by one of his best friends. He struggled against Donovan's hold on his shirt, managing to wrench himself free, then with both hands attempted to shove Donovan away. Donovan took one step back, his eyes firmly on his friend.

"Don't fuckin' try an' tell me who I can and can't lay my hands on. You ain't the boss here, Curtis!" David's tone was derogatory, his hands working at his sides.

"You're right, Dave, I'm not the boss," Donovan said, his voice not giving an inch. "But she's here with me, and that makes her my responsibility. And I'm tellin' you, you touch her again and I'll deck ya."

"So she is your piece," David said lewdly. "I asked her, but she said you two were jus' friends. Maybe she just wanted to score both of us, Pony. She's playin' you. That's how these cop groupie sluts are, man…" He trailed off suggestively.

Donovan had heard enough. He knocked David off his feet with one well-placed punch. With that he turned to Gregory, who had watched with an open mouth, like the rest of the group. "I'm sorry, man," was all Donovan said, and with that he took Jeanie's hand and led her outside.

Once in the car, Donovan started the engine with a roar and screeched out of the parking space. He didn't speak for a long time, his jaw set in an angry line. All Jeanie could think of was that she'd just ruined a friendship, all because she didn't like men touching her. She felt stupid and young and lost all at the same time.

"Donovan, I am so sorry," she said, her tone bereft.

He looked over at her sharply, then started to shake his head. "What are you talking about? Why are you sorry?"

"Donovan," she began, her voice indicating her disbelief that he didn't understand. "You just slugged one of your oldest friends because of me. Why else?"

"Yeah, and that old friend of mine was pawing you like a stray dog. It's me that's sorry." He shook his head. "He knows better than to act like that around me."

Jeanie was quiet for a long moment as she watched him. "I just… I'm sorry that I didn't handle it myself. I didn't want to offend him. I mean, he is your friend, and it was your thing and all…"

"Jay," Donovan said, shaking his head again. "You were with me, and I promised you I'd keep you safe and sound, and I didn't. I just didn't see it going on—I guess I was too involved in talking to everyone…"

Jeanie was surprised by his self-deprecation. "Donovan, you were great. I mean, hell, you just did that knight on a white horse saves the damsel in distress thing… What more do you think you could have done?"

"Kept it from happening in the first place."

Jeanie grinned. "Right, and you're omnipresent now too?"

"No, but you were there with me, and I didn't take care of you," Donovan said possessively. Jeanie heard the tone and felt warmed by it.

"You did take care of me, and you were great, okay?" she said, putting her hand over his on the stick shift. Donovan glanced down at her hand, and a smile tugged at his lips as he nodded. They pulled onto the freeway then, heading back toward his house.

"You win," he said finally. "But you have to let me make it up to you anyhow."

"It's not necessary," she said as she started to move her hand. Donovan took it in his as he looked over at her.

"It is necessary, and you're gonna let me do it, aren't you?" he said, his tone brooking no argument.

Jeanie laughed, and just then his cell phone started to ring.

Donovan reached over and hit the hands-free, still holding her hand. "Hello?"

"Pony?" Gregory said, yelling over the din in the bar. "Hey, man, you okay to be drivin'?"

"Yeah, I'm fine," Donovan said, grinning at the phone. "I only had a couple of beers and a shot, no big deal."

"Yeah, okay, I just wanted to make sure. I mean, I didn't want you leavin' here drunk and pissed off as all get out. And then we end up wiping your sorry ass off the road somewhere. Ya know?"

Donovan smiled. "Your heartfelt concern is touching, Greg, really."

"Yeah, I know. So, what is going on with you and the beautiful girl?"

Donovan glanced over at Jeanie, who discreetly pretended to be looking out the window with interest, a grin on her face. "Why do you ask?" Donovan replied sheepishly.

"Well, I figure it's something major, considering…"

"Considering what?" Donovan's tone belied the embarrassment he felt at the direction of the conversation.

"Well, considering that David is out cold, and I haven't seen you hit that hard in a damn long time."

Donovan started to laugh at the tone in his friend's voice and the horrified look that Jeanie gave him. "Look, Greg, man, I gotta go," he said when he recovered his composure.

"Alright, later," Gregory said, his tone indicating he knew he had just tipped his friend's hand, so to speak.

After he hung up, Donovan looked over at Jeanie again. "Don't worry about it, I'm sure David is fine. Hell, he probably passed out more than anything else."

"Uh-huh," Jeanie said uncertainly. "So you've hit him before?" She'd noted that Gregory hadn't seemed too taken aback that Donovan had hit their friend, only that he'd hit him hard.

Donovan shrugged. "We fight all the time, the four of us."

"Over women?"

"Sometimes. Other times about other stuff. It's not really a big deal."

"Yeah, I know, you do it all the time," Jeanie said caustically.

"Stop it," Donovan said with a grin. "Now, when are you going to let me make this up to you? And don't tell me it's not necessary, we already covered that."

Jeanie gave him a measuring look. "Well, I guess that depends on what you're planning to do to make it up to me…"

Donovan glanced over at her, surprised. Jeanie started to laugh. "I meant like dinner, movie, flowers… What?"

Donovan shook his head, as if trying to lose the thoughts he'd had. "Well, I meant like dinner, at least."

"Okay…" Jeanie said. "How about this, then. I have the sneaking suspicion that you cook, am I right?"

Donovan gave her a sidelong glance, as if trying to decide how much to tell her. "Yes, you're right—I cook. A man has to eat, you know."

"Yes, but your kitchen doesn't look like the kitchen of a man who eats just anything that comes by."

Donovan's look was narrow this time, but his grin gave him away. "Checkin' me out, were ya?"

Jeanie grinned sheepishly. "Yeah, kinda."

He smiled. "Maybe you'll make a good detective someday… Okay, so you caught me. I can cook, fairly well, I guess. Why?"

"How about you cook dinner for me, and then we're even," Jeanie said, feeling bold suddenly.

"How 'bout tomorrow night?"

"You have yourself a date, Sergeant."

CHAPTER 3

The next night couldn't come fast enough for Jeanie. She spent the day checking the clock. They'd decided she should be there about seven o'clock. Time seemed to be dragging its feet mercilessly.

Donovan, on the other hand, spent the day on a callout. There had been a major raid on a case he had assisted on, and Joe had called him to ask if he wanted in on it. Donovan had accepted happily. The raid had gone well, but there had been a great deal of evidence to catalog. He spent the day in a strange house, sifting through piles of belongings, extracting illegal paraphernalia from everyday items. On the way home he stopped at the store to buy what he needed for dinner. He got home an hour and a half before she was to be there. He rushed to take a shower and start dinner.

When Jeanie knocked on the door, she was surprised at his appearance when he answered. He was wearing black cotton slacks and black suede Oxfords, but the teal shirt he wore hung open and his hair still looked damp. He grinned sheepishly at her, shrugging. "Sorry, I got hung up at a raid that took all day long."

"No problem," Jeanie replied, trying not to stare at his chest even as he reached up to button his shirt and tuck it in. She liked how he was dressed, the color of his shirt matching his eyes perfectly; it was very distracting. She followed him down the hallway and into the kitchen. He reached over and pulled out a crystal glass, poured wine and handed it to her.

"Dinner's almost ready," he said, taking a drink from his own glass.

"It smells great," she said, sitting on the low island between his kitchen and dining room.

He glanced over at her and grinned, happy that she seemed comfortable with him. He made a face. "Well, we'll just see about that."

Jeanie tasted the wine; as usual, he had picked a great one. "How do you do that?" she said, shaking her head at him.

"What?" he asked, looking up from the stove. "Oh, the wine?" He smiled. "Practice."

When they sat down to dinner, Jeanie noticed that he had all the polite gentlemanly things down. He held her chair for her and served her. Then she tasted the pepper steak he'd made, and she was sure she'd died and gone to heaven.

"Donovan, this is fantastic," she said, astounded. "I figured you could cook, but... wow..."

Donovan grinned. "Well, I do have a little confession to make."

"What?"

"I did go to a culinary academy for about a year and a half, before I quit to go into regular college and become a cop."

"Really?" Jeanie asked, ever surprised by this man. "How much farther did you have to go to finish the academy?"

"About a semester or two."

"And how long was a semester there?" She assumed it must be different from academic college.

"Like a regular college, about four to eight months…"

Jeanie stared at him in shock. "Are you nuts? Why didn't you finish?"

Donovan looked pensive, then shrugged. "I guess I just decided I wanted to do police work instead."

"But you were so close." Jeanie shook her head. "And you graduated from college too, didn't you?"

"Yep." He nodded as he picked up his wine glass and took a drink.

"What's your degree in?" she said, realizing in all the time they'd spent together she'd never asked him that.

"Criminal science."

"That's a hard one, isn't it?"

"Hard?" Donovan tilted his head slightly as he thought about it. "I guess it's harder than your average administration of justice degree, yeah, more of the sciences and all that, but I thought it'd be more applicable, ya know?"

"Yeah, I guess," Jeanie said, her tone still indicating her surprise at his accomplishments. She ate in silence for a while, enjoying the food and the wine. When she looked up, she realized Donovan was watching her and felt self-conscious all of a sudden. "What?"

"So why don't you like to drink around men?" he said, staring directly into her eyes. So directly, in fact, it took her a moment to realize he'd actually asked her a question.

"I…" She hesitated, feeling a little bit shy all of sudden.

"You don't have to tell me. I've just been curious since last night."

"I don't mind telling you, I just… I wasn't sure how to explain. Just suffice it to say that I'm kind of gun-shy where men are concerned," she said, looking everywhere but at him, afraid he'd see exactly what she meant.

"Did you get burned?" he asked, not willing to "suffice it to say" anything.

"No… I just, well…" she started, looking for the right words. She looked up at him and saw that direct, teal-eyed stare again, and took a deep breath, willing herself to tell him the truth. "I'm just, well, I'm only willing to go so far with men, and that tends to cause me some problems. Being around men who are drinking, and then having them see me drink, makes them loosen up and assume I will too. It causes problems like last night." Her voice was soft on the last; she didn't want to make him think she was blaming him in any way.

Donovan looked at her for a long moment before nodding slowly. "Okay…" he said, his gaze falling on the glass of wine in front of her. "But you're okay with this? I'm not making you uncomfortable, am I?"

"No, Donovan, not even close to being uncomfortable. You're so great about everything. I mean, you've never even made an inappropriate comment to me. I trust you more than I've trusted just about any man I've ever met."

He grinned then, nodding. "Figures."

"What's that mean?" she said, her grin wide too.

Donovan looked up at the ceiling. "The beautiful ones always trust me…" He sighed, then looked at her again. "Like a brother."

She laughed. "Now I didn't say that."

The conversation proceeded in a different direction then. She asked him about the raid that morning, and he asked her about things in Midnight's office, how she'd gotten the job with the department, how she had liked working for Joe.

"Joe was the best to work for," she said, smiling. "He was always so cool about things—he's never gotten that 'I'm a big-shot captain' attitude. He's cool."

"Yeah, Joe's not really into rank, that's for sure. He raised holy hell with Midnight when she wanted to make him a captain. She'd already made him a lieutenant when she went to be captain of vice, but at least that was just running FORS, which he had half done already. But when she told him she needed him to make captain so he could keep watch on vice for her, he flipped. They argued for weeks over that one." Donovan shook his head, remembering the arguments.

"He actually argued with her?"

"Yeah." Donovan grinned. "Haven't you heard them argue before? Sometimes you'd think they were married."

"You know, that's something I never understood," Jeanie said, then stopped herself, realizing she was talking to Joe's wife's brother.

"What, why they aren't married?" Donovan knew it was what she had meant.

Jeanie made a face. "Bad question?"

"Not really. I wondered the same thing myself after seeing the two of them together. Joe says they love each other, but they can't live with each other. It's weird to think that they can be as close as they are and not be together, you know?"

"Yeah, makes you know that all that bullshit about men and women not being able to be friends because of the sex thing is just that—bullshit," Jeanie said vehemently.

"Now tell me how you really feel," Donovan said, his grin lopsided.

Jeanie looked back at him for a long moment, then blew her breath out in a sigh. "I guess I've just had one too many guys try to pull that one on me." Then she gave him a very explicit look. "What about you? Do you think men and women can be friends without sex being a part of it?"

Donovan compressed his lips in a sardonic smile and looked down, shaking his head. "I'm damned either way here, aren't I?" he said finally, and Jeanie couldn't help but laugh as she nodded.

"So you don't think they can be? Friends, I mean."

"I think people can do anything they want, they just have to work at it. But Midnight and Joe aren't exactly the best example of that. They have had sex, you know."

"Well, I've heard they were together a long time ago, before they met Randy and Rick…"

"And they had a short affair about five years ago…"

"Oh, during all that stuff with your sister, right?" Jeanie asked, regretting it instantly.

Donovan nodded, looking serious.

"I'm sorry, Donovan, I didn't mean to trivialize it. That must have been a really rough time for all of you."

"It wasn't fun, no. It was shortly before I applied for the department, and my family name was still mud then." He shook his head.

"It didn't make things easy."

"But your sister was acquitted."

Donovan gave a short, sarcastic laugh. "All cops know that being acquitted doesn't make you innocent," he said derisively.

"But Randy was," Jeanie said, her voice sure.

"I know that, Joe knew it, Midnight, Rick, and all of FORS knew it too, but that doesn't mean everyone did. They figured because Midnight and Joe had connections at the top, it was all a whitewash."

"People actually think the chief would let an attempted cop killer go free? What the hell's wrong with them?"

Donovan sat back in his chair, looking every bit the veteran cop and every day his twenty-seven years and then some. "People don't always think logically. People saw that one cop, a veteran cop, went down for trying to kill Joe and Midnight. The way they saw it, Randy should have gone down with him. If nothing else, for having an affair with the guy."

"For that she should go to jail?" Jeanie said, shaking her head. "These people are idiots. If people went to jail for having affairs, then half the department would be incarcerated as we speak!"

Donovan laughed at that one. "Tell me about it."

After dinner, Donovan refilled their wine, pouring the last of the bottle into her glass. They sat on his couch and talked for a while longer. She asked him about some of his more interesting cases and watched him as he talked about them. Jeanie was finding that she liked him more the better she got to know him. He was direct with her where it counted, without being rude or pushy. He talked to her like she was already a police officer, happily explaining anything she didn't understand without derision. Another thing that she liked was that he didn't talk to her like a "woman" when it came to police work; he talked to her like a fellow officer. On the other hand, when they touched on more personal things his voice softened and his eyes would fix on her. Donovan Curtis was the first man she'd ever met that could make the differentiation between the woman and the career goal. Jeanie definitely liked that.

She had long since finished her glass of wine, and as they talked she'd occasionally take his glass out of his hand and take a sip. At one point Donovan gave her a wry grin. "Like that wine, I take it?"

"You could say that." She grinned, feeling just a little tingle of a buzz in her head. She liked the feeling of having him around; it made her feel more secure somehow, knowing he was the kind of person he was. There was no fear that he'd try to take advantage of her. Though she realized that she did want him to do more than talk to her—but she wasn't sure how to make that happen. He was sitting at the end of the couch with his back against the arm, turned toward her. She was next to him in close proximity, basically within the semicircle his arm on the back of the couch had created. It was very comfortable having him this close to her. He smelled of Tommy cologne, and he looked incredible; she found it difficult to concentrate on the conversation once her thoughts had taken this direction.

As she watched, he drained his glass, and without thinking she made an indignant sound. He looked over at her and saw that she was staring bereft at the empty glass in his hand.

"Oops," he said, grinning.

"Oh sure, oops." She gave him a mock glare. "All I wanted was one more taste… you rat."

Donovan looked at her for a long moment. "There is a way to solve that…" Without another word he leaned down, kissing her gently. Her hands went around his neck immediately, as if she'd been waiting for him to do this—she had. What had started out as a gentle kiss turned more ardent immediately. Donovan slid his hand around her waist, pulling her closer to him. Jeanie moved willingly.

When the kiss finally ended his hand kept her close as he looked down into her eyes. "I have to admit," he said softly, "I've wanted to do that all night."

Jeanie looked back at him, still trying to catch her breath from the unexpected kiss. "And I've been wanting you to do that all night. And last night too," she added impulsively.

Donovan looked surprised for a moment, but then started to nod. "Yeah, I wanted to kiss you then too."

"Well, why didn't you?"

Donovan smiled. "Guess I was afraid you'd slug me."

"Well, you were wrong, Sergeant Curtis."

"Guess I was." He leaned down to take possession of her lips again, pulling her even closer than before. Her hands slid along his back, moving to the front of his shirt, sliding up his chest to his shoulders. He gripped her waist tighter, then moved his hand to her waist, his other slipping into her hair, caressing her neck. Within minutes they were both breathless.

Donovan finally pulled back to look at her again. She stared back at him, her eyes filled with the same desire reflected in his.

"I have a confession to make," Jeanie said softly.

"What's that?" Donovan replied huskily, still staring into her eyes.

"Yesterday when I was here, I wanted to check out more than just your kitchen…"

"Mmhmm…"

"I wanted to see your bedroom too," she said, then looked chagrined as she held up her hands. "Don't get me wrong, I just think a guy's bedroom says a lot about him. Where he sleeps and all… ya know?" She looked at him, hoping he hadn't taken her meaning the wrong way.

"In other words, you want to see the bedroom, not necessarily the bed. Right?" he said, a smile playing at his lips.

"Yeah…" she said, grinning shyly.

"I understand." He nodded. Then he stood up, pulling her to her feet. "Come on, I promise your virtue is safe with me." He sounded like he was half joking, but she could see he meant it.

She followed him down the hallway and into his room. At the door he flipped on the light and held his arm out to her, indicating she should precede him. She walked inside and wasn't too surprised to see that the room was as neat as the rest of the house. It was done in a lot of wood and hunter green, which seemed to fit him pretty well. She walked around, looking at the pictures on the dresser and the various things lying about. She noted that his badge, gun, and spare magazines were laid out on the dresser. The gun was, of course, holstered. She picked up his badge. The gold shone brightly on the shield, and she ran her finger over the ribbon emblazoned with the title "Sergeant." Looking back at Donovan, she saw that he had taken a seat on his bed, leaning back against the headboard to watch her.

She held up the badge. "Someday I'm going to have one of these."

Donovan nodded. "Probably higher up than that."

Jeanie set the badge down and moved her hand to the holstered weapon, then looked back at Donovan. "May I?"

"You know how to handle a gun?" he asked, his tone all sergeant.

"All four of my brothers are law enforcement—I've been around them my whole life."

Donovan nodded and she picked up the weapon, sliding it out of the holster. She surprised him by depressing the magazine release and checking the chamber by pulling back the slide and removing the bullet there. She glanced over at him, and he raised an eyebrow at her. Then she lifted the gun to point it toward the wall, looking down the sights.

"What is this?" she said, looking over at him as she set the gun down.

"HK in forty-five," he supplied, and was further surprised when she nodded in obvious understanding.

"More knock-down power, right?" She picked up the bullet she'd taken from the chamber and slid it back into the magazine, then slid the magazine into the well in the gun, clicking it into place.

"Right," Donovan said, watching her with fascination. She certainly did know guns.

"Guess that comes from having a rangemaster for a brother-in-law, huh?" she asked as she reholstered the weapon.

"Yes, it does. Do me a favor?"

"What?"

"Re-chamber my round, please," he said caustically.

"Oh, sorry," she said, pulling back the slide deftly to re-chamber the bullet she had put back in the magazine.

Donovan shook his head, never having seen a woman who wasn't already a police officer so good with a weapon. "I'd say you know weapons," he said, grinning.

"Told you," she said with a smile, realizing suddenly that she'd impressed him.

He nodded. "I guess you did."

Jeanie walked over to him, glancing at the clock.

"Ready to leave already?" Donovan asked.

"No. I just have the world's most overprotective parents. They don't allow me to stay out all night if I want to continue to live under their roof."

"Ah," Donovan said, nodding.

"Ah," Jeanie echoed, surprising him by climbing up to straddle his outstretched legs, sitting down on his lap and looking down at him. Without a word she leaned down to kiss him. His lips met hers eagerly as he pulled her body flush with his.

After a long, deep kiss, he looked up at her. "Thought we were going to avoid the bed in here," he said lightly.

"Couldn't help it," Jeanie replied, sitting back and sliding her hands down his chest. Donovan closed his eyes momentarily in response to her touch, and that made a bolt of excited electricity go through her. He was very surprised when her hands moved to the buttons of his shirt, undoing them. He continued to watch her as she pulled his shirt tails out of his pants and laid the shirt open. "That's what I thought," she said, looking into his eyes.

"What's that?" he asked, his voice husky again.

"That you had an incredible chest. I saw a little bit of it when I came in this evening—I wanted to see more," she said, surprising herself with her candor.

Her honesty was obviously affecting him too, because he reached up and pulled her down to him again, his lips covering hers hungrily. Jeanie was astounded at how affected she was by him, her body craving everything she'd run away from in the past. Eventually it became obvious to her that she wanted a lot more from him than he would presume to take. She sat up, unbuttoning her blouse. Donovan's teal eyes watched her, but she could see he was cautious suddenly. His hands rested on her hips; she reached down and moved them to the bare skin now exposed. Again his reaction to her action was to close his eyes for a moment, as if the sensation were too much to take. It served to spur her on. She placed her hands on his bare shoulders then slid them downward suggestively, her nails leaving a light trail over his skin.

"Jay…" was all he said, but the sound of desire in his voice was too much. She wanted him like she'd wanted no other man, and she wasn't sure she wanted to deny that need right now. Not allowing herself to stop and think, she removed her blouse and bra. In spite of her weight on him, Donovan sat up, sliding his hands around her back and pulling her to him. The feel of his skin against hers only made the warmth inside her grow stronger. His lips were on hers again, and she refused to think about what was happening. She wanted him, and if things got out of hand, if she didn't stop this time, she didn't care.

She was actually surprised when Donovan moved to lay her down on the bed beneath him. His lips trailed down her neck to her breasts, and for a moment she couldn't even breathe, the sensation was so incredible. When he continued farther she tensed automatically. He sensed it and surprised her by looking up at her, his teal eyes burning.

"Do you trust me?" he asked softly.

Jeanie looked at him for a long moment, thinking the last time he'd asked her that was the night before at the bar. She'd answered him easily then. "Yes," she said finally. At this point she didn't care what he did. He continued to kiss her as he removed her skirt—she'd long since kicked off her shoes, back in the living room. Before long she lay naked in front of him, but she was surprisingly devoid of any shame. He had moved to lie on his side next to her, his hand caressing her skin.

"You have the most beautiful body," he whispered against her lips before kissing her again. His hands slid over her body, and Jeanie couldn't think of anything but Donovan, his lips, his body so close to hers, and his hands. Before she realized what was happening he brought her to orgasm and she writhed next to him, feeling like every nerve in her body was screaming. Afterward, as he kissed her gently on the temple, nuzzling her hair, she thought about what had happened. They hadn't made love; he had taken her to the heights of passion without taking anything else. She looked up at him and couldn't resist the urge to kiss him again. Her body still ached at the ecstasy he'd just brought her to, and in a way she wanted to thank him, to show him how good it had felt. Their kiss was lingering, and Jeanie realized he had been cheated in all of this.

"Well, that wasn't exactly fair to you, was it?" she said softly.

"I'll live," Donovan said, his tone low. "That's what they make that 'cold' faucet option on the shower for." His smile was engaging, and Jeanie couldn't believe this man was real. She kissed him again, and this time pushed him to his back and slid her body over his. She could feel him against her, and it was obvious he was in dire need of that cold shower. As her body moved over his, she heard him groan softly. He had his head pushed back deep against the pillows, his eyes closed. She pressed her lips to his chest then, kissing him gently, feeling him respond immediately.

"Jay..." he groaned. "Babe..." His hands moved to her body, holding her firmly against him.

"Ha, so you are human," she said softly, moving to kiss his neck.

"Way too human right now," Donovan said, his voice colored with desire.

Jeanie didn't say anything. She kissed him, her mouth all but devouring his. She was surprised to realize she wanted him again already. The feel of her skin against his as well as the knowledge of how much he wanted her at that moment was a heady combination.

"Make love to me, Donovan," she said, her lips still against his. "I want you."

Without another word he moved to do as she asked. Just before moving his body into hers, he looked down at her, watching her eyes intently. "Are you sure about this, Jay?"

"I'm sure that I want you more than I've ever wanted any man in my life, Donovan. Make love to me." She sounded so sure, and Donovan didn't argue with her; he was way past the point of being able to, anyway. He made love to her then. He was gentle with her, careful to cause her as little pain as possible and quick to make her forget the pain after it was inflicted. He took them both to heights she couldn't have even imagined, and she found herself clutching him as she cried out when they reached that plateau together.

They lay together afterward, she on her back, he on his side. His head rested against her torso, his arms wrapped tightly around her waist. Her arms were around him too, caressing his shoulders and back. She couldn't believe that she had done what they had just done, but there was no turning back now. She was no longer a virgin.

"You okay?" Donovan said, his face still against her skin.

"I'm more than okay. I... I can't even begin to describe how I feel right now," she said honestly.

He looked up at her then, his eyes worried. "Are you sorry?" he asked, concern coloring his voice.

Jeanie looked thoughtful for a moment, then shook her head. "No, I guess I should tell you though that I don't usually go this far on the first date."

Donovan grinned. "I kinda guessed that, yeah."

"I can't even believe I did this with you..." she said, her thoughts swirling about in her head.

"Thanks..." Donovan said chidingly.

She laughed. "You know what I mean."

"No, I don't. Explain it to me," he said seriously.

"Well, I just... I really don't know you that well. Hell, some of the guys I've dated haven't gotten me as far as you got me in the first ten minutes in here," she said, indicating the bed. "Half the time I wouldn't let them touch bare skin for at least six months."

"Yikes," Donovan said, indicating sympathy for the other men she'd dated.

"Yeah, tell me about it. And here I go out with you one time, and have dinner with you once and I hand over my virginity just like that."

"You're awfully calm about it."

She rolled her eyes. "Oh, don't worry, I'll freak out about it in a few hours."

"Well, that puts me right at ease," he said, looking chagrined.

"Donovan, I asked you to make love to me, not the other way around. Don't feel guilty about it. I'm not sorry I did it with you— I'm just surprised, that's all. You were perfect, fantastic, better than I dreamed of in all these years of anticipation," she said convincingly.

"Alright then." He moved to lie on his back and pulled her with him so that he held her at his side. One arm was wrapped around her shoulders, his free hand caressing her cheek. "Thank you for letting me be your first. I have to tell you, I'm a little stunned myself. If someone had told me last night where we'd be tonight at this time, I would have put the person in jail for lunacy."

Jeanie laughed. "You and me both, Sergeant."

They fell asleep together for a while, and Donovan woke with a start, suddenly worried about whatever curfew her "overprotective" parents imposed on her.

"Jay," he said, touching her cheek.

She stirred, then opened her eyes. "Hmmm…" She looked up at him sleepily.

"God, you even look good when you just wake up… unreal." He

smiled. "I woke you because I thought you had to be home by a certain time."

Jeanie glanced at the clock on his nightstand. "Usually they expect me home by two, but they're out of town so I have some leeway."

"Well, I want you to stay as long as you can, but I don't want to get you into any trouble with your parents either," he said, sounding like the older man again.

"I can stay a couple more hours…" She kissed his shoulder. "The question is, can you make love to me again in that amount of time?"

"I'll do my best…" he said, moving to kiss her.

She ended up leaving three hours later. At home, she lay in her own bed, already missing the warmth of his body next to hers. It was going to be a long day…

****

Christian waited patiently outside Harrod's, garnering a number of admiring glances from women on the street. He leaned indolently on the hood of his black Jaguar, a cigarette in his mouth. He was wearing his customary black chinos and black leather ankle boots, but instead of his usual black shirt he wore a sapphire blue one, making his light blue eyes stand out more. When Geneva stepped out of the store, she caught her breath at the sight of him. Even after six months of seeing him, Christian's incredible good looks still made her feel weak, not something she was normally given to. Predictably, Christian made no move to help her with her packages, only standing when she walked over to him. He reluctantly opened the trunk of the car for her when she gestured to him with her full hands.

Once in the car she gave a frustrated sigh, leaning back in the seat and glancing over at him. She caught his wry grin and knew she had once again fallen for his bait. Christian consistently irritated her, and she had long since come to find out that he did so on purpose.

"Where to now?" he asked, not looking over at her.

"Home," she said, her voice controlled. "We have a party tonight, remember."

Christian's brow furrowed as he looked over at her. "No, I don't remember. A party where?"

"At the home of Lord and Lady Glenenshire," she said, expecting him to be impressed. She didn't see him tense.

"I have plans," he said, his tone short.

"Cancel them."

Christian's light blue eyes narrowed at her, and she could see a fight brewing. "I told you about this last week, Blue. Don't give me that look."

"Last week, you say?" Christian replied disbelievingly. "I don't think so."

"Blue…" Geneva began soothingly. "I know I told you we had a party, and I absolutely must have you there with me—Lady Glenenshire is the worst at matchmaking. She's so in love with her husband she thinks everyone should be so happy." She made a face, indicating her opinion about being "in love."

Christian gave a short, disgusted laugh, which Geneva assumed had to do with what she had said. He was actually thinking about

Lady Glenenshire's husband and how "in love" he must be with his wife. He wondered how Lady Glenenshire would feel about her dear husband's illegitimate son—would she "love" him too? Christian's lips twisted into an evil grin as a thought occurred to him. Maybe going to this party wouldn't be such a bad idea.

"Fine, I'll go," he said evenly.

Geneva looked over at him, surprised. He didn't usually change his mind that easily. Since he seemed to be in a good mood, she decided to broach another subject with him.

"Blue... I've been thinking..."

"And?" Christian said when she didn't continue.

"Well, I think you should give up your flat," she said, rushing on when she saw the look on his face as he started to shake his head. "You're at my house most of the time anyway. It would make things so much simpler, don't you think?"

Again he gave a derisive laugh. "No, I think it'd make it easier for you, but it ain't gonna happen." His voice brooked no argument, but Geneva wasn't one to take a warning.

"Why not?" she snapped, angry at his tone.

"Because I need my own place to go, and I'm not givin' it up."

"Good Lord, Blue. We've been together for six months—you'd think you would trust me by now. I'm not trying to clip your proverbial wings, I just want to simplify our lives a little. Cut down on all this running around, and all that."

"I like the running around," Christian said, his tone taking on an edge. She was pushing him, and he didn't like being pushed.

"Christian..." Geneva began, slipping. She'd finally discovered his real first name, having found it on a bill in his apartment.

His raised voice cut her off. "Don't call me that." The muscles in his jaw tensed as he clenched his teeth. "That's not my name."

"It's your given name," Geneva replied, immediately sorry she'd said it.

His eyes blazed in anger. "It's my father's name, not mine."

"I'm sorry, Blue," she said, softening her tone and placing her hand on his leg. "I just want you at the house. I want to wake up with you there." Her voice softened more as she all but whispered, "I love you…"

Christian looked down at her hand, his lips twisting in a sardonic grin as he shook his head. She had just said the wrong thing. "Geneva," he said, his tone ice cold. "We have a business arrangement. I escort you to parties, and you pay me." He looked her straight in the eye, his light blue eyes as cold as his voice. "And sometimes I fuck you. But that's all there is—you got that?"

Geneva was too stunned to reply. She had far overestimated her hold on him.

The past six months had been incredible to her. Christian had been a superior pupil. She'd taught him a number of things in the bedroom, drawing from her extensive and varied experiences. Christian had been willing to learn, not exactly the overeager youth she was used to, but moldable. He took everything she taught him and fit it to his own style of lovemaking, which tended toward the more aggressive and dominating, which suited Geneva perfectly. She was tired of the young men that basically lay down at her feet and begged her to do anything to them. Christian Collins never begged. He took what he wanted, giving back exquisite pleasure in the process. He was

101

not the tender type. After sex, he would either get up and leave or move away to the other side of the bed. He didn't "hold" or "cuddle"; he didn't have to. After sex he didn't care to be near any woman—he never had. Geneva was no exception. He also wasn't one to give compliments or use endearing names. Christian was indeed totally different from any man Geneva had ever encountered, and it made her all the more determined to change him and bring him under her control.

No more was said about Christian's flat. He dropped her off in silence and drove away. She called him once inside her house and told him to pick her up at seven o'clock. Geneva wondered idly if he'd even show up. He did appear, and again her breath caught in her throat at the sight of him. He wore a navy blue polished-silk Armani suit with a jacket that cut in at the waist, making his fantastic body and slim waist contrast his obvious build. Under the suit he wore a crisp white banded-collar shirt. His jet black hair shone in the lights of her foyer, his light eyes seeming to glow in his ever-tanned face. Geneva wanted him the moment she set eyes on him, but she knew he wouldn't make love to her then. She knew he was still angry about her comments earlier.

Christian was very satisfied with Geneva's reaction to his appearance. He had made a point of looking especially good that evening. He had an objective this night.

Christian Jeremy Sinclair, the current Lord of Glenenshire, stood greeting his guests. His friends called him Jeremy; only his parents and his wife ever called him Christian. Christian Collins walked in the front doors of his father's home, looking for all intents and purposes like the lord of the manor himself. His confidence shone in his light blue eyes, even as they lowered at the sight of his father. It was a fight for Christian to control his desire to strike the man as he shook hands with him. Jeremy had no idea who he was shaking hands with. He had long since forgotten the beautiful little Spanish maid he'd seduced and impregnated then fired. The only thought that occurred to the lord was that this young man had a rather firm handshake, even if he wouldn't make direct eye contact. Even that thought was fleeting as he saw Geneva. The Lord of Glenenshire had a long-standing lust for beautiful women, which he managed through great pains to keep hidden from his wife.

Christian recognized the look of desire in his father's eyes, exact mirrors of his own, and saw the beginnings of an opportunity.

After a moment-too-long embrace and a whispered greeting, Jeremy released Geneva, looking down at her again. Christian stood to the side, watching, waiting patiently. When Geneva joined him, his look was knowing even as he grinned.

"What?" Geneva asked.

"He's got one for you, don't he?" Christian said, not bothering to sound jealous, because he wasn't.

"Jeremy?" Geneva whispered as she steered him farther into the formal living room.

"Don't play dumb with me, Eve," Christian said coolly. "He's got a hard-on for you, and you want me around to make him jealous, right?"

Geneva looked back at him, her eyes wide. Even after all the time they'd spent in bed together, she could never adjust to his direct manner. If he thought something, he said it. After a long moment's hesitation, she nodded resolutely, thinking he'd be angry. She was astounded to see him smile brilliantly, with a glint in his eyes she didn't understand.

"I think," he said, taking her arm and pulling her closer to him, bringing her face up to his, "tonight would be a good night to take him up on the offer."

"Blue!" Geneva said, ever surprised at him. "We are in his home, and his wife is here… or have you forgotten what I told you about her?" she asked in a harsh whisper.

"I haven't forgotten," Christian replied evenly.

"But why?" She saw the irritation spark in his eyes immediately. "Fine," she said, not wanting to argue with him. "I'll have a go at him… He is a very handsome man…" She let her voice trail off, hoping to catch some jealousy in his eyes, but she saw nothing at all.

A look crossed Christian's face that she didn't understand, but before she could question him, the Lady of Glenenshire entered the room.

"Geneva, whatever are you doing in here?" the lady of the house said chidingly.

"Sarah!" Geneva said, her voice the epitome of culture as she crossed to the auburn-haired woman, hugging her. Then she turned to Christian. "Sarah, this is my friend, Blue."

"Blue?" Sarah's eyes went to Christian and widened in surprise at the handsome man standing before her.

Christian smiled, allowing it to touch his eyes, making them twinkle and making both women want to sigh. He gallantly took her hand and gently raised it to his lips, watching her eyes. "It's a nickname," he said smoothly.

"And I can see why…" Sarah said, her voice coming out a little on the breathless side. She looked to Geneva then. "So this is the dashing man you've been about with, causing an absolute uproar."

Geneva smiled and nodded, reaching over to take Christian's hand, suddenly feeling it necessary to hold on to him. She'd seen the look in Sarah Sinclair's eyes; the woman wanted him. She couldn't believe it! Sarah Sinclair was legendary for her devotion to her husband. Everyone knew that Jeremy was in love with his wife, but it was also known that he had strayed on occasion. But Sarah had always been considered a saint amongst the married set. Geneva realized Christian was causing more of a stir than she had actually wanted this time. As Sarah led them from the room, Geneva pulled him back, looking searchingly up at him. "What are you doing, Blue?"

Christian looked back at her, his eyes giving nothing away. "Just do what you were told to, and you'll get what you want," he said, his tone cool.

"What does that mean?" she asked, her voice taking on an edge.

"It means," Christian said, lowering his voice as he stepped closer to her, reaching up to stroke her breast seductively. "If you do this, I'll reconsider giving up the flat."

Geneva gasped at the feel of his hand as well as his words. She nodded blindly, not able to think past the sensations he was causing.

When they joined the rest of the dinner party, Geneva looked a little flushed, but she was smiling widely. She chatted happily with the guests, her eyes straying over to Christian, who was inexplicably deep in conversation with Sarah Sinclair. After dinner, many of the men retired to the drawing room with the customary cigars and brandy. Some women joined them, others continuing their gossip session in the sitting room. Geneva accompanied the men, making a point of getting close to Jeremy. His eyes had been on her a great deal that evening, and Geneva hadn't been able to deny the thought that it would be a welcome change to have a man that really wanted her. Christian always left her with the feeling that she had imposed upon him, and she hated it. She missed having a man panting at her feet.

A half hour into a conversation about the United Nations, Geneva saw Jeremy slip out the side door of the drawing room. After a moment's hesitation she followed. Coming through the doorway, she was surprised to find him lounging against the opposite wall, as if waiting for her. He had been.

"I've been watching you," Jeremy said, his voice low.

"I know you have…"

Jeremy watched her for a moment longer, then pushed off the wall and took two steps, bringing him face to face with her. Without a word he pushed her against the door she'd just come through and closed behind her, his lips coming down on hers in a crushing kiss. Minutes later, he took her by the hand and led her down the hallway to one of the guest bedrooms. There he removed her dress and took her on the bed. The entire time he was making love to her, Geneva could think only of Christian. It was thoughts of the blue-eyed devil that made her reach her climax, not the man inside her.

"Do you read?" Sarah Sinclair asked, glancing over her shoulder at Christian.

"I can," Christian said, his look direct, his lips set in a wry grin.

Sarah laughed lightly, turning to face him. "I meant do you like to read?"

Christian looked contemplative for a moment, his eyes on the floor, then looked back up at her. "Reading's not one of my favorite activities, no," he said, his voice screaming a come-on.

"What kind of activities do you like then?" Sarah asked, watching him. He was sitting casually on the edge of her husband's desk, his long legs stretched out in front of him and crossed at the ankles. He had removed his jacket, and his hands rested on either side of him, gripping the desk. She was pacing like a nervous animal, and Christian loved it.

"More… physical ones."

"I see…" Sarah said tremulously. She continued to move about the room, as if looking for a way out but not really wanting it.

Christian pinned her with a look, making her stop. "Come here," he said, his tone commanding. She did as he said, moving to stand in front of his outstretched legs. He pulled his legs in, grabbing her hand as he did and pulling her toward him. His lips met hers, and she groaned at the contact. He held her waist and lifted her so that she straddled him. Drawing on many of the things that Geneva had taught him, Christian made love to her. Eventually they moved to the leather couch, and he proceeded to excite her beyond all of her expectations. As he took her, his body sliding into hers, he felt a stab of guilt, but the hard knot of his heart refused to acknowledge it. As he felt her reaching her climax, he pulled back and looked down at her, his light blue eyes so like his father's.

"I want to hear you say my name, my given name," he said, his tone harsh with restrained desire.

"What is it?" Sarah asked, barely able to think coherently, her body screaming for release.

"Christian," he said, looking directly into her eyes. He moved back into her, even as he saw her eyes widen. She searched his face even as her body responded to him. Again he brought her to the very edge of her climax and pulled back, looking down at her, his eyes narrowed, breathing heavily himself. "Say it," he said, his voice a husky command, his body moving to edge her closer, making her willing to say or do anything.

He continued to move in her until her nails dug into his back as she reached her climax, crying out, saying his name over and over, not caring what it meant.

Afterward, he stood, staring down at her. She looked back at him, her eyes reflecting shame and surprise. After a long minute, Christian moved to pick up his discarded clothes, the muscles in his back rippling. When he was dressed, he turned around. She was sitting up; he tossed her dress to her. She pulled it over her head, but her eyes didn't leave his, a question clear in them.

Without saying a word he walked out of the room and through the house, a very satisfied grin on his face. He had accomplished what he'd wanted to. He made his way out to his car and lit a cigarette. He stood leaning against the Jaguar, staring up at the dark sky. The guilty feeling returned, but he pushed it away angrily.

Later that night, Christian sat on Geneva's bed, watching her get undressed. He still wore his suit pants and the white shirt, now unbuttoned and open. "So did you get him or not?" he said conversationally.

Geneva looked over at him from her dressing table. "Jeremy?"

"You fuck someone else tonight?"

"Blue…" she said, starting to chide him for his language but realizing she'd just end up in a fight with him. "As a matter of fact, I did," she said, standing and moving to the bed, looking down at him. She longed to see a flash of jealousy in his eyes, but none was forthcoming.

"Was he worth the effort?" Christian asked derisively.

"Yes…" Geneva replied, forcing enthusiasm into her voice.

Christian looked at her for a long moment, then reached a hand up, moving it down her body from her shoulder to her waist. Geneva shivered involuntarily. He pulled her down to him, sliding her body along his. His light blue eyes stared directly into hers, pinning her. "Was he as good as me?" he asked, without even a hint of jealousy in his voice but a truckload of seduction.

Geneva couldn't even think to lie to him. "No," she replied simply, giving in to her desire for him and kissing him. He spent the next two hours reminding her how good he was.

Afterward, he lay on his stomach, his arms wrapped around the pillow under his head, his face turned toward her. She lay on her side, facing him, her hand resting on his shoulder. She always tried to keep some physical contact with him, when he'd let her.

"So why did you want me to sleep with Jeremy?" she asked, raising an eyebrow at him. "Just so you could show me how much better you are than a lord?"

Christian looked at her for a long, measured moment, then shrugged. "No, so I could fuck his wife."

Geneva pulled her hand away from him as if she'd been burned, staring disbelievingly at him. He laughed, his eyes glittering in the semi-darkness of the room. "What kind of devil are you, Christian Collins?"

His eyes narrowed at her use of his given name, but then he grinned. "The one and only."

"You don't think I actually believe you slept with Sarah Sinclair, do you?" she said, sitting up and looking down at him.

"I don't care if you believe it or not. It wasn't for your benefit—it was for mine," he said, his voice cool.

"And what did you get out of it?" Geneva snapped, thinking Sarah had enticed him away with more money.

"I got to fuck my father's wife and hear her scream my name." His eyes captured hers. "And his."

Geneva stared back at him, horrified. "Your father's wife?" Christian nodded. "You're telling me that you're Jeremy Sinclair's son?"

"Yes."

Geneva looked at him for a long moment, and she knew, she knew he was telling the truth. Suddenly she could see all the resemblances, the eyes, the build, the strong jawline, and the cruelty too. "You used me," she said accusingly. A ruthless smile tugged at Christian's lips, even as he stared back into her eyes. He wasn't ashamed. "You bastard," Geneva breathed, her eyes narrowing, her hands curling into fists. She threw herself at him, her fists flailing, seeking to hurt him as he had just hurt her. She raked her nails at him, catching him on the throat before he defended himself.

He caught her wrists, holding her away from him. His hands tightened as she struggled against his grasp. His eyes were light blue pools of fire as he narrowed them at her. "Don't make me hurt you, Eve, because I will."

"You can't hurt me any more than you have, you monster," she screamed.

"I can break you in half, Eve, and don't think I won't if you push me too far." His voice was like cold steel, and Geneva couldn't believe what he was saying. She couldn't believe she actually loved this man. Maybe he was, as he had said many times, the devil himself.

"Let go of me!" she said desperately. "Please…" Her voice softened as she looked down into his eyes. She saw no caring there, no love, no emotion other than antipathy.

Christian released her, shoving her away from him. He got up from the bed, moving to pull on his pants, feeling her eyes on him the entire time. When he looked at her, she was sitting on the bed. She had tears in her eyes, but they didn't even faze him. She had used him for six months. She had used his face, his body, and his presence to make all her friends jealous. She had allowed everyone to look at him, as if he were an animal on display. She'd traded sexual comments with them, talking about him as if he didn't exist. Now she was getting her comeuppance, he couldn't even begin to feel sorry for her. Without a word he picked up his jacket and walked out of the house. He strode to the Jaguar KX8 and climbed inside, starting the car with a roar. He threw it into gear and drove away.

Christian spent the next hour speeding through the byways of England's countryside. The stereo cranked Def Leppard's dark-toned album Slang. The song "Deliver Me" captured his mood perfectly. It started out low and dark and turned grinding and angry at the chorus; the words were fitting as well.

Eventually he made his way to a London pub and drank the night away. Ironically it was the same pub Joseph Michael Sinclair had spent many a night in twenty-two years before.

Christian spent the next week alternating between the bars and lying passed out in his flat. Geneva called, leaving numerous messages on his machine. After two days he turned it off. One evening, after a long drinking session, Christian was dropped at his apartment by a cab. He went up to his flat and promptly passed out on his bed. He woke to the sensation of someone touching him. A hand trailed down his cheek, sliding down to touch his chest. Christian lashed out, grabbing the hand.

"Blue! It's me!" Geneva cried. She was kneeling next to him on the bed.

Christian shoved her away from him with enough force to make her fall to the floor with a yelp. He sat up, looking down at her in the half-light from the hallway. "What're you doin' here?"

Geneva drew herself up, narrowing her eyes at him. "I'm still paying for this apartment. I have a legal right to be here."

"Get outta here, Eve," Christian growled as he lay back on the bed.

"I own this apartment," Geneva said haughtily. "I paid for the clothes on your back, the food in your mouth, even the alcohol in your veins right now. I own the car you drive. I own you." The last was said with as much venom as she could muster. She had stood, looking down at him. She was surprised when his hands shot out, grabbing her by a handful of her coat.

Christian dragged her face to face with him, his eyes blazing, reaching up to grab a handful of her hair. "You own me, do you?" he grated, sounding more drunk than he had before. His eyes glittered as he stared into hers, his face a mask of barely controlled fury. "You own me… You have title to a great fuck, is that it?" His tone was cutting, with a tremor to it that should have set off warning bells in Geneva's mind. But she wasn't thinking about how dangerous Christian Collins was; she was thinking about how much she wanted him at that moment.

"That's right," she said, her tone still arrogant.

Christian's hand twisted in her hair, making her wince in pain, but she refused to cry out. She wasn't going to allow him to get the upper hand this time. She did own him, and she would make him do what she wanted him to. He let go of her coat and brought his hand up to her throat, staring back at her. Her eyes challenged him.

"And what is it you want now?" Christian said.

"You," she breathed, her body pressing against his illicitly.

"Of course you do," Christian replied disgustedly, even as he yanked off her coat, tearing at her clothes.

He took her a little while later, but it wasn't with the usual passion she incited from him. He was rough and hostile, hurting her. Geneva found herself pushing at him, trying to get away. Her nails dug into his chest, her breath coming in ragged gasps. She struggled against him, but he held her fast.

"This is what you wanted," Christian said, his voice a harsh whisper against her ear. "You wanted me… Well, this is me. Ain't so pretty, now is it?" His voice was as cold as ice and the look in his eyes was vicious.

"Blue, stop! Please," Geneva said, afraid of what he would do to her now. She could sense that he was still very drunk. She had learned in their six months together that he was a mean drunk. Geneva had realized too late that she had been foolish to push him the way she had, and now she was paying for that folly. His body slammed into hers, making her wince with every thrust. Her struggles only seemed to incite him more, so she gave up. Christian was much stronger than his appearance belied, and she knew he could really hurt her if he wanted to.

When it was over, Christian moved to sit on the side of the bed, panting. Anger still coursed through his veins, even as his breathing calmed. Geneva lay on his bed, watching his back. She could see his muscles tense as if he were fighting with himself, trying to reign in his emotions.

"Blue…" she said, moving to sit behind him, touching his back tentatively. She slid her hands along his shoulders soothingly, moving to kiss his back. He tensed immediately.

"You want to get me started again?" he said harshly.

"No," Geneva said, fear in her voice. "I don't want you to be angry anymore. I'm sorry I said all those things. I didn't mean them. I just couldn't stand being away from you, and that made me angry. I love you, Blue." Her voice was soft, and Christian had to swallow against the anger that welled up in him again at the sound of her lies.

"You love me," he repeated disbelievingly.

"Yes, Blue, I've told you that," Geneva replied softly.

"Yeah, you've told me." He shook his head, not in the mood to argue with her.

"But you don't love me, do you?" Geneva asked, hating the pleading in her voice.

Christian sighed, looking up at the ceiling, growing irritated again. "I don't believe in love, Eve. It's an emotion for suckers who have to find an excuse to stay with someone."

"Is that what you think I'm doing, making up an excuse to be with you?"

"Aren't you?" he said, surprising her by turning around, his light blue eyes watching hers. His face still showed the anger he was feeling, and Eve wasn't sure how to respond to his question.

"Jesus Christ, Eve!" Christian said, appalled. "I just raped you— doesn't that mean anything to you? Doesn't it make you mad? Aren't you the least bit pissed off?" His tone indicated that she had to be, and if she wasn't something was wrong with her.

Geneva looked back at him, her eyes widening when he used the word "rape" for what she would have described as "rough lovemaking." She began to see how willing she'd been to accept anything he would give her, and the thought made her ashamed and enraged at the same time.

"Yes, you bastard, it does. Does that make you happy?" she said, her voice taking on an edge.

Christian's lips twisted in a wry grin. "As a matter of fact, it does."

"Why? Why do you want me angry at you?"

"I don't want you to be angry. I want you to hate me," he said, with more emotion in his voice than she'd ever heard.

"I don't hate you…" Geneva said, her hand on his cheek.

He reached up, his hand covering hers, and then pulled it away from him, moving to hold her wrist. "You're not hearing me, Eve," he said, his voice taking on an angry edge. "I want you to hate me."

She shook her head. "I can't, Blue."

"Try harder," Christian said sharply. He started applying pressure to her wrist, making her writhe in an attempt to lessen the pain.

"You're hurting me," she cried.

"Good," Christian said venomously. "I've got your attention then. I want to hurt you, Eve. I want to make you mad, I want to make you scream, I want to hear you say you hate me."

"I can't, Blue," she said, her voice becoming desperate. He hadn't lessened his hold on her wrist and she was afraid he actually had the strength to break it. "I can't hate you—I need you."

It was Christian's turn to look surprised. He released her wrist and sat back, watching her in an almost predatory way. "Get out, now," he said, his tone dead.

"Blue…" Geneva said softly as she moved to touch him again.

"Get out!" he roared, his light blue eyes fiery.

Geneva didn't stop to think this time. She got up and, grabbing up her coat and the pieces of clothing he'd actually bothered to remove, all but ran out of the apartment.

Christian sat in the dark, thinking about what had just transpired. He hadn't been able to contain the rage he had felt when she'd told him that she "needed" him. It was a lie, he knew that. What Geneva Glasstone needed was an ego trip, and Christian Collins was the best there was for that purpose. The fact of the matter was, he was tired of being used. Tired of being treated like a mindless idiot because he looked so good. He was fully aware of his looks, and that they alone would get him quite far in this world. The idea of trading on his looks had always been alright with him, but now, because he

116

was literally making a living because of his appearance, it had become too much. He was using his looks to hurt people, and it had started to wear on him. Anger and hatred had become almost a way of life for him. He wondered mildly, as he sat there in the dark, if it was literally starting to eat away at his soul, because that was how it felt.

He fell asleep thinking along those lines, dreaming terrifying dreams of hell and death. He woke to the sound of his phone ringing. Without thinking he picked it up, realizing belatedly that it might be Geneva.

"Yeah?" he said harshly.

"Mr. Collins?" a tentative female voice said.

"Yes, what is it?"

"I'm calling from Prince William Hospital. Your mother is here. We've been trying to get ahold of you—she's very ill. Mr. Collins?"

Christian had sat up, almost gasping for breath at the size of the sudden knot in his stomach. "Is she…" he stammered, his voice almost a whisper. "She's okay, right?"

"Sir," the woman said, her voice more businesslike now. "You need to come down. Your mother's condition is precarious, and we need some information from you. Can you come?"

Christian was nodding, his mind racing. He realized then that the woman couldn't see him nodding. "Yes, I'll be there straight away," he said, and hung up. He got up, suddenly feeling a monster headache overtake him. He sat back down for a moment, then got up more slowly. He took a quick shower and threw on a pair of jeans and a black shirt, sitting down on the bed to pull on his boots. With still-wet hair, he grabbed his keys and black leather jacket and left the house. It was a blustery November morning in London, but he didn't even notice the chill as he walked to the Jaguar and got in.

He pulled up in front of the hospital a little while later. He walked inside and inquired where his mother would be. The nurse at the front desk checked her computer and told him she was three floors up. Many heads turned as he walked down the corridor toward the elevators. Christian paid them no mind; he was used to it.

Once at the floor his mother was on, he asked yet another nurse as to her whereabouts. The young woman was tongue-tied as she looked up into his handsome face. His eyes flashed impatiently at her as he was once again reminded that his looks could sometimes be a hindrance as well as an asset.

"Josephine Collins, could you look it up, for God's sake!" he finally said when it was apparent the woman wasn't going to get over herself.

"Oh!" she said, obviously regaining her senses. "Yes, sir, I'm so sorry. She's in 3B—it's just down the hall there. I'll call the doctor to come speak with you." Christian was nodding and already moving away.

Christian walked into the room and stopped, staring down at his mother. She looked very frail, lying in the hospital bed. She was pale, and her breathing looked labored as well. Christian walked over and sat down next to her, taking her hand in his. The look on his face could have melted even the hardiest of souls' hearts, but it was a look reserved only for his mother. No other woman had ever seen his face light up the way it did when she opened her eyes and looked at him.

"Christian…" she said, smiling. Her voice was very weak.

"Mum… What happened?" he said softly as he leaned down to kiss her cheek.

"I started feeling poorly a few months ago…" She trailed off, as if she had to draw enough strength to continue. "They say it's breast cancer, dear."

For a moment, Christian felt like his heart had stopped, like time and everything around him had frozen. A long minute later, he shook himself out of the shock, and forced himself to speak with a normal, calm voice. "Everything'll be fine, Mum. Don't you worry about it." Christian stood as he saw the doctor in the doorway. "I'll be right back, okay?"

He got up and went out into the hallway with the doctor.

"Mr. Collins, I'm Dr. Green." The man extended his hand to Christian. "Your mother is very ill. Her cancer is at a fairly advanced stage, and I'm afraid unless she has radical treatment soon, her chances aren't very good."

"Wait a minute," Christian said, holding up his hand. He couldn't believe this was happening. "Why—How has this happened?"

The doctor looked taken aback, his eyes blinking behind his coke-bottle glasses. "Apparently, sir, she has been experiencing pain for quite some time, but she didn't come to the hospital until it became overwhelming, and so the cancer wasn't caught as quickly as it could have been. Sir!" the doctor exclaimed when he saw that Christian had gone pale.

"Okay, okay," he said, nodding, staring unseeing as he went over what his mother and Dr. Green had said. "You talked about treatment—when can that be done?"

"Sir, it's not that easy. It isn't yet available for free in the UK, and having it done privately is very expensive…" The doctor trailed off as

Christian's eyes narrowed dangerously.

"You make the arrangements and I'll get the money, you got it?" he said, his voice a low threat.

The doctor just stared back at him, clearly intimidated.

"How much does it cost?" Christian asked, growing impatient. "The treatment, man! How much does it cost?"

"It's hard to say, sir. It could be a great deal—"

"Give me a figure." Christian clenched his teeth as the urge to hit the man welled up in him.

"A hundred thousand," the doctor said, naming the figure off the top of his head.

"Fine, I'll get it." Christian nodded, even as he his mind reeled. "How long will it take?" he said, his tone no-nonsense now, so much so that the doctor didn't bother trying to dissuade the young man any further.

"Well, fortunately, if you have the money, it's quite straightforward to source the treatment from America. It could be any time. The problem, sir, is that the ability to pay must be in place before it can be started—"

"How long do I have?"

"It could be as little as a matter of hours, sir," the doctor said, immediately seeing a hopeless look in the young man's eyes.

"I'll get it, you get the ball rolling," Christian said, turning to go back into the room to see his mother.

His mind was churning; he wasn't sure what he could do. He had some ideas, and he would resort to them if he needed to. He went in and spoke to Josephine for a few more minutes, but the need to get the money was all important in his mind.

CHAPTER 4

Christian left the hospital and went back to his flat, and after a few quick drinks, he drew up the courage to call his father. When the call was answered, Christian asked for Lord Glenenshire. The line was silent for a moment, then his father came on.

"Lord Glenenshire," Christian said, hesitant at first.

"Yes?" Jeremy said, unable to identify the voice on the end of the line.

"You and I met a week or so ago. I attended a dinner party your wife gave. I was with Geneva Glasstone..." He let his voice trail off, hoping his father would be remembering his encounter with Geneva.

"Yes, I believe I remember you."

"Yes, well, do you remember a maid you had about twenty-five years ago?" Christian asked, his tone still conversational.

"I... a maid, you say?" Jeremy said, sounding a little flustered.

"Yes, she was a Spanish maid, very beautiful. You seduced her too, I believe." Christian chose his words to show the lord he knew full well what had transpired between him and Geneva.

"I don't know what you're talking about!" Jeremy said, angry now, but Christian could hear the alarm there too.

"Oh, I think you do," he said coolly. "You got her pregnant, didn't you? And then fired her... didn't you?"

"Who do you think you are, young man? To accuse me of such acts?" The lord's voice was very aristocratic, as well as indignant.

"Who am I?" Christian said, moving in for the kill. "I'm your son."

There was silence on the other end of the line, and Christian could almost see his father's eyes narrow in thought. Indeed, Jeremy Sinclair's light blue eyes were narrowed. He was remembering the young man who had been with Geneva. He was remembering that he was very handsome, and that all the women at the party couldn't stop talking about him... Then he remembered the light blue eyes, so like his own family's; at the time it hadn't caught his attention, but now... Oh my God, was all Jeremy Sinclair could think.

"While I'm sure this comes as a surprise to you, Father," Christian said, not allowing him too much time to think, "and I know you'll be wanting that joyous happy reunion and all, I need your checkbook at the moment."

"What are you saying?" Jeremy replied, aghast.

"I'm saying I need a hundred thousand pounds. Now," Christian said, matter-of-fact.

"And I suppose I'm just to give it to you without question?" Jeremy said, regaining his wits quicker than Christian had hoped he would.

"No, but I could come down there now and we could have that happy reunion... You know, me, you, your wife..."

"If you come here, you'll be denied access to the house. I'll have you arrested for trespassing." Jeremy's voice was strong with the surety of a rich upbringing.

"I don't need to come down there. I just need to call the press—they'd be interested in this type of story."

"Try it, you little bastard, and I'll make sure you end up in jail for blasphemy."

"I don't think they jail people for that anymore, Father."

"Stop calling me that. You are no son of mine. I don't know what you're talking about, and I will not have this conversation go any further," Jeremy yelled, then slammed down the receiver.

Christian shook his head as the line disconnected. He had been pretty sure he wouldn't get the money from that end, but he had tried it just in case. He knew of another option that also had to do with his family roots but was less inflammatory. Christian was the nephew of a very rich publishing magnate, and his uncle had been very kind to his mother before she left Lord Glenenshire's home. He knew the story well; his mother had told it to him often enough.

Josephine had just come from telling Jeremy about the child she carried when, in her upset state, she'd run right into Joseph Matthew Sinclair.

"I'm sorry, sir," Josephine said, inclining her head to the man and trying to appear less upset.

"Never you mind that, miss," Joseph said, trying to catch the young woman's eyes. "And what has happened to you?" he asked kindly. Josephine looked up at him, her wide brown eyes surprised that he seemed to care. Joseph nodded, taking her hand and saying, "Come with me, dear."

He led her out into the garden, where he sat her down and talked with her. She finally admitted to him that she was pregnant with his brother's child. Joseph didn't seemed surprised in the least; nor did he accuse her of lying. She went on to tell him that Jeremy had fired her because, he said, she was lying. Joseph was very kind, asking what she would do. Josephine assured him that she could take care of herself, that she would return to the arms of her family in Spain.

"All the same," Joseph said, pulling a card out of his vest and writing on the back of it. Then he handed her the card face up. "That," he said, pointing to the name on the front, "is my barrister. And this"—he turned the card over—"is my number and address in London, if you need anything. I want you to keep this card," he said, his hand warm on hers, his light blue eyes staring into hers kindly.

Josephine had kept the card. She had never used it, but had cherished the thought that at least one of the Sinclairs had been kind. She told Christian he was in reality part of a great family of people, that his uncle was the kindest of men. Josephine had been very sad when Christian was three years old and she heard Joseph Sinclair and his lovely wife, Cynthia, had been killed in an accident. She had been upset to learn that Scotland Yard had accused their only son of murdering them. Josephine had known it wasn't true. She had seen then-seventeen-year-old Joseph Sinclair the Fourth with his parents, and had seen the obvious love and respect he held for them. She didn't believe the accusations for a minute.

Growing up, Christian had heard about the Sinclairs incessantly. Never about his father, but about his father's brother and nephew. When Christian was fifteen his mother had excitedly shown him the society pages that chronicled Joseph's marriage to Randissi Curtis. Christian had looked at the pictures with indifference. But he had taken the paper to his room later and read every detail of the

125

wedding, dreaming that someday he'd meet this rich cousin of his. He had long since given up on this dream.

Now, as he drove over to his mother's home to look for the card Joseph Sinclair senior had given her, he thought about his cousin again. He wondered idly if he was still married, aware that these society marriages rarely lasted. He knew the odds were that the money wouldn't come from this source either, and that he'd basically have to sell his soul to Geneva to get the cash, but he wanted that to be a last resort.

At his mother's apartment he dialed the number on the front of the card, thankful that Joseph senior had given his mother his barrister's card as well as his own.

A woman answered. "Hello?"

"Yes, ma'am," Christian said politely. "I need to speak with Barrister Debenshire, please."

"Hold on a moment," the woman said, obviously not surprised to receive a phone call for the barrister at home. Christian hadn't tried the office phone, figuring it may have changed after Joseph senior died. He waited, tapping his fingers on his mother's nightstand, where he had finally located the card.

"Yes, this is Robert Debenshire. How can I help you?"

"Sir," Christian said hesitantly, suddenly not sure what to say; begging wasn't something he was used to doing. "My name is Christian Collins. You don't know me, but my mother knew a previous employer of yours..."

"Yes..." Robert prompted, noting the young man's hesitancy.

"The employer was Joseph Sinclair."

"I think you might be confused, young man. I am still Joseph Sinclair's barrister."

"Oh," Christian said, realizing he had saved himself a little more work. "I meant Joseph Sinclair senior, but you're the son's barrister as well?"

"Yes, I am," Robert said, sounding surprised. "Joseph senior, you say?"

"Yes, my mother met him when she worked for his brother, Christian Jeremy Sinclair."

"Ah, yes. And what is it I can do for you, young man?" Robert asked, always ready to get down to business.

"Well, you see, sir, your previous employer gave my mother your card and told her if she ever needed anything to contact him or you. I, uh… well…" Christian paused, suddenly realizing he may be way off in looking in this direction, taking for granted more than he should have.

"Go on, son," Robert said gently, having detected the urgency in the young man's voice.

"Well, sir, she's in the hospital, and she needs urgent private treatment. We don't have the money for it, and I guess I was hoping…"

"That I could get you the money?" Robert supplied; there was no accusation in his voice that Christian could detect.

"Frankly, yes," Christian said matter-of-factly.

Robert was silent for a long moment. "How much do you need?"

"A hundred thousand," Christian said, mouthing the figure and rolling his eyes as he waited to hear a resounding no on the other end of the line.

"I need to make a phone call," Robert said, all business. "Where can I reach you?"

Christian was taken aback. He gave the barrister his mother's number, and as he hung up started to think that this was how people with a little more class told you no. He didn't figure he'd ever hear from Robert Debenshire again.

Robert dialed Joe's number in California, still feeling a bit surprised by the revelations of minutes before. He realized with a grimace that it was late in America, even as Joe picked up the phone.

"'Lo?" Joe said, his voice gruff from sleep. He glanced at Randy as she looked up at him, concern in her eyes.

"Joseph, it's Robert. I'm sorry to call so late…"

"No problem, Robert. What's wrong?" Joe asked, tightening his hand on his wife's waist.

"Well, I just got a phone call from a young man. He says that your father knew his mother. That his mother worked for your uncle."

"Okay…" Joe said, surprise clear on his face that someone from his father's past would be calling Robert. Randy sat up, looking down at him. Joe shook his head, indicating that everything was alright.

"Well, the young man says that your father told her to call if she needed anything. And it seems that she needs medical treatment and they don't have the money to pay for it…" Robert trailed off, not sure what to make of the request himself.

"Give it to 'em," Joe said simply, surprising Robert further.

"But Joseph, we don't know who these people are," Robert said, his tone cautionary now.

"Robert, they had your number, they knew who my father and uncle are. You think it's some big scam? They're not asking for a cut of my inheritance—they're asking for money for treatment. Not the usual routine for a scam. Give 'em the money, Robert. We'll worry about the details later."

"Alright then," Robert said, ever astounded by the Sinclair generosity. Joe's father had been much the same. That was why he had believed the young man's story in the first place. He had felt, however, that it was his responsibility to point out the possibility of deception to Joe.

Christian was just thinking about calling Geneva and what he would say when his mother's phone rang. "Hello?"

"Mr. Collins, it's Robert Debenshire."

"Yes, I know," Christian said, trying to mask his surprise at hearing from the man again.

"I've been given approval by my employer to give you the money you need."

"You have?" Christian said, unable to hide his shock this time.

"Yes. How shall I get the money to you?"

"My mother is at Prince William Hospital. I guess you could give it directly to them."

"That would be fine, if that's what you want," Robert said, glad he was able to help now. It was obvious from the tone of the young man's voice that he hadn't really expected to get the money. The fact that he wanted it paid directly to the hospital served to further uphold his story that his mother needed treatment.

"Yes, sir," Christian said, his voice holding as much respect as it possibly could. "Sir, thank you so much... You can't imagine... Please tell your employer, tell Joseph, thank you."

"I'll do that."

After hanging up, Christian sat staring at his mother's bedroom wall. He had a sense of unreality. He couldn't believe his cousin had just given him a hundred thousand pounds. Joseph Sinclair junior didn't even know him. He didn't know Christian was his illegitimate cousin—he had no idea at all who he was—and yet he had given him the money without question. Something his own father, who did know who he was, couldn't be bothered to do. Anger began coursing through Christian's veins. Christian Jeremy Sinclair had tossed them out like worn-out shoes years ago, not caring if they lived or died, and now he had tossed them out again. He didn't care what happened to him or his mother. And now, Christian thought, it was time for him to pay for his indifference.

After making a quick stop at the hospital to see the doctor and tell him the money end was taken care of and then going in to see his mother, Christian went back to his apartment. He drank a few shots of scotch and then, securing his SIG Sauer P220 forty-five-caliber gun in his belt, he drove to his father's house. He had every intention of killing the man. The butler answered the door and was taken aback by the young man standing there.

"Get Lord Glenenshire," Christian said.

"Sir, do you have an appointment?"

Christian brought the gun from out of his belt. "This," he said, lifting it under the man's nose, "is my appointment card. Now get

130

him."

"I will not," the butler said, starting to close the door, but Christian kicked it open with a booted foot.

"Then just get the fuck out of my way," he said, moving through the doorway. He stepped into the house and walked toward the study, as if sensing that was where his father was. He was right. Jeremy was just coming out to investigate the noise in the entryway when his son stepped up to the door.

"What is going on out here?" Jeremy said as Christian backed him up into the study.

"This is going on, Father," Christian said angrily, brandishing the nasty-looking gun.

Christian didn't notice Sarah Sinclair in the room until she gasped in horror at the gun in his hand. Christian turned to her and grinned. "Bet you thought the guy was faithful, huh?" he said cruelly. "Of course, you weren't either, were you?"

"What are you talking about?" Jeremy asked indignantly.

Christian looked at his father, his expression mocking. "That night I was here with Geneva—you know, the night you fucked her—well, I fucked your wife the same night." Jeremy just stared at him, his mouth hanging open in shock. Then his eyes went to his wife, who had gone pale. "Don't look at her, you son of a bitch. It's not like you fucking Geneva was the first time you've been unfaithful. Hell, you fucked your maid and conceived me, didn't you?" His light blue eyes blazed in an almost crazed way. "Didn't you?" he yelled, wanting an answer.

Jeremy stared at the gun pointing into his face and nodded, his eyes wide.

"Well, you finally met him," Christian said, nodding, his face contorted in rage.

"Met who?" Jeremy managed, his breath barely coming through his constricted throat.

Christian grinned evilly as he raised the gun. "The devil himself," he said, and pulled the trigger.

Later, it was hard to discern what had happened next. Christian remembered watching his father's face, seeing the look of sheer terror. He heard Sarah scream and heard the door to the study crash open. The next thing he knew, he was being taken to the ground by rough hands. He didn't resist; he'd done what he'd come to do. There were lights and sirens and people talking, but Christian didn't pay them any attention. The only thing he heard was that his father wasn't dead. Christian wasn't sure if that made him happy or not.

Two hours later he found himself in a cell. He looked out through the bars and wondered if that was what he'd see for the rest of his life. He had inquired about his mother, but no one had anything to tell him.

The next day he was astounded when he woke to see a well-dressed man in his late fifties standing in his cell, looking down at him.

"You're Christian Collins?" the man said, his accent sophisticated.

Christian nodded, his eyes narrowed.

"Come on then." The man nodded toward the now open door. Christian stood slowly and followed him to a room down the hallway.

Inside, the man gestured for Christian to sit down, and Christian, still not fully awake, did.

"I'm Robert Debenshire," the man said, extending his hand. Stunned, Christian took it. "I was contacted by Commissioner Bartelt; he told me you were here and that you claimed to be Jeremy Sinclair's son. Is that true?" Robert watched the younger man with his deep blue eyes, easily seeing the Sinclair family resemblance. He'd known the Sinclairs long enough to pick out their build, jawline, and most outstanding, their unique eye color. Christian was just a very dark version of Joe.

Christian looked back at Robert Debenshire, surprised the man was there, and further surprised that he seemed to be on his side. He nodded to Robert's question.

"Your mother is in the hospital, is that correct?" Robert asked.

"Yes," Christian said, sitting up straighter as his chief concern was addressed. "I need to know how she is, please, sir."

Robert grinned at the sudden intensity in the young man. He found it ironic that Christian's mother seemed to mean as much to him as Joe's parents had meant to him sixteen years before. Robert remembered that Joe's main concern when he awoke in the hospital had been his parents. "Your mother is comfortable, Christian. Her treatment was started early this morning."

Christian sat back in the chair, nodding, then his light eyes, so much like Joe's, turned to Robert. "Does she know about this?" He gestured to his surroundings.

"No," Robert said, again noting the relief on the younger man's face. "Why did you do it, Christian?"

133

"Don't call me Christian," the younger man said, his eyes flashing angrily. "My name's Blue."

"I see." Robert nodded. "And why did you shoot your father, Blue?"

"Because I hate the son of a bitch. It's that simple."

"Did you contact him last night? Before you spoke with me?"

Christian didn't answer; his eyes gave nothing away. This kid's as cool as Joe was when he was younger, Robert thought. He remembered Joe in his rebellious days, when he and Rick would stay out all hours of the night. Rick would come in smelling of alcohol and women. It was a scary time for Robert as a parent; he was always waiting for that phone call telling him his son was dead in an alley somewhere. Joe's parents had had the same worry over their son; he had discussed it often enough with Joseph Sinclair senior. And now Robert was sure he was looking at Joseph Michael Sinclair's rebellious youth reincarnated.

"Chris—I mean, Blue?" Robert prompted. "Did you contact your father before you called me last night?"

"If you're lookin' for somethin', why don't you come out and ask?" Christian said coldly. "Are you asking if I think I was temporarily insane at the time I shot my father?"

"I suppose I am asking your state of mind at the time, yes," Robert said, surprised by the young man's quick mind.

"My state of mind…" Christian said, pursing his lips mockingly. "My mother was in the hospital, possibly dying at the time. That bastard was sitting in his fucking castle, with all the money in the world. He'd already tossed my mother out on her backside when she made the mistake of getting pregnant with me, and now he had the nerve

134

to deny her the money to save her life. I guess you could say I was a little pissed off, yeah." Christian's voice had remained calm during his litany, his eyes focusing on Robert's face on the last line.

"Are you curious as to your father's health at this time?"

"Only if you're going to tell me that the bastard's dead," Christian said, deadly serious.

"He's not. He is, however, calling for your head on the most convenient platter available."

Christian didn't even blink, staring back at Robert. "And you're here to give it to him?"

"I'm here to try and save your life, Christian!" Robert said, his tone indicating his surprise that Christian hadn't already realized that.

Again, the young man's face didn't change, but after a minute he nodded, as if reluctantly accepting Robert's help.

"I need to make some phone calls and meet with Commissioner Bartelt," Robert said. "I am going to do everything I can to get you out of this, I promise." He sounded so earnest that Christian suddenly found himself looking at the man very differently.

His eyes widened in surprise, but then narrowed suspiciously again; he was ever a child of the streets. "Why would you want to do that?"

"Because," Robert said, sitting down in front of Christian, staring directly into the younger man's eyes, "your cousin is like a son to me, and you're his family, and therefore part of mine."

Christian was stunned into silence by Robert's words. His mother had always told him he was a Sinclair by all rights, but he had never believed it. Now here was this man, a barrister to the richest people in London, and he was telling him he was Joe Sinclair's cousin, and his family. Christian had no reply to that, so he simply nodded.

****

Joe Sinclair was enjoying a quiet evening with his wife. He and Randy had been kissing like teenagers on the couch when their phone rang. Joe dropped his head back on the couch as Randy started to laugh. She moved to get up, but Joe pulled her back to him. "Don't answer it," he said, moving to kiss her again.

"Joseph Michael…" Randy said, grinning up at him, but she allowed herself to be pulled back, her lips welcoming his.

The answering machine picked up and moments later they heard Robert's voice. "Joseph, it's Robert. Look, we have a situation here. Now… it's about that young man I called you about last evening. I do hope—"

"Robert, I'm here," Joe said, picking up the phone. "What's going on?"

"Well, it seems that there was a little more to that young man's story than he told me in the beginning."

"And what would that be?" Joe asked, sitting up again and pulling Randy back into his embrace, holding the phone with his shoulder.

"A number of things. First of all, it seems that the reason his mother came to know your father is that your uncle is the father of her child…"

"And that child is the young man that called you," Joe said, easily following the logical chain of thought.

"Yes. It's interesting, however, that he didn't tell me that information last night. It was as if he didn't want to blackmail you in any way into giving him the money."

"Yeah, honor is a Sinclair family trait, you know," Joe said, grinning. He knew what Robert was doing. "You sold me on the kid already, Robert. So what's happened?"

"Well, it seems that he contacted his father before contacting me about the money, I guess in hopes that your uncle would have the same honorability that your father did."

"He didn't," Joe said, remembering his uncle well.

"No. And after securing the funds for his mother's treatment, the young man went to his father's home and attempted to kill him."

"Oh shit," Joe said, the tone in his voice making Randy sit up and look at him.

"Well put," Robert said. "His saving grace would be luck—your luck, that is. It seems that Inspector Bartelt—do you remember him?"

"Yes, I do," Joe said, nodding. He easily remembered the name of one of the men who had accused him of trying to kill his parents so he could inherit their money.

"Yes, well, he is the head of Scotland Yard now. When he heard the story about this young man, and heard from the servants in the house that he had claimed to be Jeremy's son, he decided to contact me."

"And why would he do that?" Joe asked, his brow furrowing, confusing Randy further.

137

"I guess he still feels he owes you for the agony he put you through after your parents were killed. He contacted me and told me what was happening, and I went down to the station and spoke to the young man in person."

"And what did you find?"

"First of all, Joseph, let me assure you, there is no question as to this boy's heritage. He has many Sinclair family traits, not the least of which is your father's eyes, like you."

"Okay…" Joe said, having already accepted that the young man was his uncle's son, but reassured all the same.

"He told me that he was angry about his father throwing his mother out into the street when she was pregnant with him, and his anger was further fueled when the man refused to help with her treatment."

"So what you're saying is that you can maybe get him off on a temporary insanity plea?" Joe said, surmising Robert's plan.

"That was my thinking, yes, but an interesting wrinkle has developed. The boy has a couple of champions here in England that don't want to see this even come to trial."

"Who?" Joe asked, wondering if there was ever going to be an end to the surprises in this story.

"One is Geneva Glasstone. Do you remember her?"

"Jesus Christ. Yes, Robert, I grew up with the woman. She's one of them? Who's the other?"

"The other, oddly enough, is Sarah Sinclair," Robert said, knowing it would shock Joe.

He was right. "My aunt is defending this kid? Has she finally come to her senses about old Jeremy?"

"I think she has been more aware of Jeremy's indiscretions than any of us realized, but she has a definite desire to see this young man freed, and I'm not sure it all has to do with Jeremy…" Robert trailed off discreetly, and Joe found himself coughing as he choked back the guffaw that came naturally at the conclusion his mind had jumped to.

"You gotta be kiddin' me?" he said disbelievingly. "You're saying this kid and Sarah… that they…" He couldn't even say the words. He remembered his aunt as so proper and conservative. He couldn't even picture her with a man half her age, and certainly not in the way Robert was alluding to. "How old's this kid, anyway?"

"Twenty-five. And believe it, Joseph. I can tell you that Geneva's interest is not exactly about seeing justice served either," Robert said lightly.

Joe shook his head, grinning all the same. "Kid's doin' 'em both, eh?"

"Joseph Michael Sinclair!" Randy said, seeing the look of pride in Joe's eyes and having discerned some of the conversation from Joe's side of it. Joe laughed out loud at the look on his wife's face.

"I gotta meet this kid, Robert," he told the older man jokingly, eliciting another outraged look from his wife as well as a slap on the arm.

"Well, that's the thing, Joseph. Bartelt said that if Jeremy could be made to agree, he would happily push for the young man to be sent to the States in care of his cousin, one Joseph Michael Sinclair. That is, if you'd be willing to accept the responsibility."

"The kid's not exactly underage, Robert."

"No, but he would have to be on some sort of probationary status for at least a year. Bartelt knows that you're a police officer now, and he's willing to appoint you as Christian's probation officer, as it were."

"Christian?" Joe said, hearing the young man in question's name for the first time. "His mother named him after my uncle, even after what he did to her?"

"Yes, strange that, isn't it?" Robert replied, nodding. "He uses his mother's maiden name, though. And he hates his given name, goes by Blue."

"Interesting," Joe said thoughtfully. "Well, look, I gotta talk to Randy about this before I agree to anything. Can I call you back?"

"Certainly."

They hung up a few moments later. Joe looked at Randy for a long minute, not sure where to start. He had told her the evening before about the phone call from Robert, but now things were definitely more complicated.

"Talk to me about what?" Randy said, watching his eyes.

"Well, first of all, that kid that called Robert isn't some stranger as we thought—he's my cousin," Joe said, his tone indicating that he wasn't totally comfortable with the word yet.

"Your cousin?" Randy said, surprised.

"Yes, remember my uncle Christian? We called him Jeremy, and I had to explain that there was really only one uncle, that his name was Christian but he preferred Jeremy? I told you he looked a lot like my dad?"

Randy nodded. "Yes, I do remember him. He was very nice."

"Yeah, well, he was really nice to a lot of women that weren't his wife. Including this kid's mother, a maid that worked for him."

"Oops," Randy said, understanding now.

"Yes, oops." Joe grinned. "Well, he kicked the woman out when she got pregnant. Thinking on it now, I remember something happening when I was about eleven. My father, mother, and I had gone to visit my aunt and uncle and we had to come home early. My dad had been all time pissed off at my uncle and I never knew why. I think this was probably it. I think I might remember the maid too—she was a beautiful Spanish girl, if I remember right. Had my eye on her at one point..." He let his voice trail off as Randy punched him on the arm. "Sorry, love, it was long before I met and fell in love with you. Anyway, now I guess the kid has gone and tried to kill my uncle, and now he's in jail."

"And..." Randy prompted when he didn't continue. She knew there was more to the story.

"And Robert thinks he can get him off, but there's a condition to it. He wants to send him here."

"To what, live with us?"

"Yeah..." Joe said, knowing this was a lot to dump on her.

"He tried to kill your uncle and now Robert wants to send him here?" Randy stated disbelievingly.

"Randy, that's oversimplifying things a little bit, wouldn't you say?" Joe said quietly.

"Yeah, okay, maybe. But Joe, we don't know anything about this young man. We don't know that he's not just plain unstable."

"Randy, he's family," Joe said, doing some oversimplifying of his own. "My family, and he needs help. I gotta give it to him."

"Why?" Randy asked, her question not accusing in the least.

"Because that could have been me, Randy, years ago. I could have been in that kind of trouble, and I would have needed someone to bail me out."

"You would never have tried to kill your father, Joe."

"No, but I could have managed to kill someone else in any one of my drunk stupors. I could have gotten into a lot of trouble, maybe something as bad as this…" His light blue eyes looked down into hers, searching for understanding. He had told her many times that she would never have recognized the man he had been in London before his parents were killed. Randy could see now that he was identifying with this young man and was doing his damndest to make her see that.

Finally she nodded, ever trusting of her husband's judgement. "Okay, Joe, if you think it's something we should do, we'll do it."

Joe smiled, pulling her into his embrace. "Thanks," he whispered softly into her hair. "I love you."

Randy pulled back just enough to look up at him. "And I love you for being able continue to amaze me even after ten years of marriage."

Joe gave her a questioning look. "Amaze you?"

"Well, first you give this kid a hundred thousand dollars without question, and now you're bailing him out of a serious problem. You don't even know him, you just know he's family, and he's not really that… but I know how you think, and to you he still is, right?"

Joe nodded seriously. Randy just shook her head, smiling and handing him the phone he had set down on the coffee table minutes before.

Joe called Robert and told him to go ahead with whatever he needed to do to get Christian out of jail.

Four hours later, Christian was surprised to find himself standing outside the jail he'd been inside minutes before. Robert walked out the double doors and over to him.

"How'd this happen?" Christian asked, too shocked to be cool.

"Your cousin made this happen," Robert said simply. "But there are some conditions to your release."

"And what would those be?" Christian was still too surprised to be aloof.

"You have to leave the country for a while, and you have to stay away from your father," Robert said, almost grinning on the last part.

"Great, and where the hell am I supposed to go?" Christian said, his voice taking on an edge. They'd dealt him right out of his homeland.

"That's all been arranged, but first I thought you'd like to go and see your mother at the hospital."

"Yes." Christian was still curious about these "arrangements," but figured Robert would tell him when the time came.

It was his mother who told him; Robert had been to see her that morning. He had told her everything, having been assured by her doctor that it wouldn't be too much for her to hear. She had been upset to hear that her son was in jail and more so when she heard what he had done. Robert had assured her that he was seeing to getting Christian out and that no charges were going to be filed. Josephine had been amazed. Robert had explained to her about Christian's phone call to him, and that Joseph Sinclair senior's son had been the one to pay for her treatment at her son's request. Josephine had been taken aback by such generosity and had bid Robert thank Mr. Sinclair very much for her. She was further amazed when Robert told her about the conditions of Christian's release, and that his cousin had agreed to allow him asylum in America to avoid charges of attempted murder.

Sitting at his mother's bedside, Christian was just happy to see his mother looking more comfortable than she had the last time he'd seen her. The doctor had assured him the treatment was going quite well and they were optimistic for her future.

"You look worlds better, Mum," Christian said, holding her hand and brushing her hair back with his fingers. He now looked far different to Robert, who had noted the change on the young man's face. He knew he hadn't been wrong, comparing Christian to Joe in his earlier days. Joe's face had lit up the same way when his mother was around.

"Thanks to you," Josephine said to her son. "I heard what you did…" She trailed off to indicate that she'd heard everything.

Christian immediately looked contrite, but he shook his head. "I had to, Mum. I couldn't let the bastard get away with it twice."

"Christian…" Josephine said sorrowfully as she shook her head. "I know why you think you had to do that, and I can't really blame the way you feel. I just wish things could be different for you."

"Well, I guess they're gonna be right now," Christian said hesitantly, not sure how to tell his mother that he had to leave the country because of what he had done. He was surprised when she started to nod.

"Yes, they will be. I understand that you're going to America to live with your cousin for the time being."

"I am?" Christian said, looking up at Robert for affirmation. The older man nodded. "I didn't know," he said to his mother.

"Well, Mr. Debenshire told me this morning. I want you to promise me, Christian Joseph Collins, that you will give your cousin all the respect he deserves for his generosity in this. He didn't have to do a thing for either of us, you know."

"Yes, Mum, I know," Christian said obediently. Robert doubted that anyone aside from his mother ever warranted that tone from this young man.

She was right about Joe's generosity; she didn't know how right. Joe had further ordered Robert to make sure Josephine had a decent job with benefits to go to once she was ready, to ensure her future financial comfort, even if that job was at Sinclair Publishing. "Hell," Joe had said, "I don't care if you make her a vice president, just make sure she wants for nothing again." To Joe's way of thinking, Josephine Collins was family too, and he knew it was what his father would have done if he'd known the dire straits she had slipped into after leaving his uncle's home. Robert hadn't talked to her about the job or any of that as of yet; he was waiting until her mind was settled about her son having to leave.

Three days later, Christian Collins was on a plane headed to America.

The morning after Randy and Joe agreed to allow Christian to come live with them, they were surprised when Susan showed up at the breakfast table with an announcement. She walked in beaming from ear to ear. "I have something I need to tell you both," she said, looking a little hesitant.

Joe looked up from the report he was reading, lifting his coffee to his lips and nodding. Randy moved to sit down at the table, looking at Susan.

"I'm getting married," Susan said excitedly, showing them her left hand, which had a rather large engagement ring on it.

Joe just about choked on his coffee. "You're what?"

"You heard her, Sinclair," Randy said, shaking her head at her husband.

"To who?" Joe asked disbelievingly.

Randy and Susan looked at him as if he'd just gone off the deep end. Randy said, "Duh."

"I'm marrying Warren, Uncle Joe," Susan said, using the familiar name as she had when she was younger.

"Oh," Joe said, trying to look enthusiastic, but Randy could see he didn't like the idea one bit. She questioned him about it as he drove her to school that morning.

"So what's up with you?" she said softly.

"Whaddya mean?" Joe's mind was already on the office.

"I mean your total lack of enthusiasm for Susan's announcement this morning," Randy said, looking at her husband's profile. "Are you worried about her still working for us, because she's already assured me she has no intention of quitting anytime in the near future."

Joe shook his head. "No, that's not it. I know she wouldn't do that to us. I just... I don't like it."

"What do you mean, you don't like it? What's not to like?"

Joe looked over at his wife, his eyes narrowed as if trying to see something in her expression. "How much do you love me?" he said, surprising her.

Randy replied without hesitation. "With everything I have. Why?"

"And would you say that you've felt that way about me from the beginning?"

"Yes."

"Do you think Susan feels that way about this guy?"

Randy hesitated, thinking about the question, and after a long moment had to shake her head.

"That's what I don't like."

Randy looked back at her husband of over nine years, ever surprised by his way of thinking. She hadn't thought about it that way, and she wouldn't have expected Joe to either. But upon reflection she realized Susan was like Joe's niece, and he was protective of her just as Rick was. So it did make sense that he would be concerned about her making a poor choice when it came to marriage. Reaching over, she took his hand, feeling very fortunate to be married to a man that thought the way he did. Joe looked over at her, seeing her love for him reflected in her eyes, and smiled.

He thought of the moment again a number of times that day and always smiled to himself. In the time that Susan had been with them, his and Randy's marriage had become more like it had been originally, and Joe was thankful for that. He loved his wife more than he could put into words, and any distance between them always made him feel lost. He knew it wasn't exactly a tough cop way of seeing his marriage, but when it came to Randy he didn't care how he looked. Joe and Randy had been through too many things in their lives together and had come too close to losing it all to allow even a fleeting thought of trivializing it, and Joe wouldn't do that.

Joe was busy trying to get month-end reports in from all his lieutenants when Rick walked into his office and sat down. Joe looked up, his face all captain until Rick tossed FORS' month-end report on the desk between them. Joe smiled then, and Rick laughed.

"I knew I wasn't allowed to have a conversation with you till this was in," Rick said, pointing to the document on the desk.

"Got that right," Joe said, grinning at his oldest friend.

"Yes, Captain." Rick said the rank as if it were a bad word, his grin wide. Joe had taken a lot of flak from the members of FORS for allowing himself to be promoted to captain of vice and therefore out of the unit. Rick had been the most vehement, since it had left him in the position of being in charge and eventually promoted to lieutenant, whether he liked it or not. His wife was the chief, after all.

"So, I hear tell you're getting a care package from England," Rick said, his voice becoming friendlier, but his look pointed.

"Yeah, and I hear you're gaining a nephew," Joe shot back.

"Aww, yes, young Warren…"

"You mean boring Warren."

"What's wrong with him? He's from a good family, he's been courting the girl since the day they met."

"Good family?" Joe said, his face indicating his disgust with the term. "You're starting to sound like our parents, man."

"Yeah? Well, just wait till Kat gets old enough to talk about guys, then see how fast you change your tune. You'll keep her away from guys like us, that's for sure."

Joe laughed. "Great, what does that say for our wives?"

"Their parents weren't around to speak up for them," Rick said, shaking his head ruefully. "We got lucky. But I'm tellin' ya, man, Kail's been hangin' out with some older kids, and now she's askin' about guys and stuff. It's makin' me crazy!"

"Shit, Rick, she's only ten… Maybe she's got more of her mother in her than you thought, huh?" Joe said, grinning widely.

"Shut the fuck up!" Rick said, grinning too.

"Hey!" said a voice from the doorway. Both men looked up to see Midnight standing there. She walked in, kicking the door closed and moving to sit in the chair next to Rick's. "I don't want to hear that kind of language in my old office," she said with a grin.

Rick smiled at her. "If you'd heard what he'd just said, you'd know I was just defending your honor."

"I see," Midnight said, looking at Joe. "And what was it you were saying?"

Joe shrugged innocently. "Just that I thought Mikeyla was probably a lot like you. Can't understand why that would be an insult to your honor."

Rick was laughing by this time, seeing that Midnight was buying it. Joe managed to hold a straight face long enough to get Rick punched in the arm, and then he broke out laughing too.

Midnight watched them both, shaking her head. "I think you two need a vacation. Hey, look, I came down to get the scoop on this kid you got comin' in from England," she said to Joe.

"Christ, how did you two hear all this so fast?"

"Dad," Rick said, at the exact same time Midnight said, "Robert."

"He called this morning," Rick explained. "Having received Susan's little announcement telegram this morning with the paper. He called to make sure she'd told us, and then told us about your… cousin, is it?"

Joe nodded. "Yeah, I guess he's my uncle's son…" He trailed off, indicating that he didn't really doubt it. "Anyway, he got into some trouble and now your dad is sending him here to cool out."

"What kind of trouble?" Midnight asked with a pointed look.

"Robert didn't tell you?" Joe said. Midnight shook her head. "Well, he kinda tried to off my uncle." His voice was chagrined as he looked back at his partner of thirteen years, knowing she wouldn't take something like that lightly.

"Kinda tried to off him?" Midnight repeated, with an expression that indicated she thought Joe was euphemizing the situation a little bit.

"Look," Joe said, putting his hand down on his desk. "You don't know my uncle, Night. The guy's a real bastard. Christian's the son of a maid that my uncle slept with, got pregnant, and then canned. The kid snapped, that's all. Do you think I'd actually let him live with

150

my family if I thought he was dangerous?"

Midnight shook her head, knowing full well Joe's priority was that his family remain safe above and beyond everything else. She blew her breath out. "I guess if you trust him, we will too."

Rick nodded his agreement, and Joe smiled at them both. They were like the siblings he'd never had. They were his family, as far as he was concerned. Midnight and Rick were his best friends in the world, and he prized them right up there next to his kids and Randy in terms of importance. It felt good knowing that his "family" approved of his acceptance of Christian, and he knew it would make things easier on Christian as well.

"Okay, now on to the next topic of discussion," Midnight said, sitting forward and looking at Joe. "What's goin' on with my student and your brother-in-law?"

"Huh?" Joe said, his face blank.

"Oh, come on, Sinclair! Wake up! Haven't you seen Jeanie lately? She's like in a daze, and I think it has a lot to do with that brother-in-law of yours. And you're telling me you know nothing?" Midnight shook her head at him, as if he were slipping.

"Well, we haven't seen a lot of Donovan lately…" Joe said, trying to think of the last time they'd seen him.

"Yeah," Rick said, getting into the discussion finally. "I heard he busted one of his best friends in the mouth at 10-7 a couple of weeks back."

Now Midnight looked concerned. "Who?"

"Uh-oh," Rick said, looking over at Joe, who had also gotten a serious look on his face. "I see the chief and the captain coming, and

I think I need to go back to work. Let's just forget I said that, okay?" He stood up and moved to Joe's door. "It's been real," he said, and walked out.

Midnight and Joe looked at each other, concern clear on their faces.

"Think it was another cop?" Midnight asked.

"If it was a citizen we would have had a complaint by now," Joe said, not wanting to think about this too much. He knew what could happen, and he knew Randy was not going to like it if it did.

"Maybe not. I mean, if it was a friend of his… Maybe the guy didn't care, or maybe he was just drunk or something…"

"Or maybe Donovan was," Joe said, aware of his brother-in-law's penchant for going out with his buddies and getting drunk and stupid. Another thought occurred to him, not one he wanted to think. "Most of Donovan's friends are cops."

Midnight nodded, her lips twisting in an unhappy frown.

"Find out from Rick where he heard it, and I'll talk to Donovan after you do," Joe said. He knew this could be a problem for both of them.

Two days later Donovan sat in Joe's office. Joe and Midnight had found that another lieutenant had told Rick about the incident and that the lieutenant wasn't the only ranking officer in the bar that night. Donovan knew by the look on his brother-in-law's face that this was definitely not a social visit.

"What happened at 10-7 a couple of weeks ago?" Joe asked, his tone all business.

Donovan closed his eyes for a second, then opened them to look back at Joe. "David Jones and I got into it," he said evenly.

"Why?" Joe said.

"He was being rude to my date."

"Rude?"

"Yes, he kept putting his hands on her and grabbed her rear end."

"So you 'got into it'?" Donovan nodded. "And did he hit you first?"

"No. I hit him."

"How many times?"

"Once," Donovan said, almost tonelessly.

"Do you know that you dislocated his jaw?" Joe asked, his voice deepening.

Donovan looked surprised. "No, sir, I didn't know that."

"Do you know that there were a number of ranking officers in the bar that night?"

Donovan winced ever so slightly. "No, sir." He suddenly felt like he was back in the academy.

"Do you know how far my ass is hangin' out here, Curtis?" Joe said, almost sounding like a drill sergeant now. "Do you know the position you've got the chief in? Don't you know by now how close these people watch how you're treated, how Rick's treated, or Randy?"

Donovan was silent in the face of Joe's wrath, his eyes trained on the floor. He had no response to what Joe was saying. He hadn't been thinking like a cop when he hit David Jones; he'd been thinking like a boyfriend defending his territory. Bad move.

Joe paced behind his desk, feeling the need to walk off some of his anger, his light blue eyes blazing. He looked over at his brother-in-law again, shaking his head. "You gotta be better, Donovan. Better, smarter, stronger, faster, and most of all more professional, because you're related to me and because you're friends with Midnight. You can't give them a reason to ruin us all. We can't have this crap, not from you. Do you get me?"

Donovan didn't trust his voice to speak, so he nodded, all the while feeling like hell.

Jeanie knew something was up with Donovan the minute she saw him later than morning. She had to wait until lunch to speak to him about it. When they walked to his car, she could tell he was mad. She waited until they got in to try and ask him, but Donovan immediately cranked the stereo and drove like he was in a pursuit, opting for a restaurant as far from the department as he could get. He played Rick Springfield's greatest hits album, his propensity for '80s music coming through. He cranked the song "Rock of Life," singing the words and drumming his fingers on the steering wheel, a miserable look on his face. Jeanie listened, wondering how the lyrics related to what was going on.

When the song ended, she reached over to turn the radio down. She was beginning to get worried. In the months they'd been together, she'd found that Donovan was usually pretty open. There were a couple of subjects he was closemouthed about, one of which was his parents, but she was sure this didn't have anything to do with them.

"Donovan, tell me what's wrong, please," she said finally, seeing that he wasn't going to be forthcoming.

"What's to tell?" he said, shaking his head ruefully. "I fucked up and now I'm gonna have to pay for it."

"Fucked up how?" Jeanie considered him a pretty good cop, and not just because she was going out with him.

"That night at 10-7 when I punched David out," he said, looking over at her, his face drawn and angry. She nodded. "Yeah, well, I forgot to consider the fact that David's a cop too, and that there might be repercussions to punching out a fellow officer."

"What kind of repercussions?" Jeanie asked, realizing she hadn't thought of it that way either.

Donovan shrugged, shaking his head angrily. "Oh, just little ones like losing my career, that's all." The look on his face belied his casual tone.

"They wouldn't do that!" Jeanie said, aghast.

Donovan looked over at her, giving her a rueful grin and shaking his head. "They won't have a choice if David decides to file a complaint," he said, aware she had been referring to Joe and Midnight.

"But…" Jeanie said, trailing off as Donovan shook his head again.

"It's my fault, Jay. I didn't think. I reacted like I would have when we were all teenagers. It never occurred to me that other cops would see it as an attack on another officer." He stopped at a light then and rubbed his eyes with the heels of his hands "I am so goddamned dumb sometimes!"

155

"Donovan, I'm sorry." Jeanie reached over to pull his hands away from his face, her expression devastated.

Donovan looked over at her and shook his head. "Jay, I'm not. I mean, I'm not sorry I hit the guy. I'm just sorry I didn't drag his ass out back and do it where no one would have seen it. I still feel fully justified in hitting him, I just should've been smarter about it."

Jeanie grinned. "Kicked his butt at recess, huh?"

"Yeah, or waited for him at the bus stop after school," Donovan said, the beginnings of a smile on his face. "Will you still go out with me if I'm unemployed?"

"Stop it, you're not going to get fired. David won't actually file on you, will he?" She'd realized she didn't know.

Donovan shrugged. "Who knows." Then he looked chagrined. "Joe says I dislocated his jaw."

"Yikes!" Jeanie said, her grin impish. "Betcha that made it a lot harder to talk his trash then, didn't it?"

Donovan gave her lopsided grin, then put the car into gear and drove to the restaurant. Lunch was a little easier to eat after that. Jeanie made a point of keeping his mind off the trouble. She told him stories about her brothers, how they'd gotten into law enforcement. Donovan went back to the office feeling a bit better, but the thought of losing his job weighed heavily on his mind. He was reeling at the thought that one stupid mistake could ruin all he'd been working toward for almost seven years. He wondered idly if he should have finished his culinary class; maybe then he'd have a job to fall back on.

CHAPTER 5

Midnight Chevalier waited at the end of the gangway. She felt foolish; she wasn't even sure who to look for. All Joe had told her was that according to Robert, his cousin was a dark version of him. She remembered the late-night phone call from her partner of thirteen years. She and Rick had been fast asleep when the phone rang.

"Tell Joe it's too damn late to be callin'," Rick had said as she reached for the phone. He had promptly snuggled up to her back and gone back to sleep, used to late-night calls from his best friend. They were rarely for him.

Midnight had answered the phone, and Joe had sheepishly told her that he had a raid scheduled for the morning and that Christian was due in shortly thereafter. And could she please do him a huge favor and pick him up. Midnight had grinned in the darkness, knowing her partner well, and also knowing that it had probably been Joe's wife who had reminded him about over-scheduling himself. She was right; Randy had been the one to remind Joe that Christian was due in at 8:00 a.m. the next day. Randy had a final that morning and was therefore unavailable to pick Joe's cousin up, so the next likely candidate had been Midnight.

Now, standing in the terminal, Midnight looked out at the cold November morning. Great day to travel, was all she could think. Midnight caught the attention of many of the men in the airport. She was dressed casually, wearing her old uniform of jeans, boots, and a hunter green Oxford, as well as her leather FORS jacket. Even as the Chief of Police she insisted on keeping a hand in on the action. She was scheduled to go on a raid with one of her former members of FORS, Tiny Ako—now a sergeant with the homicide unit—later that afternoon. Her mane of copper-blond hair was still worn long; Rick wouldn't allow her to cut it. She still looked every bit the beautiful, fiery leader of one of the most effective gang task forces in the country. She began pacing when the passengers from the British Airways flight started to trickle through. Midnight was just beginning to wonder if she had indeed missed Christian when a black-haired version of Joe walked up the gangway. He looked straight at her, and Midnight knew instantly that this was Joe's cousin. She walked up to him, smiling.

"Christian Collins?" she said, her tone friendly.

"If I wasn't, I am now. And it's Blue, not Christian," he replied, his face lit with a very intense smile.

"Okay… Well, I'm Midnight Chevalier. I'm your cousin's partner," she said, thinking Christian was probably pretty devastating to most women. And Robert had been right; he was definitely a dark version of Joe.

"Partner?" Christian said as she began to lead the way down to baggage claim.

"Yes, thirteen years now," Midnight said, glancing over her shoulder; Christian had fallen in behind and to the left of her. She wondered if he was used to doing some sort of protection work, since the habit was standard for cops and bodyguards, and she knew he wasn't a cop.

"So you're a cop?" Christian asked disbelievingly.

"That's right, for sixteen years now." Midnight grinned as they reached the baggage area. She turned, and was surprised to find him standing very close. She looked up at him, her cat-like eyes narrowing slightly. Christian made no move to step back; he simply stared down into her eyes. Midnight figured any other woman would probably have dropped dead at that moment, but she simply continued to look at him, everything about her saying she was far from any other woman. Christian was taken aback by her reaction—she didn't react. For a woman, this was a first. He finally dropped his eyes, his lips twisting into a wry grin as he nodded and stepped back.

Midnight was surprised to find that he only had two pieces of luggage.

"They're shipping my other stuff," Christian said by way of explanation when she gave him a pointed look.

A few minutes later Midnight led him to the classic Corvette she still drove. She'd had a new engine put into it in the last couple of years and had some electrical work done, but she still loved it. Rick was after her constantly to buy a new one, or at least get a more updated version, but Midnight refused staunchly. Christian ran an approving hand over the rear fender as she opened the trunk.

"Sixty-three?" he asked, his eyes running along the body of the car.

"Yep," Midnight said proudly.

"Fantastic," he said, awe in his voice.

"I think so." She unlocked his door for him and moved around to the driver's side. Christian got in, looking around and nodding appreciatively. The interior was completely original.

Midnight pushed a CD into the player Rick had had installed for

159

her the year before for her birthday. The Spice Girls' first album, Spice, started; the first track was "Wannabe," and Christian couldn't help but grin. Midnight knew every word and sang them with her usual enthusiasm. Christian found himself watching her in fascination. It had been many years since a woman had actually captured his attention. This woman not only captured it but was holding it for ransom. The moment he had seen her in the airport he had been very attracted to her. He'd had no idea who she was, but had made eye contact as soon as possible. It had been a major plus to find out she was there to pick him up; he'd been expecting his cousin. At the baggage claim, he'd been attempting to make her react, and she'd shut him right down. That had secured his interest for a while. He did notice the ring on her left hand, but he'd been with enough married women to know that didn't always matter.

"And you're really a cop?" he said after the first track had ended and Midnight turned the radio down a little. He was watching every move she made.

"Yes, I really am." She raised an eyebrow. "You wanna see my badge?"

"Pass," he said coolly, holding her gaze.

"My gun then?" she asked with a wry look.

"Only if you have to take something off to show me."

Midnight surprised him by laughing. It wasn't a coy come-hither laugh; it was a disbelieving one. She shook her head in answer, and was still grinning to herself when her cell phone rang. She reached over, touching the hands-free button.

"Yes?"

"And just where the hell did you creep off to this morning?"

160

Rick's voice came through the speaker, his tone warm and languid. Midnight could almost see him sitting in their kitchen with his feet up on a chair, elbow on the table, phone in hand. She smiled.

"I had something to do for Joe."

"Uh-huh. That have anything to do with that phone call last night?"

"It had everything to do with that call, yes." Midnight looked over at Christian to find that he was watching her. She met his eyes, directly without it being a come-on in the least.

"Okay…" Rick said, and Midnight could almost feel his shift in modes. She pursed her lips, closing her eyes slowly. She knew what was coming. "And what were you wearing when you left this morning?" His even tone didn't belie the point to the question, but Midnight recognized it and knew where he was going with it. Christian had begun to wonder if this was some sort of obscene phone call.

Midnight looked down at her jeans, then glanced back at the phone with a lopsided grin. "How the hell do you do that?" she asked after a long pause.

Rick laughed lightly. "Your FORS jacket is gone—you never wear that without the rest of the uniform." Then his voice grew serious. "What's goin' on, Night?"

"Oh, just the usual…" Midnight trailed off, hoping he'd drop it.

"Don't play games with me, Midnight," Rick said, his tone cautionary. "You're going on a raid, aren't you?"

Midnight rolled her eyes, sighing. This was not a conversation she wanted to have with him. "Yes."

"No," he said, his tone still very serious.

Christian watched in fascination, wondering how she'd react to what was obviously her husband telling her what to do.

"Rick," Midnight said, her voice now much more commanding. "I'm not goin' through this with you this morning. So let's just skip it, okay?"

Rick was silent for a long moment. "Who're you going out with?"

"Tiny's team."

"They're fucking kids, Midnight! No, this ain't goin'. You wanna go on a raid, you can wait till FORS goes out again."

Christian watched as Midnight's face changed. He was willing to swear that she'd turned to stone. What he didn't know was that her independent gang leader side was coming out now.

"No, I'm goin' today," she said. "And you're getting off this subject or we're getting off the phone."

"Midnight…" Rick had recognized the tone in his wife's voice easily; it was the digging-her-heels-in tone.

"Richard," Midnight replied, the slightest bit softer.

Rick sighed, knowing he was fighting a losing battle. There were some battles with his wife he was willing to fight, and others he knew to let go. This was one of the ones destined to be set free.

"Fine," he said, his tone indicating that giving in to her was the last thing he wanted to do.

Midnight smiled. Being married to Rick was a constant challenge. That was what kept their relationship alive and well. He was an even match for her, loving her on the one hand and fighting her with the other. It was definitely a stimulating relationship, and it had come nowhere near to settled over the nine years of their marriage. Their battles were just as fiery as the ones years before, but now they were secure in the knowledge that they were always going to be together. The nightmare of five years before had taught them that they belonged together; having come to within days of being legally divorced had made them realize they couldn't live without each other. They'd accepted the volatile nature of their relationship, even determining that it was exactly what each needed in another half to continue to thrive in the marriage.

"I'll see you in the office later, okay?" she said, her voice warm again.

"Do you have a choice?" Rick still sounded stubborn, but Midnight could sense the slow grin starting on his face.

"Not likely," she replied, grinning as well.

"Not likely," Rick repeated, smiling now.

They hung up, and Christian found that his interest in Midnight had just been increased rather than discouraged. He had seen a great deal of fire in her eyes during the short argument, and he liked it. Midnight glanced over at him, rolling her eyes.

"Sorry you had to hear all that. My husband is a bit protective," she said, saying the last word as if it were an expletive.

"If you were mine, I would be too," Christian said directly.

"Yes, well," Midnight said equally directly, "I'm his."

"For how long?"

"Nine years now."

Christian narrowed his eyes, as if looking at her for the first time. "That's where I've seen you before. You're married to Debenshire's son, aren't you? Why'd you say your name was Chevalier?"

Midnight glanced over at him, surprised. "Yes, I am married to Robert's son. Chevalier's my maiden name—I use it out of habit. But… where've you seen me before?"

Christian nodded. "I saw your wedding pictures."

"Where?"

"In the London society pages, when I was fifteen. My mum was showing me Joe's wedding, and you were married in the same ceremony. I saw the photos. I thought you were beautiful then, but those pictures didn't do you justice."

Midnight looked back at him, her eyes narrowed slightly, a look she used when she was trying to figure someone out.

"Why did your mother care about Joe's wedding?" she asked. "I mean, I know that Joe's uncle is your father, but…"

"My mum adored Joe's father. I guess he was really great to her when my bastard of a father fired her. And because Joe was his father's son, she followed what he did, especially after his parents were killed." Christian's voice was lowered on the last, as if he were remembering.

"You were pretty young when his parents were killed. What, about three, right?" she asked, trying to assimilate what she knew about him with her partner's past.

"Yeah, but my mum told me all the stories. She told me about Scotland Yard investigating him and everything, and how he moved to America and became a police officer and all that…"

Christian trailed off, realizing he was talking a lot more than he was comfortable with. But she had that kind of effect on him. He was shocked to realize that he had probably told her more about himself in the last five minutes than he'd told Geneva in six months. Odd, that, he thought.

"And now you're here. It's gotta be kind of weird for you, coming here to live with a cousin you've never met," Midnight said inquisitively.

Christian looked over at her, wondering why she would care, but found himself answering her nonetheless. "I adjust quickly, always have."

Midnight gave him a measured glance. "Survival instinct?"

Christian nodded, a hint of surprise showing in his eyes. He was wondering what she knew about survival instincts.

Midnight's phone rang again, and she made an impatient sound as she hit the hands-free button. "Yeah?" she said, sounding a little irritated this time.

"Good morning to you too," replied an English-accented voice. Christian wondered mildly if half the damn country had come to San Diego. His curiosity was satisfied a moment later.

"Good morning, Joe," Midnight said, smiling and glancing over at Christian, who realized she had used his cousin's name to let him know who was on the line.

"Not really," Joe replied.

"Uh-oh," Midnight said, her face darkening just a bit. "What happened?"

"Well, the damn raid went south is what happened." Joe sounded frustrated and weary. "The bastards came out shooting, and

165

a couple of the younger guys lost it."

"Okay…"

"I got one down," Joe said seriously.

"Down?"

"Yeah, I think he's gonna be okay. Dumb sonofabitch hit a door without back up." Joe's voice had taken on a depreciating tone that Christian didn't understand.

Midnight understood it perfectly. Her face softened, as did her voice. "He knew better, Joe. You and I both know that. He was trained by the best rangemaster around."

Christian heard his cousin blow his breath out in a frustrated sigh. "I don't feel like the best right now, Night."

"Hey, you can't keep the bad guys from pulling a few punches, Sinclair. That's why they call it police work and not police fun."

Joe laughed mildly. "Yeah, okay, you win. You are all knowing and seeing."

"'Bout time you realize that," Midnight said, grinning. "Who's down, by the way?"

"Hobson."

Midnight nodded, narrowing her eyes in thought. "Wife and two kids, right?"

"Yeah," Joe said quietly.

"But he's okay, you think?" Midnight said, chewing her lip in thought.

"He was talkin' when they took him to the hospital."

Midnight nodded. "You want me to call his wife, or do you want to?"

"I'll do it," Joe said, then his voice took on a chiding tone. "That is my job, you know, not yours anymore."

"Yeah, yeah, save it," Midnight said, grinning all the while. "Look, keep me posted, okay?"

"You got it, boss. And uh… could you keep Christian entertained for a while longer? I'm gonna be here for another couple of hours at least…" He trailed off, knowing she had more important things to do than babysit his cousin.

Midnight smiled. "You'll owe me."

"I already do," Joe replied easily.

"So double it."

"Great… I'll see you soon then."

"Okay. Bye." Midnight broke the connection.

Christian was surprised at Midnight's obvious vehemence on Joe's behalf. She had been determined to make him feel better about having someone hurt on his team; that had not escaped Christian's notice. It made him curious about their relationship, but he figured he'd get that story from his cousin if anything.

"He called you boss," Christian said, having picked up on that as well. "Why?"

Midnight shrugged. "Probably because I'm his boss."

"You're his boss…" Christian repeated, as if unable to fathom it.

Midnight shrugged again. "No big deal. I'm my husband's boss too."

167

"So what does that make you?"

Midnight looked over at him as she drove into the parking lot at the police department and pulled in to her reserved spot, her gold-green eyes sparkling as she smiled. She turned her head and looked pointedly at the sign in front of her car: "RESERVED, CHIEF CHEVALIER-DEBENSHIRE"

Christian coughed as he read the words, his eyes widening as he looked back at her. "You're the fucking Chief of Police?"

Midnight inclined her head, grinning all the while.

"But I thought San Diego was a pretty big department," Christian said, having heard that from his mother over the years.

"Fourth largest in the country."

"And you're the chief," Christian said, dead pan, his face still indicating his disbelief.

"Right."

"Unbelievable."

Midnight laughed, getting out of the car. "Come on," she said, canting her head toward the building.

He followed her inside, waited as she signed him in, then followed her to her office. He spent the next hour watching her work. He, like many before him, was impressed with her way of handling people. Even as the chief she never really talked down to anyone.

Midnight was on the phone when Rick walked in. His eyes went to Christian immediately. He walked over, extending his hand. "You gotta be Christian," he said, smiling. "I'm Rick Debenshire. It's good to meet you."

Midnight was watching the exchange, and she saw the look on

Christian's face as he nodded. "Ah, the lucky man," Christian said, looking to Midnight and seeing her shake her head and roll her eyes.

Rick looked at his wife, and then back at Christian, furrowing his brow. "What?"

Christian shook his head. "Never mind. So you'd be my cousin's best friend then?"

"That would be me." Rick nodded, then inclined his head in his wife's direction. "Or you could be describing my wife."

Christian was surprised by that.

Midnight hung up the phone then, leaning back in her chair with a wry grin. "So you've met…"

"Yeah." Rick moved to sit on the edge of her desk. "So what's this lucky man shit?" he asked, not one to forget something easily.

Midnight gave Christian a look that said, "Go ahead, explain it to him."

Christian laughed. "I just meant you're lucky being married to such an incredible-looking woman."

Rick's expression was self-assured. "Luck has nothin' to do with it." The look in his deep blue eyes was challenging. Christian met it with one of his own.

Midnight stood up and walked around her desk to stand in front of her husband. "Let's try to keep the testosterone at a manageable level in here, okay?" she said with a meaningful look, her grin wide.

Rick returned her grin, closing his eyes for a moment as he nodded. "So what time's this raid?" he asked, moving on to what he felt was more important.

"Two o'clock," Midnight said cautiously, wondering if he was going to hassle her again.

"And it's Tiny's crew?"

"We covered this, Debenshire," Midnight said lightly.

"Well, I'm coverin' it again, Chief." Rick sounded serious, but his grin was in place again. Then his expression turned meaningful. "You damn well better be careful. And don't even think of having him put you on the entry team, because you can bet that beautiful ass of yours I'm gonna warn him off."

Midnight looked at him with calm acceptance as he spoke. When he was through, she leaned forward, kissing him softly on the lips, staring into his eyes even as she did so. "I only do entry when I have you or Joe as back up, you know that," she said gently.

"Yeah, well…" Rick looked stubborn, but his eyes showed how easily he was affected by his wife's words and actions. He stood up, his hands on her waist, and pulled her to him. He kissed her then, his intensity telling her everything he didn't say, but Midnight recognized the signs of possessiveness in it as well. She knew he was sending Christian a very definite message that she belonged to him without question. When their lips parted, Midnight looked up at him, her expression telling him she knew what he was doing. His own basically said, "Yeah, so?" He left a few minutes later.

Midnight glanced over at Christian and saw that, predictably, he was watching her. She grinned. "The testosterone level got a bit high again, huh?"

"As did my blood pressure," Christian said seriously.

Midnight looked at him for a long moment, then shook her head. "Hopeless," she muttered as she moved to sit behind her desk. She reached over, switching on her computer. When the screen came up she started to cuss.

"Problems?" Christian craned his neck around to try to see the screen.

"Just that this computer is a piece of crap and my system's always down."

To Midnight's surprise, Christian stood up and walked around her desk. He glanced at the keyboard, then around the back of the computer.

"Do you mind?" he said, gesturing to the machine.

"No." Midnight shook her head, moving her chair back to give him room.

Christian touched a few keys, bringing up new screens. "This a three-eight-six or a two?"

"Three-eight-six," Midnight said, surprised. "You know computers?"

"Yeah, some." Christian shrugged. "I studied it at school for a while, but I decided it wasn't going to make the kind of money I needed to make at the time."

"I see," Midnight said, having learned from Joe about Christian's "colorful" past—what Joe knew of it, anyway. "Know anything about programming?"

Christian glanced at her. "Some. Why?"

"Think you could do an assessment of a system I have for my inventory?"

Christian gave her a measured look, turning around to sit on the edge of her desk. "You'd trust me to do that?"

Midnight nodded.

"You don't know anything about me," Christian said, his tone indicating his surprise at her lack of caution.

Midnight looked back at him for a long moment. "I do know you're my partner's cousin—by definition you're practically family. I figure that means I have to trust you."

Christian couldn't begin to think of a reply. No one had ever given him that sort of credit before. Here she was, the chief of a police department; she'd known him all of two hours, and she trusted him. She'd called him family, Joe's family… It hit him again that these people really thought of him as Joe Sinclair's family. They didn't seem to care that he was illegitimate. Being a bastard had been the torment of his life; it had made him feel less worthy and he'd used his looks to compensate for that. And now here these people were, treating him as if he had always been a Sinclair. It just didn't jibe.

So he didn't have to reply. He turned back to the computer, his thoughts swirling in his head. Eventually, he had all the information he needed to determine the problem. He checked the back of the machine, made a few adjustments, and corrected a few lines of machine language that had somehow become skewed. He stood back. The program came up as it should, and Midnight clapped like an audience at a performance.

"So, whaddya say, Blue. You want a job doin' this or not?"

Christian turned around. "Doin' this assessment, right?"

"To start with, but then I figure I'll want you to fix the problems you find too."

"First thing would be to upgrade to at least fourt-eight-sixes," Christian said, nodding toward the computer. "That'll cost ya."

Midnight nodded. "Well, why don't you check everything out and give me a figure as to what it would cost to make everything run better."

"Better being faster? Or more efficiently?"

She grimaced. "Is both too much to ask?"

"No, but that will definitely cost."

"Cost I can deal with; it's damned computers that don't do what I want that I can't deal with."

"Well, that I can fix," Christian said, pleased to have a job after only two hours in the States.

It was almost eleven before Joe finally made it into the office. Christian was sitting at Midnight's terminal, trying to familiarize himself with the system. Midnight was sitting on the other side of her desk, reading through a month-end report. Joe stood in the doorway, surveying the scene before him with a bemused grin on his face.

"Well, that didn't take long," he said finally.

Christian turned around, and Midnight looked up. "What?" Midnight asked.

Joe walked over, extending his hand to Christian and shaking, then looked at Midnight with a gesture to his cousin. "He's been here, what... three hours, and already he's taken over your job?" He grinned widely.

Midnight rolled her eyes. "I could be so lucky. He's going to do some work on our computers. Thankfully the recessed computer-phobic Sinclair gene skipped his generation."

Joe looked at Christian, who had stood by this time. "You know computers, man?" he asked, surprise coloring his voice.

"Yeah." Christian shrugged. "Doesn't everybody?"

Midnight laughed. "Blue, if there was a place on this earth where everyone knew computers, your cousin would be in the place on the planet furthest from it."

"Ah," Christian said, understanding dawning.

"Yeah, well…" Joe looked recalcitrant. "I know a lot of people that know a lot about computers and wouldn't know the business end of a gun if it was pointed at them."

Christian looked pensively up at the ceiling.

"What?" Joe said, mockingly irate. "You're gonna say you know guns too?"

Christian's lips twisted in an apologetic grin. "When I carry, it's a SIG P220, with Black Talon ammunition, seven rounds in the clip, one in the chamber, two spare clips, and TRITIUM night sights."

"Shit," Joe said, shaking his head, as Midnight started to laugh. He grinned. "Shut up, Night." Then he looked back at Christian. "You ready for lunch?"

Christian nodded. "Okay."

"Night?"

"Rain check. I've got a raid this afternoon, and I'm determined to get this report read before then."

Joe raised an eyebrow. "Rick know you got a raid?"

"Yes, Sinclair, he knows," Midnight said, exasperated.

"Gave you shit, didn't he?"

"Doesn't he always?" Midnight didn't sound angry in the slightest.

"You gotta be gettin' used to it by now."

"You'd think so. I'll see you two later."

"Yeah, later," Joe said.

Outside, Joe led Christian over to the Jaguar he was driving that day. He had anticipated having Christian with him on the way home that evening, and he had to pick Randy up from school. He took note of Christian's appraising look at the car. "I usually drive a Porsche, but I gotta pick Randy up…"

"Jaguar's cool," Christian said. "Had one back home."

"Yeah? What model?"

"KX8."

Joe nodded. "Badass car."

"Blew more than a few doors off."

Joe reached over to dial a number on his cell phone. The line rang, and a woman answered.

"Hello?"

"Hey," Joe said smoothly.

"Hey yourself," Randy replied, a smile in her voice.

"How'd the final go?"

"Fine. How'd the raid go?"

"Not fine."

"Uh-oh… What happened?"

"I'll tell you over lunch. Are you free?"

"Oh, I suppose for you I could manage to be…"

"Well, Christian and I would appreciate it."

"You say that now…"

Joe laughed. "We'll pick you up outside the psych building in ten, okay?"

"You got it, handsome."

Ten minutes later Joe pulled up to the psychology wing at the University of California at San Diego. Christian got out to let Randy sit in front with Joe. He was taken aback by how beautiful she was in person as well. Don't the women in this country age at all? he thought. He extended his hand to Randy, taking hers gently.

She smiled. "Christian, it's very nice to meet you." She was taken aback by his appearance as well. He really was a dark version of her husband. His looks would be considered movie-star handsome.

In the car, Christian listened as Joe and Randy talked, watching the way his cousin acted with his wife.

"Have you seen Donovan lately?" Randy asked at one point, and saw a strange look cross Joe's face. "What?"

"Why do you ask?" Joe asked, his tone cautionary.

"It's just been a while since he's come by, and I wondered if he's on assignment again, or something…" she said, her eyes narrowing. She knew her husband well, and she could see he was debating telling her something. "Why did you think I was asking?"

"I just thought you might have talked to him or something…" Joe said cautiously.

"Okay…" Randy sounded a lot like Midnight when she was waiting for more information.

176

"Look, I didn't want to say anything till I knew what was going to happen."

"Happen about what?" Randy asked, her voice taking on an edge.

Joe looked up, gritting his teeth. He could already hear the lioness coming out in his wife and he hadn't even told her anything yet. He was silent for a long moment, then blew his breath out in a frustrated sigh. "A couple weeks back he got into it with a friend of his at 10-7. He hit the guy and a couple of LTs saw it. I talked to him about it yesterday." He kept his voice purposefully casual, but Randy wasn't fooled by it.

"You held a corrective interview with him over a bar fight?" she asked incredulously.

"It wasn't just a bar fight, Randy," Joe said, his voice becoming a little edgy. He knew what was coming. "The other guy was a cop too."

"Okay, so now what happens?" Randy said angrily. "Now you hang him from the highest flagpole for doing the same damn thing other cops do?"

"Randy! I'm doin' my job. You know damn good and well that I can't let something like this go. He injured another officer, it has come to my attention, and now I have to do something about it. That's my job."

"Oh yeah, and when it comes to my brother you really do it, don't you?"

"I'm not gonna get into this with you, Randy." Joe made a cutting gesture with his right hand. "So let's just fucking drop it, okay?"

"So what's going to happen to him?" Randy asked, as if she hadn't heard what he had just said.

Joe took a deep breath, blowing it out and shaking his head. "It's real simple. If the guy files on him, he's gone."

Randy stared at him, a horrified expression on her face. "You can't do that," she said, as if he had just pronounced a death sentence on Donovan.

"I don't have a fucking choice."

"That's not fair, Joe, and you know it."

"Fair?" Joe repeated, his voice low, his expression disbelieving. "And I suppose it's fair that I catch hell every time your brother does something stupid?"

"No, just when you treat him differently than other officers."

"I give up," Joe said coldly. "I'm not going to argue this with you, because there's no winning with you. To hell with it." His phone rang then, and he hit the hands-free button without hesitation. "Yeah?" he barked.

"Jesus," Midnight said. "What's wrong with you all of a sudden?"

"Sorry." Joe closed his eyes momentarily. "I'm just on the receiving end of a lot of shit right now."

Midnight was silent for a moment. "Let me guess… It has something to do with your wife and her brother?"

"How'd you guess?" Joe said, angry still. Randy looked over at him, narrowing her eyes.

"Randy," Midnight said, obviously knowing she was on the speaker.

178

"Yes," Randy said after a long moment. She still looked irritated.

"I don't know what Joe's told you—"

"He told me that Donovan's in trouble for getting into a bar fight and that he could lose his job over it, and that's just plain bullshit, Midnight."

"It's not bullshit, Randy. It's procedure."

"Yeah, and it always goes double for Donovan, doesn't it?"

"As a matter of fact, it does," Midnight said calmly. "Randy, do you have any idea the fine line Joe and I walk every day? We have to balance everything—we have to keep everyone happy. And believe me, since half the fucking department still thinks Joe and I are together, and the other half isn't totally convinced that I didn't sleep my way into this job, or that your acquittal for attempted murder wasn't a departmental whitewash to save Joe's reputation, keeping people happy around here is a full-time job. Furthermore, Joe is Donovan's supervisor—Joe is doing his job. And I'm doing my job. When I hear that one of my officers hauled off and coldcocked another officer, it is my responsibility to see that it doesn't happen again. And if it happens to be your brother that was stupid enough to do it, then I have to make sure that he gets exactly the same treatment every other officer in the department would get. 'Cause I guarantee you one thing, Randy—everyone is just watching and waiting for me to screw up, and they're watching for Joe to screw up so they can write us off. I won't let it happen, not to me and not to Joe. We've worked too fucking hard for this department to lose it over hurt feelings—yours, to be exact. Do you understand?" Midnight's voice had become strident during her tirade, and even Christian could almost feel her anger crackling through the speaker.

179

Randy was silent for a long moment. It was obvious she was digesting what Midnight had said. Joe was looking over at her, having driven into the parking lot of the restaurant and parked during Midnight's maelstrom. His face held no apology; it was drawn and serious. It was obvious to Christian that this was an ongoing issue with them, but he doubted Midnight had ever addressed it directly with Randy. He was right. Joe had told Midnight about Randy thinking he was too hard on Donovan. Midnight had always threatened to "straighten her out," but Joe had always told her he'd deal with it.

Randy glanced over at Joe, a pained expression crossing her face at the look on his. She nodded to him, and Joe closed his eyes for a long moment.

"Randy?" Midnight said, her tone all chief.

"Yes," Randy said. "I get it."

"'Bout goddamned time," Midnight said. She sounded only half joking, and Randy knew it.

Midnight and Randy's relationship had been very different since Randy's affair with Dick Dickerson five years before. Midnight had become more of a friend, but also more of an adversary. Whereas before Randy's dalliance Midnight would excuse any foolish or naive thoughts of Randy's as her youth or innocence, now she was quick to point it out when she thought she was being difficult or irrational.

Midnight's main concern was always Joe. The agony her best friend had gone through, inflicted on him by his wife, had been burned into Midnight's memory, and she was determined to keep it from ever happening again. For that reason she was ever watchful for anything that made things hard on Joe. She guarded his spirit like a sentinel, determined to keep him from being hurt like that ever again.

Just as Joe was there for her anytime Rick failed to be, Midnight was ever Joe's back up. That conviction made her more vocal, like she had just been. Randy appreciated it, because as determined as Midnight was to keep Joe from being hurt, it was matched by Randy's determination to keep from hurting him ever again like she had five years before.

Lunch after that was a more sedate meal. Joe dropped Randy back at school, telling her he was headed home for the rest of the day. He had been up since four o'clock that morning and it was starting to wear on him. At the college, Joe pulled up to the curb and stopped the car. Randy had been quiet all through lunch and even more so on the drive back. Joe looked over at her, reaching across to touch her hand. She turned to him, the look in her eyes pained. Joe shook his head and leaned over to kiss her softly. "We'll talk later," he whispered against her lips.

Randy nodded and got out of the car.

On the drive to Joe and Randy's house, Christian looked over at his cousin. He'd been surprised by the argument between the couple, but he'd been pleased to note that Joe didn't seem to have been pussywhipped in the slightest. He had stood his ground, and Christian had been further surprised by Midnight's vehemence. It was obvious to him that there was a history there, and he was curious as to the nature of it.

"So what's the story with Midnight?" he asked.

"Pertaining to what?" Joe said, his tone guarded. Christian picked up on it.

"You."

Joe gave the younger man an assessing look, as if trying to judge how much to tell him. Finally he shrugged. "We've been partners for-ever. She's married to my best friend, and she is my best friend."

"And you were a couple once," Christian added wisely.

"Yeah, that too," Joe said, his grin slow.

"She is incredible." Christian shook his head. "And I don't say that kind of thing about women."

"She is pretty great," Joe said, thinking of his partner. "And very taken," he added, seeing the look on Christian's face.

Christian waved Joe's statement away. "Taken is a temporary condition, easily curable."

Joe looked back at his cousin, surprised at first, then started to laugh. "I'm warning ya, man, Rick may seem easygoin', but Midnight is the one thing he will fight to the death for. And I'm deadly serious about that."

"Yeah, but what if she decides she wants me?" Christian said, testing his boundaries.

"Don't hold your breath," Joe said confidently. "She's in love with him deep. Besides," he said, changing tactics when he could see he wasn't convincing the younger man, "that woman is more than two handfuls, and she's getting more difficult as she gets older, not easier."

"That's why she needs a younger man to take care of her."

Joe gave his cousin a long look, then shook his head. "Make your best play, man. But I'm not gonna be responsible for what Rick does to ya, or for that matter Midnight."

Christian nodded, his grin wide. "I could be so lucky. So what's the story with your wife? She got a mother bear complex or what?"

"I guess in a way she does. She's been the only mother Donovan's had since he was eleven—that tends to make her protective."

"She always jump your shit like that?"

Joe shook his head. "She gets a little bent when it comes to Donovan, yeah."

"So why didn't you marry your partner instead? At least she's on your side."

Joe laughed. "Not always. In fact, half the time she sides with Randy. You just happened to catch the argument she's on my side in."

"Yeah, but Midnight is so…" Christian held his hands up as if trying to think of a way to describe her. "What possessed you to break it off with that?" He sounded aghast.

"Falling in love with Randy is what possessed me. You haven't had a real good first impression of her, but believe me, she's the one I want."

Christian shrugged. "Okay…"

"Trust me, Randy and I have been through a lot together, and she's been worth every second." Joe looked out the window for a long moment, then back at Christian. "So what was the story with you and Geneva Glasstone?"

Christian looked over at him, his eyes showing mild surprise that Joe knew about Geneva. After a long moment he shrugged, looking away. "It was business."

"Business?"

Christian glanced back at his cousin, a leering grin starting on his face. "That and sex."

Joe widened his eyes. "She's older than me, man…"

"You know her?" Christian said, surprised.

"Yeah, me and Rick and her used to attend a lot of the same parties, and they weren't all society gigs, if you get my meaning."

"I believe that. Well, she used me, I used her—it was mutually beneficial."

Joe looked surprised, but didn't question him further.

"Look, man," Christian said, his tone changing. "I gotta tell ya, what you did for me, for my mother…" He trailed off as emotion welled up in his voice. "I can't begin to thank you. To do that for someone you didn't even know, on the word from some guy that your father knew his mother." He shook his head as if he couldn't begin to comprehend it.

Joe looked back at him seriously. "I recognized my father's way. And I believed you. You're family—that's what family does."

"Yeah, but you didn't know me."

"And how much desperation had to build up to get you to call me? You didn't know me either," Joe said somberly. "I figured you weren't in the habit of going through all that you did to get to me as a scam. You were legitimate, and so was your need."

Christian grinned "Legitimate."

"You're a Sinclair. I don't care what you call yourself," Joe said simply.

Christian just stared back at him; hearing him say it made it seem true. He didn't know what to make of these people. They were so different from the people he'd dealt with his whole life. They didn't seem to want anything from him, and were willing to accept him into their circle without a price. He knew it wasn't possible, he just didn't know when he'd find out he was wrong.

Two nights later, Christian was sitting in Joe's living room. He was watching television, his mind still trying to adjust to being there. It was just after nine o'clock when Randy came in. She had one night class this semester and it kept her out late two nights a week. Christian had kept to himself over the last two days, trying to make the assimilation to being dependent on someone for his livelihood without giving anything in return. It was a difficult leap for him.

"Hi there," Randy said, surprised to see him sitting in the living room. She had noted his isolation from them and had wondered if that was how he would always be. She hoped not; she knew Joe liked the young man, and she sincerely hoped they could become friends.

Christian glanced up, looking chagrined at having been "caught" in the living room.

"What are you watching?" Randy asked, making a point of keeping her tone friendly. She knew she had made a bad impression on him the first day she'd met him, and that had also bothered her. She didn't want Joe's cousin thinking she was a shrew.

Christian looked down at the remote in his hand, then at the TV, and shrugged. "A movie."

"Well," Randy said, sitting down on the opposite end of the couch. She smiled. "That narrows it down."

Christian grinned, not really looking at her.

"I owe you an apology," Randy said quietly.

Christian looked up at her. "For what?"

"For the other day, for the fight that Joe and I had in front of you…"

Christian looked down at his hands, shrugging. "It was your car—you have a right to fight with your husband in it," he said, his tone belying his discomfort at the position he was in.

"That bothers you, doesn't it?" Randy asked, zeroing in on his concern easily. "That you imagine yourself to be at a disadvantage here."

Christian glanced up at her, his light blue eyes clearly indicating that he didn't think she had a good grip on reality at that moment. "Imagine? No, I don't imagine anythin'," he said coolly.

"You're wrong, Christian," she said softly. "Joe doesn't look at your being here as an imposition, or that he's doing you a favor. He looks at it as family doing for family. It's what he'd do for his aunt, or his uncle if it came to that. You're his family and you needed something—he provided it. Nobody's keeping score here." She looked at him frankly. "But you."

Christian narrowed his eyes slightly "Nothing comes for free. I've been around long enough to know that."

"Well, you haven't been around my husband," Randy said, her face taking on a faraway look. "Since I've been married to him, he has done so much for my family, my brothers. He bought the house we grew up in and gave all three of us the title. He paid for Donovan to go to school. He helped Darrell, my older brother, with the capital to start a construction business. He's done so much… and he never asks for anything in return. He doesn't remind you of what he's done for you, he just does. We've been through so much together, and there were some really bad times, but he stood by me. And he loved me when I didn't deserve it. I love him all the more for that now." She turned back to Christian, looking a bit abashed. "I'm sorry, I'm going on and on. I guess I'm still hammering myself for the fight the other day. We were supposed to talk and we haven't had a chance yet. But I don't want you to think Joe is expecting anything from you. Neither am I. Okay?"

Christian had watched her during her speech and begun to wonder if his judgement about her had been a bit hasty. Rethinking his first impressions was not something Christian Collins was given to doing, but things seemed to be changing a lot since he'd reached America.

"Midnight said something the other day about you being on trial for attempted murder?" The question had been mulling around in Christian's head since that day.

Randy couldn't help but smile. She wondered if he'd even taken to heart one word she'd just said. She rubbed her forehead as she tried to think of a way to put her answer. Finally, she just nodded, not sure what to say.

"Who did you try to kill?" Christian asked, his tone reminding her that was what he had done to get arrested.

Randy shook her head. "I didn't try to kill anyone. I was accused of trying to kill Midnight and Joe." She said it so simply that Christian had to think about it for a minute to understand that she'd been accused of trying to kill his cousin and his cousin's partner.

"Whoa..." he said, his face showing his disbelief. "What happened?" Then he looked a bit chagrined. "Or is it none of my business?"

Randy shrugged. "It's common knowledge around here. About

five years ago I decided to become a police officer, much to Joe's dismay. He fought the idea and I ended up foolishly rebelling against his adamancy. That rebellion led me into the arms of another man. Another police officer with the department. Little did I know that the guy was as dirty as they come and he and his friends had had his sights on getting rid of Joe and Midnight and their unit, FORS, for a long time. I fell right into the trap. First he attacked Midnight in my presence, almost killing her when he threw her up against a wall. Then he and his friends kidnapped Joe and tried to kill him too. Because I was involved with this dirty cop, I was accused of masterminding the whole thing."

"But you were acquitted?" Christian said, surprised by her story.

"Yes. And to this day, I'm sure that what convinced the jury the most was the fact that both Joe and Midnight testified on my behalf. They'd both been hurt so much by this man I'd been involved with, and yet they stood by me." Randy closed her eyes, shaking her head. "You can see why I'm devoted to my husband now. He loved me enough to believe in me, and trust me, even when some of the evidence was pretty damning. Even when I cheated on him."

"And Midnight testified for you too?" It was clear Christian couldn't believe that.

"Yes. She almost died because of what Dick had done, while I was standing right there, and yet she testified for me. In fact, she hid the fact that I had been there at all from Joe when she woke up, because she knew that for whatever reason, Joe still loved me. She wanted Joe to be happy, and she thought he would be if I would just regain my senses. I did in a hurry."

"Jesus Christ…" Christian said, almost awestruck. "Who are

you people?" He shook his head. "I can't even begin to fathom having that much faith in anyone."

"Hang around this family long enough, we'll get to you," Randy said, her smile wide.

The following morning, Christian sat in Midnight's office, working on her computer. Midnight was at the table, reading and writing notes. Joe walked in and again was taken aback by his cousin sitting at a computer. He couldn't get used to the fact that the young man had a knack for the machine.

"Where've you been?" Midnight asked, glancing at her watch and looking back at the man she still considered her partner.

"Had to drop Susan off at school," Joe said, leaning against the doorjamb.

"She's going to school in the daytime now?" Midnight asked, surprised.

"Just on Mondays and Wednesdays. Her and Randy are doing a sort of a trade-off for a semester. Susan wants to finish her child psychology degree, and Randy had a night class to take for a lab."

"Okay..." Midnight grinned at her partner. "Speaking of Susan," she said, taking on a conspiring tone, "Rick told me what you thought about her and Warren, and I have to tell ya, I agree with you. The guy's about as dullsville as they come."

Joe nodded, rolling his eyes. "Did Rick tell you what he told me?" Midnight shook her head. "He said that Warren was from a 'good family.'" Joe's tone indicated what he thought of that.

"I'm not surprised. He's been getting real protective of the young women in his life lately. It's all these guys that are hanging around Keyla right now that's doin' it."

"Yeah, well that doesn't mean Susan should marry some drip. She's gotta live with the guy. Have you seen them together? The guy's about as demonstrative as a radish, and has the personality to match."

Midnight laughed at Joe's description, but nodded all the same. "Hey, who knows, maybe Susan likes radishes…"

"I'll buy her a salad," Joe said seriously, but his eyes glittered humorously.

Midnight shook her head, grinning. "If she thinks she wants to marry the guy, what can we do? It's her life, her decision."

"Yeah, yeah, women's lib and all that crap. I've heard it all before," Joe said, waving his hand disdainfully.

Christian, who had been listening in, laughed.

Midnight looked over at him. "Is that another country heard from over there?"

Christian grinned, shaking his head, indicating he was not entering into this discussion.

Midnight turned back to Joe, her face taking on a more serious expression. "So did you have that meeting with Jones yet?"

"No, I'm on my way now, boss," he said, returning her grin, but with a pointed look.

"So why are you still here?" she said jokingly.

"I'm not," Joe said, and turned and walked out of the office. Midnight's laughter followed him.

CHAPTER 6

Donovan was called into Midnight's office later that day. Walking in, he felt his stomach tighten; this was the last place he wanted to be. Steeling himself, he knocked on her inner door.

"Come," Midnight called.

He went in. "You wanted to see me, Chief?" he said, ever respectful.

Midnight looked up and smiled. "Yes, Donovan, come on in." She looked over at Christian. "Christian, could you excuse us for a few minutes, please?"

Christian looked surprised for a moment, then nodded. He had been surprised that she had asked him, rather than telling him to get out. It was refreshing to be treated with respect instead of disdain or tolerance. He left the room, closing the door quietly behind him.

"Have a seat, Donovan," Midnight said, gesturing to a chair as she moved to sit behind her desk. She could easily see that the situation was wearing on him. "How much sleep have you had in the last few days?"

"Oh… some," Donovan said vaguely.

"Not enough, I'll bet."

Donovan looked back at her seriously. "If your career was on the line, would you be able to sleep?"

Midnight knew he was right. "Well, thankfully that is no longer an issue. Jones doesn't want to file a complaint." The relief that flooded Donovan's face was almost painful to witness. "But next time you decide to be gallant, try to be a little less public about it, okay?"

A lopsided grin tugged at Donovan's lips. Her statement told him that while she thought what he had done was wrong, it was also admirable. Midnight knew full well where Donovan had come by his chivalrous ways. He'd been hanging out with one Joseph Michael Sinclair too long. It had been difficult for Midnight to find fault with what Donovan had done after Jeanie told her the whole story, but it had been her responsibility to respond officially. She was very happy, therefore, to be able to "officially" let him off the hook.

"Now, the next thing I called you in here for is that I need a favor," Midnight said.

Donovan nodded. "Okay."

"I need you to take Christian over to the warehouse so he can see the inventory logs there."

Donovan looked back at her for a long moment, then nodded slowly. Midnight could see a question in his eyes, but she liked the fact that he seemed willing to do whatever she asked. It was the loyalty that she needed from him at the moment.

"He's going to work on a new inventory system for me, and I want him to have an idea of how things have been tracked in the past," she explained.

"A new system?" Donovan asked, surprised.

"Yeah, I've been thinking about it for a long time now, and then come to find out that Joe's cousin happens to be a computer whiz—it seemed a perfect opportunity."

Again Donovan nodded, his faith in Midnight's judgement as set in stone as that of any veteran member of FORS. "When do you want me to take him?"

"Now, if you have time."

"You got it boss." Donovan stood to leave.

Midnight walked around her desk, reaching up to hug him. "I'm glad everything worked out."

Donovan hugged her tightly. "That makes two of us," he said, his grin wide.

When they parted, Donovan looked down at the petite woman he respected more than anyone in the world. "Thanks, Midnight."

"What for?" Midnight asked, her voice reflecting surprise. "We were busting your butt, Donovan, just like we would have on anyone else."

"I know, but I also know that neither you nor Joe liked it much. I'm just really sorry I put you two in that kind of position, ya know?"

"Hey, I know where you got that damn valiant streak from. I've had to deal with that for fifteen years—you think I'd be used to it by now."

Donovan smiled.

Ten minutes later, Donovan led Christian to his Mustang, parked in the department lot. Once in the car, Donovan flipped through radio stations and finally pushed in a CD. Skipping through the tracks, he settled on one and turned the volume up. The eerie keyboard and guitar intro to The Cars' "Moving In Stereo" came through the speakers, filling the car. The electric drum and keyboard kicked in as Donovan accelerated out of the parking lot and down the street, exercising the high-performance engine. He couldn't get over how relieved he was at having been cleared of the incident in the bar; he was ecstatic. His fingers drummed on the steering wheel as the song played on and he sang to the words. Christian observed, his light blue eyes taking in the expensive leather interior of the car, and wondered idly if Joe had bought it for "Randy's brother."

After the song ended, Donovan lowered the volume and glanced over at Christian apologetically. "Sorry, I just had a need to do that. Blowin' off some steam, ya know?"

Christian nodded, narrowing his eyes slightly. "So you're clear, then?"

Donovan looked surprised for a moment, but then realized Christian had probably heard Joe and his sister discussing the matter. "Yeah," he said simply.

"So was it over a broad?" Christian said derogatorily as he watched Donovan for a reaction. He got one.

The muscles in Donovan's jaw tightened and his eyes narrowed as he stared straight ahead. "The broad is my girlfriend," he said, his tone indicating that Christian was out of line. But Christian knew that.

The Englishman shook his head disdainfully. "Ain't found a woman yet worth fighting over."

"Well, I have," Donovan said, his anger under control now.

"She good-lookin'?" Christian asked with a leer.

"Incredibly," Donovan said, refusing to rise to the bait again.

"She good in bed?" Christian asked then, knowing he was pushing it.

Donovan looked over at the other man, his eyes narrowed. "That's none of your fucking business."

"Careful," Christian said, his eyes twinkling with barely suppressed delight. "You just got out of a jam. I don't think even your sister could get you out of another one right now."

Donovan looked back at Joe's cousin, his mouth open in appalled anger. He wasn't even able to come up with a retort that would fit. Finally he shook his head, looking back at the road. Christian laughed lightly to himself, shaking his own head. Americans were even easier than the English, he thought wryly.

They were silent for the rest of the drive to the warehouse. Once there, Donovan showed Christian the records and stood by as the Englishman looked at them.

"Archaic," Christian muttered to himself as he leafed through the written documents. He shook his head. "Too fucking easy to cheat."

"That's what's been happening," Donovan said.

"Ya got rats, eh?"

Donovan nodded. "Lots of 'em."

"And that's what you're working with Midnight on?"

"Yep. Gotta clean house, and right now she's only trusting family to do that," Donovan said, aware he was now including Christian in that.

Christian didn't miss the comment, and he was again taken aback by it. Here he had purposely baited the guy a half hour before, pissing him off no end, and yet even Donovan considered him "family." It irritated him more than he could say that it made him feel good. The last thing he needed to do was go soft. Instead of replying to Donovan's statement he simply nodded.

On the way back to the office, Donovan's car phone rang. He hit the hands-free button.

"'Lo?"

"Hey there," Jeanie said, making Donovan smile instantly. Christian knew it had to be the "broad" they had discussed earlier.

"Hi," Donovan said, his voice softening just a bit.

"I heard the good news."

"Yeah, I was gonna tell you when I got back. Midnight told me about an hour ago."

"Well, she just told me. I guess she figured she would probably get more work out of me if I wasn't worried about the demise of your law enforcement career thanks to me." She sounded chagrined on the last.

"Jay, we've already had this discussion," Donovan said lightly even as he rolled his eyes.

"I know, I know. Anyway, are we having lunch today or what?" she asked, her tone changing slightly.

Donovan picked up on it instantly. He grinned. "What did you hear?"

"Damn it, how do you do that?"

"Talent. You heard from them, didn't you?"

"Yep." Jeanie was almost dancing. "My physical agility is next Saturday at ten. Can you be there?" she asked, her voice almost begging him.

Donovan smiled again. "I'll do you one better. I'll take you over the course this weekend."

"You can do that?"

"I happen to know the Chief of Police—I think I can manage it."

"That would be so great, Donovan. I'll owe you so big."

"I'll collect eventually," Donovan said suggestively. "Look, I'll be back in ten. We'll go and celebrate."

"I'll be waiting, Sergeant," Jeanie replied, her voice low now, giving no indication of whether she meant for him to collect or for him to get back. Donovan laughed as he hung up.

"That's the one, huh?" Christian asked with an open look.

Donovan nodded, his smile wide. "That's the one."

Back at the office, Donovan walked in with Christian right behind him. Jeanie was sitting at her desk, but stood up when he came in. Donovan went over, pulling her into his embrace. After a few moments, she leaned back, looking up at him with a brilliant smile on her face. Christian watched the exchange and saw immediately what Donovan thought was worth fighting for. Jeanie was beautiful. Her long chestnut hair, her brown eyes, her smile—she was incredible. Christian was beginning to wonder if San Diego had any ugly women in it. And it seemed the Sinclair-Debenshire clan had the corner on the fucking market for beautiful women.

"Jeanie," Donovan said, finally remembering Christian standing just off to the side. "Have you met Christian?" He knew she'd been out of the office that morning and hadn't likely met him before that.

"Nope," Jeanie said, glancing at Christian. She was taken aback by his looks; his coloring was so dark, and in direct contrast to his light blue eyes. He was breathtaking. "So you're the other Sinclair," she said, her smile friendly, but much like Midnight, it was nowhere near a come-on. She extended her hand.

He took it in his, staring directly into her eyes as he smiled. "Actually, it's Collins, Blue, but I'm pleased to meet you all the same." His voice was a caress, and Jeanie didn't miss it; neither did Donovan.

"Jet back, man," Donovan said, his tone light but his eyes narrowed. "She's well and truly taken right now."

Christian didn't look at him. He continued to stare into Jeanie's eyes, the look in his own triumphant. Jeanie saw it and narrowed her eyes slightly as she grinned. She had figured out that he was trying to get to Donovan, and it had worked.

"Well," Christian said to her, his tone not changing, "when you get done with him, give me a call."

This time Donovan actually took a step toward him, an action that made Christian start to smile delightedly. Jeanie shook her head, moving to take Donovan's arm and steer him toward the door. "Come on!" she said to her boyfriend, glancing back at Christian as they went out. Christian was still grinning as he sat on the edge of her desk, watching them go. She shook her head at him, but her grin too was intact.

Joe showed up in Midnight's office at four thirty, looking harried. "Christian," he said, poking his head in the door.

Christian looked up from the computer. "Yeah?"

"Look, can you do me a favor? I need someone to pick Susan up from the college. I gotta go out to a raid site and I'm just not gonna make it."

Christian nodded. "No problem."

"Thanks, man. Midnight can give you directions. I gotta go. I'll see ya at home later."

"You got it," Christian said, feeling again the beginnings of the warmth he felt every time Joe treated him so familiarly, like they'd known each other for years instead of days.

An hour later Christian pulled up to the building Midnight had told him about. He waited behind the wheel of the black Jaguar Joe was having him use until he got a car of his own, garnering a number of interested gazes from female passersby. He had the radio on, but he couldn't find a song he liked. Finally he pushed in Matchbox 20's Yourself or Someone Like You. The song "3AM" came on. He drummed his fingers to the music as he waited for Susan.

Not too much later, she walked up with a man right beside her. She looked surprised to see him; they had met briefly the day before, but she certainly hadn't expected him to be picking her up from school that day. The man with her looked at him as well. Christian read the suspicion in his eyes easily. He and Susan had a quick conversation, and then he took her into his arms, kissing her. Christian saw the look of surprise on Susan's face and started to grin.

When she got into the car he was still grinning, and by this time shaking his head. The man she had been with stood on the sidewalk, watching them. Christian put the car into drive and, giving him a cocksure look, drove away. He reached over to turn up the song that had just started, "Push," and started to sing along.

Susan was surprised to find herself watching him in fascination, further surprised that he had an extremely nice singing voice. She had reacted to Christian the day before in the way most women did—tongue-tied and nervous. Christian had run into her in the hallway of the house. She had been rushing off after one of the children, but had stood stock still in front of him, dumbfounded.

"You must be Christian," she had said finally, her voice coming out cracked.

"I must be," Christian had replied, enjoying having the advantage. His light blue eyes had stared down into hers, making her squirm noticeably.

A moment later there had been a crash in the living room and Susan had had to rush off to find out what the children had gotten into. Christian had stared after her, grinning to himself.

Now, she watched him sing, his head moving with the slow rhythm of the music, his light eyes watching the road ahead. The words to the song were inflammatory, to say the least, but Susan could see that Christian liked them, and it made her wonder who the woman he was singing about was.

As the song ended, Christian turned the volume down. He glanced over and noted that Susan was watching him; he just gave her a knowing smile then looked away.

After a long silence, Christian surprised her by saying, "So that was him, huh?"

It took Susan a moment to reply. "Him, who?" she asked, looking perplexed.

"The guy," Christian said, his tone indicating she should know.

"What guy?" Then understanding dawned. "Oh, you mean

Warren?"

"Yeah, Warren," Christian said, using the man's name as if he found it distasteful.

"Yes, that was him. Why?"

Christian shrugged. "Looks like a real pansy," he said, so casually that it took Susan a moment to realize he'd just insulted her fiancée.

"Excuse me?"

"I said, he looks like a pansy. Hell, he looks more English than I do."

"Well, you hardly look English, now do you?"

Christian grinned, aware he was irritating her. "If you wanted English, why didn't you just go back home and buy one?"

"Buy one?" Susan repeated, her voice reflecting her lack of understanding, but a few moments later she began to work it out. She grew angry then.

"How dare you," she said, her English accent sounding very high class, especially to Christian. "I will have you know that Warren and I are in love and that is why we're getting married. As for his looking English, well that's just icing on the cake."

"Not in this case, love," Christian said derogatorily.

"What is that supposed to mean?"

Again Christian shrugged, his expression infuriatingly serene even as his words were maddening. "You could do better."

"Better?"

"Yeah, the opposite of worse."

"I know what it means," Susan snapped. "Warren is from one of the best families in America. They own four large corporations with offices all over the world."

"So that's what gets you off, is it?" Christian said evenly.

"Off?"

"It gets you hot, all that money and power."

"No!" Susan exclaimed. "I mean… That's not… I…" She trailed off when she realized she was making no sense. Then she narrowed her eyes at him. "What right do you have, talking to me like this?"

"I'm just makin' an observation," Christian said calmly, even as his eyes twinkled at having gotten to her so easily.

"Well, keep your observations to yourself."

Christian was silent for a long few minutes. "Joe don't like it, you know," he said finally.

"Like what?"

"You marrying this guy."

Susan was taken aback, not sure whether or not to believe him. "How do you know?"

Christian looked over at her, his light blue eyes disconcerting her, then shrugged. "I heard him talkin' to Midnight."

Susan looked worried. "What did he say?"

"Just that he thought the guy was boring."

Susan didn't reply, her thoughts swirling. She hadn't known that Joe didn't like Warren; he hadn't said anything. Christian ejected the tape and put in another, fast-forwarding to his favorite song on it— the title track on Def Leppard's Slang. He liked the words a lot, and it had a fast-driving, harder-edged melody. He turned the volume up again and once more sang along. He looked for all intents and purposes like he meant every word, staring directly at Susan as he sang the first verse, disconcerting her further as she took in the words.

When the song ended, Susan looked at him pointedly. "What does 'slang' mean?"

Christian looked back at her openmouthed, then started to grin, shaking his head. "If you don't know, he ain't doin' it right."

"What?" Susan said, aghast at the insinuation in his voice.

"Sex," Christian said, loudly and clearly. "It's sex, okay?"

"Good Lord," Susan said. Her sensibilities were being severely tested on this ride. She saw Christian shaking his head and immediately became angry again. "What?"

"Nothin'," Christian said, his tone indicating disgust.

"What?"

"He's the only guy you've slept with, ain't he?" It was clear he thought she really didn't need to answer.

"What business is it of yours?"

Christian looked at her for a long, measured moment, then shook his head again. "You don't have to marry the first guy you fuck, you know."

Susan couldn't even begin to think of a reply. She sat staring out at the road ahead, feeling very impotent. Christian knew he'd hit home, and wondered if she'd even get past her injured dignity long enough to actually think about what he'd said. He figured he owed Joe a little bit of an effort, and he'd been trying to clue her in, but he also knew her sensibilities had been offended. "Diplomatic" was never a word anyone used to describe Christian Collins.

Later that day, Jeanie was spending her time with Donovan as she had many evenings since their first night together. They were lying on his couch, watching a movie, when his phone rang. Donovan reached up over his head and picked up the cordless phone.

"Hello?" he said, glancing down at Jeanie apologetically. She watched as he listened for a moment, then saw an irritated look cross his face.

"Look, Allison," Donovan said, obviously straining to be patient, "I can't, okay?" He listened for a couple more minutes, shaking his head and looking up at the ceiling. "No, alright, I just can't." He blew his breath out in an irritated sigh, glancing down at Jeanie again. "Because, Alli, I have a girlfriend now, okay?" Alli obviously went off on a tangent then, because Donovan listened resignedly with a very closed look on his face. When she was through he said, "Well, that's how it is, okay? No, you don't have to believe me, you just have to stop calling, okay?" He hung up a few minutes later. He looked down at Jeanie and saw that she was still watching him.

"Troubles?" Jeanie asked wryly.

Donovan grinned at her. "No, just an ex-girlfriend that doesn't want to get the hint."

"How many of those do you have?"

"How many of what?"

"Ex-girlfriends. A lot, huh?" she said, seeing the hesitant look on his face.

"A few, why?"

"Any of them really serious?" she said, ignoring his question.

"Why?"

"I'm just curious…" Jeanie's voice took on a playful timbre. "About how many scores of women you've devastated along the way."

"Funny," Donovan said, moving to kiss her. A few minutes later, Jeanie's questions and his answers didn't matter nearly as much.

Two hours later they were in his bed, Jeanie lying over him, her hair fanned out across his chest. Donovan stroked her hair with one hand, gripping her waist with the other.

"So?" she said, her voice still reflecting the effects of their love-making.

Donovan grinned. "What? You want something else now?"

"Yes, I want to know if this is how you go about avoiding a simple question."

Donovan looked back at her for a long moment, and she thought she saw the merest hint of irritation in his eyes. She was about to tell him never mind when he started to speak.

"Yes, one serious girlfriend. And yes, lots of others, hundreds, thousands," he said, shrugging and rolling his eyes. "Maybe even millions. I lost count."

Jeanie narrowed her eyes. "You rat. You know what I meant. One serious one, huh?"

Donovan sighed, looking up at the ceiling as if beseeching help from God to get him through this one. "Why do girls always want to talk about this stuff?"

"It's genetic. So tell me about the serious one. Who was she?"

Donovan was quiet for a few moments, obviously debating whether to tell her, but then shrugged. "We got together halfway through our senior year in high school. She had her whole life planned, and it was kind of cool being with someone who had goals for a change."

"What was her goal?"

He grinned. "To be a world-famous chef."

"That's where culinary classes came in?" Jeanie said, surprised. Though hearing it now, it made sense; he'd gone because of a woman.

"Yeah… that's why I went. But I actually liked it too, for a while."

"What happened?"

"Well," Donovan said hesitantly, "I decided to go to the police academy, and it didn't fit what she had planned for us."

"And what was that?"

"She had us going to Paris after graduation and working in a very exclusive hotel there. She thought the police academy was a hideous idea." He shrugged again, but Jeanie noticed that the look in his eyes had become very distant.

"Where is she now?" she asked, feeling jealous but not sure why.

"Still in Paris, as far as I know," Donovan said nonchalantly.

"But she was serious, huh?"

"Yeah." Donovan surprised her by turning onto his side and closing his eyes, signaling an end to the conversation.

Jeanie lay next to him, wondering at his mood. Was it talking about this particular girl that bothered him, or something else? After a long time, she got up and walked over to the pictures on his dresser. She was curious now. After looking at a few, she came to one of Donovan and a young woman. She had reddish-brown hair and ivory skin. Donovan was behind her with his arms around her waist. She was holding on to his arms, laughing up at him; Donovan was smiling too. Jeanie was just starting to take a closer look when she heard Donovan's voice.

"What're you doin?" he asked tiredly from the bed. He had opened one eye and was looking at her.

Jeanie shrugged. "Just looking."

"At..."

"This is her, isn't it?" She turned the picture around to him. Donovan looked at it for a long moment, as if reliving the time when it had been taken. Finally he nodded. "What's her name?" Jeanie asked doggedly.

"Serena."

Jeanie examined the picture and saw again what she thought she'd seen before Donovan spoke. She looked up at him, her eyes widening a little bit. "Were you engaged to her?"

Again he hesitated, as if not sure how much he wanted her to know, but after a few moments he nodded.

Jeanie was stunned. She didn't know exactly why she was so surprised about a guy like Donovan having been engaged before. God knew he was gorgeous, and funny, and everything else that attracted her to him, but engaged?

"When were you two supposed to be married?" she asked when she found her voice again.

"After graduation."

"You were supposed to be married that year?"

"It was a long time ago, Jay," Donovan said, irritated now.

"Yeah, but…"

"But what?" Donovan said sharply. "It's over, okay? What's the big deal? We wanted different things and it's over. Can we just drop the subject now?" Donovan sat up and took the picture out of her hands, tossing it aside and pulling her to him. As if to make up for his tone, he kissed her softly on the lips. "When do you have to be home tonight?"

"Same as usual, by two," Jeanie replied, already grinning at him.

"Someday I'm just going to kidnap you and never let you go home again," he said as he began to kiss her again. He threatened to kidnap her just about every night.

Later, as they lay together having made love again, Jeanie looked over at him. "Why does it matter so much to you that I stay here after two o'clock? Most guys would probably be happy…"

Donovan raised an eyebrow. "Do I seem like most guys?"

"No," Jeanie answered resoundingly. "But why does it matter to you?"

"Because I'd like to wake up to you in the morning, okay?"

"I can live with that," Jeanie said. She left as usual at 1:30.

At 6:30 a.m. Donovan woke to the sensation of someone kissing his shoulder, his back, and then the other shoulder. He was lying on his stomach with his arms around his pillow. He tensed when he felt the lips on his skin, but then relaxed as the scent of Jeanie's perfume came to him. Grinning, he turned over, grabbing her around the waist.

"What are you doing back here so soon?" he said, glancing at the clock on his nightstand.

"I said I was playing tennis," she said with a sly grin.

"Jay," Donovan said chidingly. "I don't like you lying to them about me."

"Donovan, you know I have to sometimes. They just don't understand about, well, you know… this."

"They don't know we're sleeping together," Donovan supplied, shaking his head, showing his disapproval of her concealing the nature of their relationship.

"Donovan, if I told them that, I'd never get to see you. They'd probably make me quit the department altogether."

"And what, lock you away in a tower?"

"No, just disown me and kick me out of the house," Jeanie said, her tone indicating that was much worse.

"Okay, okay." Donovan held up his hands in surrender. He kissed her again. "You win. I'll just enjoy this unexpected visit."

A little while later she snuggled under the blankets with him. They didn't make love again, just enjoyed being together. Eventually they fell asleep. Donovan lay on his stomach with one leg and an arm thrown over Jeanie. She lay on her back with one hand resting on his shoulder, the other stroking the arm that lay across her.

They woke to the sound of a male voice yelling "Pony!" down the hallway.

"Darrell, stop!" Donovan shouted, putting his hand out in a halting gesture.

Darrell paid his little brother no mind whatsoever, striding into the bedroom. Luckily, Jeanie was still dressed.

"Hi," Darrell said to her, his smile wide.

"Hi," Jeanie replied, a little less enthusiastically since she felt quite embarrassed.

"I'm Darrell, Pony's big brother." He gave her an inquisitive look. "And you are?"

Jeanie didn't answer, unable to muster her voice.

"Darrell," Donovan said, sounding irritated, "this is Jeanie. Jeanie, as you can tell, this is Darrell."

"Ah, Jeanie." Darrell nodded. "The girl worth fighting over."

Jeanie turned a few shades of red, and Donovan craned his neck around at his brother, giving him a narrowed look. "What is it you came here for?"

"Oh," Darrell said, looking like he had just remembered himself. "I need to borrow a three-eighths wrench. You got one?"

Donovan looked at his older brother for a long moment, then nodded. "You know where my tools are."

"Cool," Darrell said, looking down at Jeanie and canting his head to the side. "Boy, I'll tell ya, my baby brother does have a penchant for attracting beautiful women." He grinned wryly. "Course, then he can't get rid of 'em."

"Don't start, Darrell," Donovan said, lying his head back on his pillow.

"What?" Darrell asked innocently, though he was grinning almost evilly now. "You see, Jeanie, the difference between my baby brother and me is that when I break it off with a girl she hates my guts. When Pony there breaks it off, they just all sit around waiting for him to come back. It's disgusting. He never seems to know how good he's got it either. Shit, Pony, remember Paris? Can't believe you blew her off—she was beautiful!"

"Darrell!" Donovan said, levering himself up on his arm and looking at his brother as if he were ready to strangle him. "Shut up, okay?"

"Oops," Darrell said, not bothering to look the least bit chagrined. Then he started to grin, his eyes twinkling with humor. "Just hold on to him with both hands, Jeanie. There's hundreds of them out there waiting to take him back."

"You can go find your wrench now, Darrell, then I'll stuff it down your throat." Donovan looked very definitely like he meant it. Darrell just grinned as he walked out of the room and back down the hall.

"Charming, isn't he?" Donovan said.

"In a brutish, Neanderthal way, yes," Jeanie replied, her grin lopsided.

"Yeah…" Donovan made a face. It was obvious to Jeanie that he was sincerely hoping she wouldn't comment on what Darrell had said. She wondered what had caused Donovan to break it off with someone he was obviously serious enough about to ask to marry him. She wasn't ready to ask him, though; she didn't want to irritate him again. But it did make her wonder.

Frank Devereaux sat in the restaurant booth, his brown eyes surveying the area as he waited for his friends. He thought about what had brought him to this stage in his life. He'd been a police officer for

211

twenty-one years and was still only the rank of sergeant. That fact irritated him no end, but he didn't take into consideration that he was consistently late with his reports, when he did turn them in they were frequently returned, and he had been late for shifts a number of times over the years; sometimes he didn't turn up at all when he went on a drinking binge. Of course, he didn't know that Midnight Chevalier-Debenshire was also aware of his propensity toward violence against his wife, who happened to be her secretary. As far as Frank was concerned, his father had always hit his mother to keep her in line, as well as him and his two brothers, so it was okay to knock his wife around when she got mouthy. And much like his father, he had discovered buying on time early on in his career. He was proud of the Mercedes Benz he drove, as well as the four-bedroom house in Bonita, the boat in the marina at Seaport Village, and the best in home theater and electronic equipment for the house. It was a constant race to pay all the bills he'd racked up, which was why he and Cassandra had never had children—they couldn't afford them. Life had been getting desperate until five years before, when Frank met Rico Gaston and things turned around.

Rico Gaston was a drug dealer, plain and simple. He was considered very high level in the Puerto Rican branch of the cartel. He also dealt in stolen vehicles and weapons. He had learned from his father that the best way to keep the cops at bay was to buy them. That's what he'd done—he'd bought the best. He had also set up a nice little side business that his father didn't know about, which was turning out to be rather lucrative. He had had no idea how greedy cops could get when it came to money. He and Frank Devereaux, the property sergeant for the department, had devised a plan. Drug evidence was a major part of the inventory for the police department, and Frank Devereaux had discovered early on that the record keeping was hideous at best. When drugs came in as evidence they were weighed and labeled, but no one ever weighed them again. Devereaux skimmed a small amount of the "evidence" and, utilizing departmental supplies, repackaged it using the original tags. Then he got the drugs to Rico, who sold them and gave him a cut of the money.

They'd begun branching out into guns and drugs two years before, right as the new chief took office. Devereaux thought, like some of the other men in the department, that Midnight Chevalier had fucked her way up the chain of command. So he had no use for the female chief; he also figured her for an idiot and that she wouldn't notice. He had found out from Jerry McCaffery that morning that the chief did indeed notice the inconsistencies in the reports he fed her.

Jerry McCaffery was another veteran of the department with connections throughout. He was Internal Affairs; he knew everything. As a lieutenant he had access to the most classified of files, and he knew when something was up. Something was up in the chief's office now, and what bothered him the most was that the bitch was using her own people to conduct an investigation. He disliked Midnight Chevalier intensely. She had denied his promotion to captain the year before, citing his lack of efficiency and habitual insubordination to ranking officers, including herself.

She'd had problems with him as a captain of vice when some of her officers had been involved in a shooting. McCaffery hadn't been used to the captains standing so staunchly behind their officers until he'd run into Midnight Chevalier. Two of the officers involved had been members of her old unit, along with three from narcotics. She'd read every report he'd written, pointing out inconsistencies in witness stories as well as statements from the shooting review board that had been marginally or literally biased. In the end the officers had been cleared when Midnight went through the chief, who had forced him to work with another Internal Affairs lieutenant to clear up the discrepancies. He'd hated Midnight ever since. Her denial of his promotion had only served to set his hatred in concrete.

Another reason he despised her and her friend Sinclair was their money. Jerry had grown up the hard way, having to struggle for everything he ever had. After two marriages and two nasty divorces leaving him paying a fair share of his salary in alimony and child support, he was still struggling to make ends meet. When he got to talking to Devereaux one night at the bar, Frank had let him in on his little money-making scheme. Devereaux figured that having someone in IA involved made it virtually impossible to get investigated without some forewarning. Neither of them had figured on Midnight Chevalier or that she did things her own way, using people she trusted.

Devereaux, McCaffery, and Gaston were meeting to discuss what to do. McCaffery arrived first, giving Frank the whole story on what little he'd been able to find out.

"She's got that brother of Sinclair's on it, and that little tease that used to work for Sinclair, the one that wants to be a cop," McCaffery said with a sneer. He'd had any number of fantasies about Jeanie Franco, but of course she'd never even given him a second look. At forty-five he wasn't much to look at, with brown curly hair that always looked like it needed cutting and ordinary brown eyes, the rest of him as nondescript as the suits he wore. Sure, she'd always smiled at him and been nice when he'd requested reports from Sinclair's files, but that was all. He'd never been fool enough to make a pass at her, knowing that Sinclair had a soft spot for her. Yeah, McCaffery had always thought crudely, he's probably fucking her too.

McCaffery, like Devereaux, was sure Midnight and Sinclair were still an item, and that Sinclair screwed every woman he came into contact with. Why else would they all defend him tooth and nail whenever a word was said against him?

McCaffery had had to deal with Jessica Ako again that day. She'd been working with Internal Affairs in an effort to gain experience for her sergeant's exam. McCaffery knew better than to mess with that one either way; he'd had one run-in with her husband, nicknamed Tiny. The huge Samoan had been displeased about a sexual comment he'd inadvertently made to Jessica on their first meeting, something pertaining to her being a "natural redhead." She'd mentioned it to her husband. Tiny had cornered Jerry in the parking lot one night after work, shoving him against his car and staring down at him, every inch of him the gang member he had once been.

"You made a comment to Jessica Ako today," Tiny had rumbled. "You make a comment like that to her again and I'll hand you your lungs. You got that?"

Jerry had stared up at the big man, terrified. He had never been a very brave cop, but in the face of such naked fury he had merely nodded meekly, praying the big guy wouldn't decide to remove a less necessary but still painful-to-remove body part.

"Yeah?" Devereaux was saying irritably. "Well, watch the rest of 'em. You know she's got that damned gang of hers willing to lay down and die for her..." He trailed off as he thought of his own run-ins with members of FORS, when he'd made the mistake of voicing too loudly his dislike of Chief Chevalier. A particularly nasty-looking Laotian and an equally dangerous-looking white guy named Dibbins had backed him into an interview room minutes later when no one was looking.

"You got a problem with the chief?" Spider Nguyen had said, his eyes narrowed.

"Yeah," Dibbins put in, leaning far too casually against the door, "'cause we kinda like her."

"And we're not real fond of assholes like you mouthin' off about her," Spider said, looking like the gang member he'd been years before.

"Everybody's gotta like someone, now don't they?" Devereaux said, his bravado strong.

"Yeah, well there's a little sayin' we like," Dibbins said. "Opinions are like assholes—everyone's got one."

"And if you don't want yours jacked up, you better watch your step where Midnight's concerned," Spider said very seriously.

Devereaux hadn't replied to that, not willing to push his luck. After a long, threat-laden pause, Dibbins had pushed away from the door to the interview room, gesturing in an exaggeratedly polite manner for Devereaux to proceed him. After a moment's hesitation he had, watching his back the entire time. He'd avoided vice for a while after that.

"So Curtis is working with her. Well, that figures," Devereaux said, clearly annoyed. "Hell, considering who his sister is, he's probably dirtier than we are." He laughed.

"Yeah, maybe we should bring him in," Jerry said, laughing too. "That'd really piss Chevalier off, if one of her own fucked her over."

"Yeah." Devereaux shook his head. "But it's too risky—you never know, that good-cop bullshit might be real."

"Don't count on it, his ass was almost up on charges."

"For what?" Frank asked, always interested when the "best and brightest" got into trouble.

"For punching David Jones out at 10-7," Jerry said, having read the file just that morning.

"No shit?" Devereaux said.

"Yeah, but of course he got off. Ain't nothin' Chevalier won't whitewash for Sinclair, ya know," Jerry said, conveniently forgetting that it was Chevalier and Sinclair that had initiated the investigation into the incident.

Rico Gaston arrived a few minutes later, shadowed as ever by his bodyguard. He wore a black suit with a deep-purple banded-collar shirt, and too much gold. He stood at a mere five foot seven inches, so wore high-heeled leather boots to appear taller. He sat at the booth, looking disgusted by his surroundings. "We could have met somewhere decent," he said, his nose twitching.

"Look, we don't got time to go runnin' down to the marina to your daddy's yacht every time somethin' comes up, okay?" Devereaux said, getting tired of the Puerto Rican's superior attitude.

"So what is it now?" Rico asked.

"Well, there's a potential problem," Jerry said, still intimidated by Gaston; he'd seen one too many episodes of Miami Vice.

"Chevalier's runnin' some sort of investigation," Devereaux said.

"Well, why don't you know what sort of investigation?" Gaston asked. "I thought you were cops? The best... right?" His tone indicated he thought anything but.

"Yeah, well normally Jerry would, since he's IA," Devereaux

217

said. "But she's not runnin' it through IA, which is not normal."

Gaston nodded. "How close do you think she is?"

"Nowhere near," Devereaux said. "I think she's just fishing at this point."

"Good." Gaston narrowed his eyes as he thought about what to do. "I think we should send Chief Chevalier a message, don't you? Maybe if she thinks this investigation might be detrimental to the health of someone close to her, she might just quit while she's ahead."

"What kind of message?" Devereaux asked, looking cynical. "You don't know this broad—she's like a fucking pit bull when she wants to be. It'd have to be a pretty serious message."

Gaston looked back at the veteran cop calmly, his almost-black eyes indicating no emotion. "So make it a serious message."

Devereaux looked back at the man for a long moment, then nodded, sure he knew what the Puerto Rican meant. He and Jerry McCaffery left a few minutes later.

Christian and Susan's second time together in a car wasn't quite as adversarial as the first. Christian wasn't feeling well, having caught a cold from someone at the department. It had been a month since he'd come to America, and he was finally feeling more acclimated. He'd gone out a number of times, as usual attracting extreme amounts of attention, including from men who were irritated that he received the attention from all the women in the club. He'd gotten into a few fights, easily able to hold his own. Randy had been appalled when he'd come home very early in a morning looking worn out, with a cut or a bruise. Joe laughed, reminded of his mother years before. He shook his head at Christian as the younger man looked to his cousin for assistance.

"You're on your own, man," Joe would say, still grinning.

Randy had proceeded to make sure he cleaned the cut or went off to bed after having eaten something. She had turned into quite the mother since the children had been born. Even though Christian was only seven years younger than her, she still felt the need to watch over him.

Now, Christian was driving Susan to the store to pick up some items that were needed at the house. Randy had a paper to write and Joe was still working on paperwork from the hiring process he was conducting, so Susan had decided to help out, and since she still didn't have a driver's license she had found it necessary to ask Christian to take her. Sitting in the car next to him, she waited tensely for the comments to start. They didn't come. After a long while she realized something was amiss. The stereo was low, and he was quiet. He did sing when a song he liked came on; she noted that he had a very nice singing voice. One song in particular caught her attention. Especially disconcerting were the words; they were of a direct sexual nature, and considering the conversation they'd had the last time they were alone together, she couldn't help thinking about those words. It made her wonder who he was thinking of as he sang along. It was a song by Meredith Brooks called "What Would Happen?"

When it ended, Christian glanced over at her and noticed she was watching him. He caught her look and widened his eyes slightly, as if asking, "What were you thinking about?" But he said nothing. They pulled into the store parking lot and Christian opted to stay in the car. When Susan returned she was surprised to find him asleep. She touched his shoulder gently, whispering his name to wake him.

He was slow in responding, and she began to suspect that he was indeed feeling sick. On the drive home she watched him. At one point she reached over, touching his cheek gently.

"Christian, you're burning up. You shouldn't be out," she said, her voice that of a mother's.

"Too late," he said drily.

When they arrived back at the house, he went to his room, which was in the old carriage house at the edge of Joe and Randy's property. The building had been used by the previous owner for his butler's quarters. After the first week at the house, Christian had talked to Joe about moving out to the separate building. He had explained that he was used to living alone and that suddenly being with so many people was a little too close for him. Joe had understood completely, offering to help him clear out the carriage house. The two men had spent a weekend dragging out old furniture and boxes and tidying up in general. It had been hard work, but it had also been good bonding time for the two men.

Christian lay on his bed, one arm thrown over his eyes. He'd taken the time to kick off his boots and pull off his sweatshirt. He hadn't bothered to remove his jeans; he just didn't have the energy. He was almost asleep when he heard a soft knock on his door.

"Come," he said, his voice gravelly.

The door opened and Susan stepped inside. "Christian," she said hesitantly. "I brought you something to take for your cold." She walked over to the side of the bed, holding her hand out. She held two green gel caps.

"What's that?" he asked, regarding her hand but making no move to take the pills.

"It's Nyquil. It'll help you sleep."

"I don't need help sleepin'," he said, curling his lips in wry grin. "I need help breathin' and keepin' my head from exploding."

"This will help," Susan said solicitously.

Christian looked at her for a long moment, narrowing his light blue eyes as if indicating that she was getting on his nerves. "Fine," he said finally, getting up. He took the pills and went to a cabinet at the far side of the room. He reached inside and pulled out a bottle of Jack Daniels. Popping the pills into his mouth, he washed them down with a long drink from the bottle as Susan looked on aghast.

"Christian!"

"What?" he said, taking another drink from the bottle then replacing it in the cabinet.

"You're not supposed to take medication with alcohol. It's dangerous."

Christian rolled his eyes as he moved past her, throwing himself on the bed. He looked back at her cynically.

"You don't believe me?" she asked, disbelieving.

"Not really."

"Christian Collins," she said, placing her hands on her hips and sounding very much like his mother. "It is a clinical fact that alcohol and medication can cause a myriad of traumatic stresses on your circulatory system."

Christian was laughing by the time she was through with her tirade. "Good God, I guess I really am walking on the wild side, aren't I?" He widened his eyes dramatically.

"Christian…"

"Susan, I'll be fine." He rolled to his side and glanced up at her. "Thanks for the medicine." He closed his eyes then, as if dismissing her.

"I don't think so," she said, shaking her head.

Christian opened one eye. "Well, you're cordially invited to wait around to see if I'll die, but I'm goin' to sleep."

"Fine," she said, crossing her arms in front of her chest defiantly.

Christian woke an hour later to find her sitting on the bed next to him.

"What're you still doin' here?" he muttered.

"Watching to see if you'll die," she replied curtly.

He shook his head and closed his eyes again. A little while later, he moved closer to her, reaching out to rest his arm over her legs. Susan looked down to see that his eyes were still closed; she wasn't sure if he was asleep or not. She put a hand on his shoulder and found that his skin was cold. Moving carefully so as not to wake him, she pulled the covers over him as best she could; they only reached the middle of his back.

Susan sat with his arm draped over her legs for almost an hour. At one point she shifted in an attempt to get more comfortable. Christian stirred, moving closer to her, actually resting his head on her stomach. Susan looked down at him again, surprised by his action but intrigued too. She moved her hand over his hair, stroking it as she would one of the children's if they were sick. His reaction was to tighten his arm around her, putting his hand on her waist. It was a reaction so unlike what she'd have expected based on what she thought she knew of him; it appealed to her in some strange way she didn't understand.

She knew she should be appalled that this man, who was at best a stranger, and an adversarial one at that, was treating her so familiarly. Of course, he was probably deeply asleep, considering the medicine he had taken. She wasn't sure why she was making excuses for his behavior, but she found she didn't want to move away either.

Eventually Susan found herself dozing off, the combination of his warmth next to her and the rhythm of his breathing lulling her. In an attempt to get more comfortable again, she found it necessary to shift Christian carefully. She moved down ever so slightly and leaned her head against the headboard, closing her eyes.

Susan woke a couple of hours later, forgetting at first where she was. She stirred, disturbing Christian; she realized belatedly that her hands were on his shoulder and back, and when she stretched her arms, flexing her fingers, her nails grazed his skin.

It was the sensation of nails on his bare skin that roused Christian from his deep sleep. The hand that rested on her waist tightened, as if to keep her from moving away. His other arm, which now rested under her back and around her, tightened as well. Susan stilled, trying not to disturb him further. It didn't work; Christian continued to stir. Susan shivered when his hand slid from her waist up her side, pulling with it her blouse, which had come untucked from her skirt. It disconcerted her to note that his hand now rested on bare skin. As if even in his sleep he sensed her thoughts, his hand slid back down her side, making her shiver again. She thought she'd die when he moved his head, his lips nuzzling her skin intimately.

He obviously thinks he's with someone he knows, she thought. Again, however, she found that she didn't want to stop him. His words from days before were still hanging in her mind.

She thought about what he had said then. She thought of her relationship with Warren, the man she was engaged to marry. Christian had been right about Warren being the first man she had slept with. It had irritated her that Christian assumed their sexual relationship must be dull if she didn't understand a strange term like "slang." She also knew that he had meant much more than that when he'd said what he'd said. Her relationship with Warren was comfortable. They shared a lot of the same interests and got along well.

She had met Warren in her child psychology class. He confided to her that he had taken child psychology as one of his sciences because he figured it would be easy. She'd laughed at him, telling him he obviously didn't spend very much time with children. The friendship had begun there. It had moved on to her helping him study for exams. Eventually he had asked her out. They'd had dinner and gone to a movie. After the second date he had asked if he could kiss her, and she had agreed happily. His kiss had been fair, not what she had expected, but she'd chided herself for expecting too much.

When they had moved to making out, she had convinced herself that she wanted him to make love to her. They'd made love for the first time at his parents' house, in his room. It had been painful and not anything close to what she had always dreamed lovemaking would be. But she had consoled herself with the thought that no one really enjoyed their first time. The subsequent unions had been better, but still not the fireworks she'd always heard sex was. She figured everyone had been exaggerating. Or that maybe things would improve after she got to know Warren better. Things had gotten a little better after he asked her to marry him. She'd been so happy and was so sure that she loved him that it had translated to their lovemaking. It still hadn't been fireworks, but it had been better; she'd finally

224

achieved an orgasm after a great deal of effort from Warren. She'd begun to wonder if something was wrong with her.

Now, sitting in Christian's room with his breath warm on her bare skin, she was feeling a sensation that she was sure she shouldn't be feeling. She shifted uncomfortably at the thought, once again disturbing him. This time he groaned, grasping her waist and pulling her down so that she lay next to him. He kept his arms around her and put his head against the hollow between her neck and shoulder, snuggling against her body. She shuddered at the feeling of his breath against her neck as it became even again.

"Christian," she whispered, not sure what to do. He didn't respond. She started to get up, but his arms tightened around her, holding her fast. "Christian," she said again, but he still didn't respond. Eventually she gave up, realizing she wasn't in any real danger and that she was just reacting to her own thoughts. After a while she allowed herself to relax against him. She found herself looking down at the bracelet he wore on his left wrist. It was a series of flat links, and handsome, with a very masculine style. The gold metal was a sharp, bright contrast against his bronzed skin. Susan touched the bracelet gently, sliding her fingers between it and his wrist. She examined it for a while, then slid her hand up his arm, tracing a pattern absently with her nails.

Christian stirred, sliding his left hand up her bare midriff, his thumb brushing the lower part of her breast. Susan sucked in her breath sharply at the sensation, even as he compounded it by nuzzling his lips against her neck.

"Christian!" she exclaimed, shocked by the excitation he'd incited so easily.

He stirred again then. "What?" he said, his voice a tired whisper.

"Must you?"

Christian woke a little more and took stock of their bodies and where his hands were. She was shocked to feel him grin against her ear. "What's the matter? Too hot for you?"

"Being pawed by you isn't enough to get me excited," she said haughtily.

"No?"

"Hardly," she bit back.

Susan expected him to back off then. He didn't. Instead, his lips brushed her ear as he whispered, "Let's just see."

With that his left hand moved to pull the collar of her blouse away from her neck as his lips moved from her ear, brushing her neck in a sensual kiss. His right hand slid into the top of her blouse and bra, touching her breast. He continued to caress her midriff with his other hand.

Susan was sure she was on fire, she was assailed with so many sensations at the same time. Each feeling made her writhe, her body responding of its own volition. If she'd wanted to stop him, she wasn't altogether sure her body would allow her to. She couldn't stifle the moan that escaped her lips. She turned her head away from him to avoid looking at him, but inadvertently gave him better access to her neck. He took advantage of it. His lips burned a trail from her ear to the hollow at the base of her throat. She felt his tongue slide from her throat back to her ear and again she couldn't stop the excited cry that came from deep inside her. Her body was on fire, and every movement of his fingers on her breast made her shudder against him. She felt his jean-clad leg draw over hers as he pulled her back against him. She felt his hardness pressed against her then, and the idea that he was excited too made her moan and turn her head to look at him. His light blue eyes stared down into hers, burning with reined-in passion. As their eyes locked, she felt his left hand slide downward, moving smoothly under the waistband of her skirt and panties. She closed her eyes as he continued downward, his finger sliding in to touch her very core.

Susan cried out as her body erupted like a ball of fire. She shuddered convulsively against him, not caring about who he was or whether or not he should be doing this to her. She clutched at his arms and moaned, moving her head from side to side as if the ecstasy he was causing was too much.

As her orgasm ended, she lay panting in his arms. She refused to look at him for a long minute. When she did gather her nerve, she turned to him, her eyes narrowed angrily.

"Who do you think you are?" she grated indignantly.

Christian stared back at her, a knowing look on his face, his grin almost vicious. "I'm the guy that just made you come with little or no effort." His expression changed to an informative one then, even as his voice cooled considerably. "You know, the one that doesn't excite you."

Susan stared back at him, aghast at what she perceived as his vulgarity. In fact, what he had said was true, but she wasn't willing to admit that to herself, especially not at that moment.

"Fact of the matter is," Christian said, pinning her with a look, "that's just the beginning of what I can make you feel." Then he shrugged as if indicating that he was letting her off easy. Susan said nothing, her body having shivered in response to his words.

After a long moment, he narrowed his eyes at her. "Now, you better get out of here, before you get yourself into more trouble than you can handle."

Susan agreed with his advice wholeheartedly and moved out of his embrace as quickly as possible. Christian watched her, his grin sardonic, his look direct. She avoided his eyes as she adjusted her clothing, then without a word she turned and walked out of the room.

Christian lay in his bed thinking about what had transpired. Her reaction to his touch had excited him. Her response had been so intense, it had only incited him to continue. If she'd been any other woman, he would have taken her as she lay in front of him. But even he had morals. She was engaged, and more importantly, she was his cousin's best friend's niece. Christian wasn't ready to step over that line just yet. Part of him knew she had captured his sense of intrigue. The thought dragged at him as he attempted to go back to sleep. It took a long time.

CHAPTER 7

Susan managed to avoid Christian altogether the rest of the weekend, mainly because he stayed in his room most of the time. She also managed to avoid being alone with him until the following Wednesday. That was when Joe had an early morning raid and couldn't drive her to school; Christian was duly elected to do so.

In the car, Christian had the stereo on, and other than glancing over at her a couple of times, he didn't speak. Finally Susan couldn't stand it anymore.

"Are we going to discuss the other day?"

Christian looked over at her, his grin wry. "What's to discuss?"

Susan looked back at him, her mouth hanging open. "About what happened…"

Christian gave a short laugh, shaking his head. He looked over at her seriously. "Babe, what I do in bed, I don't discuss."

"Even if you had no right?"

"No right to what, Susan?" His voice dropped an octave. "No right to drive you crazy, or no right to get you off?"

Susan made an appalled noise in the back of her throat. "Must you be so crude?"

He shrugged. "Works for me."

Susan shook her head, not sure what else to say. She stared out

229

the window, wondering what she had been thinking to bring up that weekend at all.

They arrived at the college ten minutes later. When Christian pulled up in front of the psychology building he saw that Warren was waiting for her.

"And there's the man of the hour," he said caustically.

Susan looked at him sharply, her eyes narrowed.

Christian returned her look, his eyes cool.

Susan simply shook her head, reaching for the door handle and getting out.

"Who's that?" Warren asked, looking at Christian suspiciously. Christian simply stared back at him, nonplused.

"He's Joe's cousin," Susan said, her voice still showing the effects of her anger at Christian.

"And what did he do to you?"

Susan looked at him sharply as Christian drove away. She was afraid for a minute that Warren knew somehow, but then she realized he was responding to her obvious bad mood. "Nothing. He's just irritating, that's all," she said, reaching up to kiss him.

She was very relieved later that day when it was Joe and not Christian that picked her up from school. On the drive home she noticed that he seemed quiet. "Is everything alright?" she asked.

Joe looked over at her. "Yeah, fine. Just not feeling real hot right now."

"You're sick?" she said, surprised. In the seven or eight months she'd been with them, she'd never seen him sick; Randy said he never was, for the most part.

Joe grinned at her. "I'm not sick, I have a headache, okay?"

"Okay…" she said skeptically.

When they arrived home, Joe went off to his and Randy's bedroom, saying he was going to lie down. Susan went to relieve Randy so she could get ready for school. After telling Susan what the children had had to eat and how they were mood-wise, Randy went to look in on her husband.

"And what's going on in here?" she said, standing in the doorway to her and Joe's room and looking her husband over with an appreciative eye. He had taken off his jacket and shoulder holster, but that was it. He lay fully clothed on the bed, boots still on.

"A headache," he said, his accent as clear as ever.

She walked over, sitting down next him. She kissed his forehead gently. "Well, you don't have a fever—that's good. Do you want me to stay home tonight?" she asked, not sure how bad his headache was.

He opened one light blue eye. "Don't you have a test tonight?"

Randy looked at him for a long minute. It still astounded her that he managed to keep so many things going on at work and still remembered trivial things like her tests at school. It was indicative of how much he loved her that he was so involved with what she did, knowing it was important to her. "Yes," she said softly. "But I can make it up if you need me."

"No, babe," he said tiredly. "It's just a headache. I'll lie here a while, and when it goes away I'll be fine." He reached up to touch her cheek softly, looking up into her eyes. "You be a good girl and go to school."

"Alright," she said, knowing she wouldn't get anywhere with

231

him. He didn't like to be sick, and she was sure that was why he was poorly so rarely; he abhorred the condition.

After a few quiet minutes with him, she reluctantly got ready for school, kissing him softly on her way out. That night when she got home he was asleep. She crawled into bed next to him and snuggled back into his arms as he moved closer.

"How was your test?" he asked tiredly.

"Fine, how's your head?" she whispered.

"Fine." He kissed her softly behind the ear, then nuzzled his lips against her hair.

The next morning, Joe was up and gone before Randy even woke. She spent her day at school and the library, working on a paper for her abnormal psychology class. When she took the time out to call him, she was told that Captain Sinclair was in the field. She left a message for him to call her on her cell phone when he got back. Her phone rang two hours later in class; she picked it up, glancing apologetically at the professor as he gave her a sour look. She walked to the back of the room and out the door, leaning against the wall in the hallway while she talked to him.

"Hi there," she said, smiling.

"Hello yourself," he replied softly. She knew he was sitting in his office with his door closed. He didn't like everyone to know what a big softy he was when it came to his wife. "I know I caught you during class, but I'm on my way back out in a minute or two as soon as Rick gets up here."

"What's going on?"

"Just some troubles with a new gang in town," he said mildly.

"So why does that involve you, Captain?"

"Because, Officer, I'm still part of FORS, even if I'm over the boss now, and Rick needed some backup. You know Night feels better if she trusts his backup."

"And God knows she trust you," Randy said with no anger in her voice, but there was concern. "I just don't like you going out on that stuff still..."

"I see," Joe said, grinning, as Rick walked into his office. "Think I'm too old now, huh?"

"Stop it, Sinclair," Randy countered, smiling. "I just worry about you, okay?"

"You always worry about me, babe. That doesn't change anything." Rick was watching him, having realized Randy was giving him the same lecture he gave Midnight all the time.

As if Randy knew what Rick was thinking, she said, "I thought when you got promoted you'd be in less danger, ya know?"

"Yeah, I know," Joe said placatingly. "And I am in less. It's Rick's ass on the line—I'm just backup."

"Uh-huh." Randy didn't sound convinced in the least. "And I also know how you and Mr. Debenshire love to relive the old days..."

Joe smiled. "Ah, yes. But not today, alright? I'll be fine, you'll see."

That night he didn't come home until ten thirty, with ten new stitches in his abdomen to show for his efforts. "Oh, yes." Randy nodded as she unbuttoned his now bloody shirt and examined the bandage, then touched the bruise on his cheek. "Fine, I see that now," she said as she narrowed her eyes up at him.

Joe grinned, his light blue eyes looking tired. "Okay, so 'fine' may have been the wrong word," he said, moving carefully to lie down on the couch after kicking off his boots and throwing his jacket aside.

"'Fucked up' may have been the phrase you were looking for," Randy said mildly, but her eyes showed her concern.

Christian, who had been sitting with her in the living room, laughed at that.

"Hey," Joe said lightly. "Whose side are you on, anyway?"

Christian held up his hands, indicating that he planned to stay out of this. Susan walked in a moment later, having heard Joe come in and knowing what had happened from Randy.

"Good lord," she said, seeing Joe's cheek.

"That's not the half of it," Randy said, indicating the bandage on his upper abdomen.

Joe looked up as Susan came around the couch, her expression as concerned as Randy's. "It's a scratch, for God's sake," he said, rolling his eyes.

"A scratch that took ten stitches to close," Randy said drily.

"You know," Joe said, pretending to look angry. "For this kind of grief I can stay at the office."

"Midnight was after you too, wasn't she?" Randy replied dauntlessly.

"Well, she was after both of us…" He looked a bit guilty. "Rick got cut too." He shook his head, sighing. "I'm just gettin' too old for this, I guess."

Randy smiled. "Oh, God, here we go."

"That's what Midnight told me," Joe said haughtily.

Randy crossed her arms. "That's because she's tired of writing up injury reports for one of her captains."

"Yeah, yeah…" Joe said, looking tired suddenly.

"Come on," Randy said, noting the change. "Let's get you to bed before you collapse out here."

Joe nodded but made no move to get off the couch, resting his head against the cushions and closing his eyes. Randy stood up and looked down at him. "Babe," she said softly.

After a long moment, Joe opened his eyes slowly. Taking a deep breath, he heaved himself up, wincing when he bent too far and stretched the cut. Randy looked at him, grinning wryly. "At the rate you're goin', I'm gonna have to trade you in on two twenty-year-olds."

Joe laughed softly as he followed her to their bedroom, nodding to Christian and Susan on the way out. Susan watched them go; then her eyes fell on Christian, who was looking at her.

"What?" she asked, her tone instantly defensive.

"Nothin'," he said, looking at her as if she'd gone off the deep end. Christian got up from the couch, and Susan watched him warily. Noting her look, he made a point of moving close to her, making her look up at him. "'Scuse me," he said, his tone low and somehow making common words sound like a come-on. When she didn't reply, because she was trying to think of something to say, he bent his head, putting his lips very close to her ear. "He's hers, you know."

Susan sucked in her breath, both for what he'd said and for the sensation caused by him being so close to her again. Her whole body tingled. She surprised him by turning to look at him. Their faces were a mere inch apart; she could smell his cologne and feel his warmth. Her deep blue eyes stared into his light ones defiantly, but inside, her body was screaming opposing messages at her. One part of her kept telling her to get away from him, the other part hoped against hope that he'd kiss her. "I'm aware of that," she finally managed, sounding stronger than she felt.

Christian's eyes widened triumphantly at what he saw in hers. He knew there was desire there, but also that she was distrustful of him; he enjoyed both reactions. Moving just a bit closer, bringing his mouth almost to hers, he said, "Do you?" His lips grazed hers ever so slightly, then he turned and walked out of the room, leaving her staring after him.

The next night, Joe got home from the office and went to bed early. Randy, who'd been at the library that evening, doing more research on her paper, got home and found Christian in the living room. He had gotten into the habit of being in the house in the evenings if Joe wasn't home. Nothing had been said or requested, but Christian had taken to thinking that he was the other man in the house. Because of that it was therefore his responsibility to protect the "women and children" when Joe was gone. Randy had asked him about it once; he had shrugged. "I'm lookin' after family," he'd said, surprising her. It made her happy to note that he now included himself as a member of their family, as she herself did. On this night, however, she had expected Joe to be home, and Christian was usually at least getting ready to go out by this time; it was 9:00.

"Where's Joe?" she asked, looking down at him as she set her leather carry sack down on the couch.

"He's here. He's in bed though," Christian said, sounding chagrined.

"Why?" Randy asked suspiciously, though she was pretty sure she knew.

"He's sick," Christian said simply, but it was obvious he felt guilty about giving his cousin his cold.

Randy grinned. "Serves him right. He doesn't sleep enough, eat right, or take care of himself. This is just his body's way of telling him to slow down, Christian. Don't feel bad."

"Yeah, but you said he rarely gets sick."

"That's right, and when he does, he's forced to take it easy for a while. It's sometimes a good thing, being sick. I'll go and check on him." She raised an eyebrow. "Aren't you going out tonight?" He went out most Friday nights, and half the time on Saturdays too.

Christian looked up at her for a long moment, then a slow grin spread across his face. "Maybe..."

"Go on," Randy said, smiling. "Joe's here, and I don't care how sick he is—he'll protect us. You've been working your ass off all week on that computer program for the office, you need some rec time." Randy had come home a couple of times that week to find him working at her computer, writing the program for Midnight's new inventory system. He'd taken it upon himself to upgrade her computer, making it faster and giving it a higher memory capacity, and he'd paid for it too. She also knew he worked on it late into the night sometimes, hearing him tapping away in the room next door to hers and Joe's. She was still astounded at his abilities on the computer, so used to Joe's absolute aversion to anything "high-tech."

"You win—I'll go," he said, getting to his feet.

An hour later he knocked lightly on Joe and Randy's door.

"Come in," Randy said.

Christian opened the door and saw that Joe's head was resting in her lap, her hand stroking his hair. Joe was fast asleep. "How's he doin'?" he asked quietly, not wanting to disturb Joe.

Randy glanced down at her husband, a contemplative look crossing her face. "Well, considering he didn't even stir when you knocked, I'd say he's pretty sick."

"Is that odd? Does he usually wake up that easily?"

Randy grinned. "Yeah, he's like a motion sensor. I can never get out of bed without waking him up." She saw the hesitation on Christian's face. "Go on, Christian, we'll be fine. If you'll recall I am a fully fledged peace officer too, and since my husband's one of the best rangemasters in the country, I'm a pretty damn good shot as well."

Christian grinned, having forgotten that she was a cop too, even if she wasn't working as one at that point. "I'm goin', I'm goin'. Jesus," he said, smiling. "You'd think you were tryin' to get rid of me or somethin'."

"That's it, I'm trying to get rid of you. Now go, before all the hot women are taken."

"There's always more," Christian said irreverently. Randy laughed and settled back against the pillows, looking down at her husband again and gently touching his face. Christian closed the door quietly and headed for the front door.

He met Susan coming in from her date with Warren. She looked the same as she usually did. Her hair was back in a loose bun and she wore a beige dress that did absolutely nothing for her. It was as if she wanted to remain nondescript; she didn't even have makeup on. Christian didn't understand how a woman could not want to be noticed, but that seemed to be Susan's wish. In contrast, Christian was dressed in perfect-fitting black chinos, black ankle boots, and a sapphire blue shirt that set his light blue eyes off magnificently. He said nothing to her as they met in the doorway, merely inclining his head derisively. Then he walked past her, leaving in his wake the scent of Havana cologne. It was a spicy, sexy scent that fit him perfectly, as if it had been created with him in mind.

Susan stared after him for a long time, watching him get into the black Jaguar and drive away. She was sure her heart had stopped when she'd seen him; he looked so incredible, his dark good looks enhanced even more by the perfect cut to his pants, which emphasized his trim waist and long legs. The blue shirt outlined his well-muscled chest, which she remembered all too well from the day he'd accosted her. She'd remembered that day far too many times in the last week, and seeing him looking fantastically handsome didn't help to place that memory farther back in her mind.

Christian drove down the hill, heading for the bars in Pacific Beach. He'd gone to some of the ones in La Jolla but found that he always ended up with women like Geneva who thought they owned everything and everyone. Tonight he was looking for something a little bit different. He listened to the radio on the way. Chumbawamba's "Tubthumping" came on, and he turned it up. The song was strange but he liked it. The chant about getting knocked down and getting right back up again fit him pretty well.

Once at the club, he headed straight to the bar. He proceeded to knock back three shots of tequila, then ordered a beer, tossing the blond bartender a five-dollar tip. He turned to look around him. There were the usual bar flies and a lot of college kids. He emptied his beer, and when he turned back to order another he found that the bartender was watching him. He took another good look at her; she did have a nice body, and a nice face to match.

"Beer or shot?" she asked, embarrassed at having been caught watching him.

Christian grinned, staring directly into her eyes. "Both," he said with a smile, his light blue eyes sparkling. Tara Camden found herself catching her breath. He had to be the best-looking man she'd ever seen, and she was sure every woman in the place was ready to fight it out for him. She was pleasantly surprised when he sat down at the bar. After a few minutes she turned to him and saw that he was watching her; it made her feel self-conscious.

During the course of the evening she got used to him sitting there, and eventually felt comfortable enough to treat him like any other customer. At one point she leaned over the bar toward him.

"So what part of England are you from?" she asked, having recognized his accent.

"London," Christian replied simply, but he stared straight into her eyes, making the answer seem like more.

"Are you visiting or staying?"

"Not quite sure yet, actually."

"Okay…" she said, smiling and shaking her head.

She went back to taking drink orders. Every now and then she'd turn around and see that he was still there. It wasn't like she didn't have guys hanging out at the bar a lot, but if they were interested they usually tried to hit on her. This guy didn't; he just sat there drinking his beer, alternating between watching her and other customers in the mirror behind the bar.

Once, Tara saw a woman walk up to him. She'd seen her before; she was in the bar a lot, and she seemed to score with a lot of men. Tara found herself making a point of sticking close to the Englishman just to hear what was said.

Christian turned as he saw the redhead walk up. He'd seen her watching him in the mirror, and had known she'd approach him eventually. His expression was cool, almost bored. The woman was good-looking from afar, but when she drew closer, Christian could see that she was probably in her early forties and trying desperately to hide it. Probably why she hangs in bars, he figured. Bad light helps.

"So," the woman said, her dark eyes looking up at him seductively. "Are you as good as you look?"

Christian looked back at her for a long moment, a slow grin starting on his face but not reaching his eyes. "Better," he said cockily.

With that he turned his back on her, his eyes going directly to Tara, who was standing right in front of him. Tara was trying desperately to stifle the laugh, but ended up ducking her head so the woman wouldn't see. The look on the redhead's face when the Englishman had turned his back had been hilarious. Tara had never seen someone annihilate her like that before. She guessed most men liked the woman's direct approach. When Tara looked up she saw that his light blue eyes were still on her, and he was grinning.

"Nice work," she said.

He smiled. "Ya think?"

Tara nodded, laughing again as she went to take another drink order.

At the end of the night, Tara closed up as usual. When she walked out the back door of the bar, she was surprised to see the Englishman leaning against the wall, smoking a cigarette.

"Hi," she said, too surprised to think of anything clever to say.

Christian looked back at her, grinning.

"You waiting for someone?" she asked, not sure why he would be back there. She wondered belatedly if she was in some kind of danger, but she didn't think so.

"You," he said casually.

"Oh yeah?" She smiled in spite of herself.

"Yeah," he said, dropping his cigarette and pushing off from the wall.

He walked over to her, reminding her vaguely of a black panther. Without a word he touched her face, turning it up toward his, and leaned down to kiss her. It had been a long time since she'd been kissed like that. Tara found herself putting her arms around his neck, wanting the moment to last. When their lips parted, he looked down at her, his eyes burning into hers.

"Where do you live?" he asked, his tone indicating that he wasn't expecting her to say no.

"Couple miles down the street." She motioned in the direction of the beach.

"I'll follow you," he said evenly.

Tara nodded mutely. As she walked over to her car she saw him waving down a passing cab. Driving down the street, Tara started thinking again. She realized she knew nothing about this guy; he could be a nut, or worse. Here she was leading him to her apartment. "What am I," she said out loud. "Crazy?" She made the decision then that once she got to her apartment building she'd tell him she'd changed her mind and make him leave. She made sure her cell phone was handy in case she needed to call 911. When she got to the building, she got out of her car, and a moment later the man walked up.

Christian could see the hesitation in her eyes, and he knew what she was about to say. He leaned against the side of her car and watched as she gathered her courage. He grinned when she started to speak, his light blue eyes reflecting humor.

"Look," she began. "I just... I'm really tired, and I think that..."

"That I'm some kind of nut out to kill you or somethin'," he finished for her, his voice low.

"No," she said, but he started to laugh.

"Yes," he countered, nodding. "Well, I'm not, but you don't have to trust that. You're probably smart for being cautious."

"Yeah, and I'm probably blowing a big opportunity," she said, looking thoughtful and sounding wistful.

"You are," he said confidently, but his eyes still reflected humor. He moved toward her then, touching her face gently again and looking down into her eyes. This time she kissed him, not able to resist his closeness.

An hour and a half later they lay in her bed. She lay over him, her body still entwined with his, and his hands were in her hair. After catching her breath, she moved to his side, lying on her back. He turned over to face her, propping himself up on his elbow and looking around the room.

"So this is your place, huh?" he said, his voice still a little husky.

She smiled. "Be it ever so humble."

"Hey, it's a place to live, and it's nice."

"So where do you live? And oh yeah, what is your name?" She sounded abashed at having to ask that piece of information after they'd had sex.

"I live at my cousin's right now," Christian said lightly. "And my name's Blue."

"Blue?" she replied, looking interested. "Because of your eyes?"

"Yeah."

"So what's your real name?" She glanced up at him, still astounded that she was in bed with this incredibly gorgeous man.

Christian looked at her for a long moment, obviously debating telling her. "Christian."

"Hmm…" she said, as if trying to reconcile the name with him. She shrugged. "Well, I was just going to call you London if I didn't get your name."

He smiled. "Uh-huh."

"So, I'll bet you do this a lot, huh?"

"I guess."

"Well, I don't. One-night stands aren't exactly my forte. Being a bartender and all, I tend to become pretty jaded on sleeping with anyone from the bar."

"So, how did I rate?" Christian surprised himself by asking.

"You were too goddamned gorgeous to ignore," she said forthrightly.

"I see."

"So how did I rate?" she asked, knowing he'd had his choice at the bar.

"You were too gorgeous to ignore," he replied with a sly smile.

Tara laughed. "And if I believe that, I'm sure you'll tell me another one."

Instead of replying, he leaned down to kiss her. When their lips parted he looked down at her. "Actually, I'm tired of women like that redhead thinking all they have to do is give me a come-on and I'll drop dead at their feet. You were cool, I liked that."

"That and I gave you enough shots and beer to make an elephant pass out."

Christian laughed. "You think I'm drunk?"

"Are you?"

"Not even close."

"Jesus…" She shook her head. "I take it you drink a lot, huh?"

"Enough."

"Well, after this, maybe you can come into the bar and see me every now and then. No strings attached," she said, holding her hands up on the last. "The last thing I need right now is another relationship."

Christian looked back at her, pleasantly surprised. "That makes two of us. I don't do relationships myself."

"Well, sometimes I wish I hadn't done my last one." Her voice had taken on a different edge, which made Christian curious in spite of himself.

"What happened?" he asked softly as he dropped his head to be on the same level as hers.

She shrugged. "He was my husband and he hit me. It was manageable until we had our daughter, and then he made the mistake of hitting her, once. That was it—I kicked him out."

"How old's your daughter?"

"Three."

He grinned. "She look like you?"

"Yes, blond hair, blue eyes."

"Bet she's cute as hell, too," he said softly.

"Oh, yeah, and ornery as hell." They laughed then. "So, what do you do, besides this?" She said the last indicating their bodies still close together.

Christian grinned. "Right now I'm workin' with the police department."

She looked surprised. "Are you a cop?"

He shook his head. "Not hardly."

"Then you're a criminal?"

"Sometimes. But right now, I'm working on their computers."

"You don't look like a computer geek," she said, narrowing her eyes at him comically.

"That's because I'm not a geek. I'm a hacker—get the label right, will ya?" he said, laughing.

"Oh, gee, sorry."

They lay together for a while, not talking. It was a comfortable silence. Christian had been telling the truth when he'd said he thought she was cool. He liked her easygoing manner, and he also liked that she didn't seem to think that because they'd slept together it meant they automatically had a relationship. He hated that part of the night, when he had to extract himself from whatever woman he was sleeping with. He usually did it quickly, getting out as soon as possible, but since she seemed cool about everything, he didn't mind hanging around.

"So, I guess I can take it that you won't be around for breakfast?" she said lightly.

Christian shook his head. "Gotta get back." Then, feeling like she deserved more of an explanation, he said, "My cousin's sick, and I want to be around in case his wife or kids need something."

"Sick?" she said, not sure if he meant terminally or what.

"Yeah. Just a cold, but his wife looked pretty worried when I left, so I wanna be around, ya know?"

"You expecting trouble?"

"Well, my cousin's the cop in the family. And yeah, I always expect trouble—that way I'm never surprised."

"Your cousin's a cop?" She grinned slyly. "Does he look anything like you?"

"No," he said, pretending to be jealous. "Actually, he does have the same color eyes, and about the same build, but that's it. He's got light hair and all that."

"Hmmm," she said, still grinning. She reached out, touching his cheek and running her finger along his jawline. She kissed him, moving her hand to his hair, which now reached an inch past his collar. After a few minutes, he pulled her over him, but she shook her head

"I want you over me," she said, her voice a husky whisper.

"Why?" he whispered back.

"Because," she said, more softly, "I haven't let anyone over me since my husband. It's this whole domination psycho crap, but I want you, okay?"

"Okay," he said, making a point of taking it slow and making sure she orgasmed long before him. Afterward he fell asleep, his body half-covering hers.

He woke hearing her whisper in his ear. "Hey, London…"

"What?" he said, grinning at the name.

"Not that I mind you being here, 'cause I really don't, but you said you wanted to get home early…"

Christian looked over at the clock on her nightstand; it was four thirty. "Yeah, I should get going…" he said tiredly.

"Do you want some coffee or something to help wake up?"

"Nah, no point in you havin' to wake up too." He reluctantly got up and got dressed, Tara watching him as he did. He walked over to her, kneeling down by the bed. She lay on her side, facing him, her eyes tired, but she was alert as he moved close. He kissed her gently. "Don't be surprised if you see me in your bar again."

"I'll buy ya a beer myself," she said, smiling.

He returned the smile. "You got it."

"This was… great," she said hesitantly, not wanting to sound too dumb.

"Yes, it was," he said sincerely. "I'll see ya, okay?"

She nodded. "Okay."

****

Randy had had a long night. Joe had slept deeply at first, which actually worried her, because he rarely slept that way. When he woke at 2:00 a.m., he was shivering. Randy immediately covered him better, pulling him closer to her and stroking his hair. Touching his forehead, she realized his fever was high. She got out of bed, moving carefully, and went into the bathroom to get some Tylenol. She filled a glass with water and went back into the bedroom. She was loath to wake him, but she knew she needed to get his fever down too.

"Joe, babe," she said softly as she touched his cheek.

It took him a long time to even respond, and when he did, it was obvious he wasn't all there. She had him sit up and got him to take the pills. Randy put the glass on the nightstand and then pulled him down against her again, stroking his hair and holding him.

She spent most of the night listening to his breathing, and she knew something wasn't right. That was when she was sure he had pneumonia again. He'd only had it one other time since they'd been married; she'd always been careful to make him slow down when his health seemed bad or he started to cough. She'd finally gotten him to quit smoking altogether when she'd been pregnant with Kat, citing that it was bad for her and their unborn child to have smoke anywhere near them. Not that he'd ever smoked around her anyway; anytime he'd started up again, always during very stressful times, he'd smoke on the deck outside. Now, having him sick again worried her; she knew he'd been overdoing it, but she'd been so busy with school and the kids she hadn't kept after him as she had before. She felt guilty that she hadn't taken care of him the way she should. Lying there all night, she had a good opportunity to thoroughly berate herself. By morning she was exhausted.

When Christian arrived back at the house he stopped at Joe and Randy's door, knocking softly. Again, it was Randy's voice that told him to come in. He opened the door and saw that Randy was lying still, holding her husband. It was obvious she'd been awake a lot during the night.

"How is he?" Christian whispered, walking over to the bed.

"He's not real good. I think he's already got pneumonia. I'm going to take him to the hospital first thing this morning. And don't look like that, Christian—he's real susceptible to it, and it may not have had anything to do with your cold. He'll be fine, they just need to treat him for it, okay?"

Christian nodded. "If there's anything I can do…"

"You just getting home?" she asked, though she already knew the answer.

"Yeah," Christian replied, not bothering to look embarrassed—because he wasn't.

"Then you need to go to sleep, 'cause I know you didn't wherever you were this morning," she said, smiling at him. She knew from what Joe had said that she was basically seeing what Joe had been like in his much younger days, before his parents had been killed. Christian was young, handsome, and free from any entanglements of the heart, and enjoying it to the fullest.

"All the same," Christian said, undaunted, "if you need me for anything, let me know."

Randy nodded. "Okay."

Christian left the room and went down the hall, intent on checking everything out before he went off to bed. When he got closer to the children's rooms, he noted that Kat's door was open. He saw her lying on the floor with her pillow and blanket. Kat heard him approach and sat up, smiling and holding up her arms. Christian couldn't resist stepping over the gate in her doorway and picking her up. Since the day he had set foot in the house, Kat had taken to him. She had never treated him like a stranger. It tugged at Christian's heart, even if he didn't want it to. He'd always had a weakness for children anyway, seeing them as innocents. Since this little girl also happened to be related to him, it made her extra special to him. JT liked him too, but it was Kat that climbed up into his lap every chance she got. Even now, she rested her head on his shoulder and reached up to touch his black hair.

"Kissgin," she said, trying to say his name but, as always, not quite getting it right.

"What?" He craned his neck to look down at her, smiling in spite of himself.

"Out?" she said, pointing past her door and the gate that kept her in the room when she got up before her nanny.

Christian thought about it for a minute, but knew he didn't have the heart to put her down, knowing she'd cry if he did. "Yes, out, little love," he said, turning and stepping carefully back over the gate.

Susan found him three hours later, sitting in the living room with both Kat and JT putting together blocks. He still wore the outfit he'd had on the night before, so she was able to surmise that he hadn't been to bed as of yet. "I'm sorry," she said, aghast that it was so late and that he was in essence doing what would normally be her job. In actuality it was normally her day off, but Randy had asked her to take care of the children that morning because of Joe's illness. "I guess I overslept—I never heard them wake up. They didn't make the usual amount of noise they do when they get up."

"That's my fault," Christian said. "Kat was lying on her floor when I walked by this morning, and I picked her up and brought her out here. She decided to wake her brother, so I brought him out here too." He shrugged, not realizing how much he was surprising Susan at that moment.

"And that's been since when?" Susan asked, surprise evident in her voice.

"'Bout five this morning."

"You went out last night, didn't you?"

"Yeah."

"So you haven't slept yet, have you?"

Christian just shrugged, shaking his head.

"Well, I'm up now, so you can go ahead and go to bed," she said, her voice friendly.

"No, I want to wait and see if Randy's gonna need help with Joe."

"He's not better then?"

"No, Randy says she thinks he's got pneumonia."

Susan nodded. She knew about Joe's history of being really susceptible to it since his youth. "He had scarlet fever when he was really young," she explained. "It weakened his lungs just enough to make it easier for him to get things like pneumonia."

"Yeah, Randy told me something about that."

"Well, why don't you go lie down and I'll wake you if she needs you," she said, suddenly seeing how tired he was.

"I'm alright," he said, his voice surprisingly easygoing.

"Yeah, death warmed over, but alright," she said critically as she lifted her eyebrow at him. "Look, go to my room and lie down. I swear, I'll wake you if we need you."

Christian looked at her for a long moment. Finally he nodded and got to his feet.

He walked down the hall to her room. He kicked off his boots and pulled his shirttails out of his trousers, then lay down on the bed. It bothered him to note that the bed smelled like her and that his body responded even to that. Get a grip, he thought. You just got done sleeping with a very hot blonde—why're you thinkin' of this one already?

It took him a while to clamp down on his churning thoughts, to allow himself to relax enough to actually sleep, and he found himself looking around the room. It was very plain, except for a few personal things. There was a picture of Susan, her sister Elizabeth, Deborah, and Wilson. Christian saw that Susan definitely—fortunately—favored her mother; her father looked a lot like the guy Susan was engaged to. Classic pasty-faced Englishman type, was how Christian classified them. He scanned over the other pictures and saw what must have been a real "family" portrait; it contained a fairly decent-sized group, including Robert and Anabelle with all five of their children. Just in front of Rick sat Midnight and Mikeyla, and Deborah had Wilson in front of her with Susan and Elizabeth. Next there was Allison and her husband, as well as Mandy and Kathcrine, who were still unmarried.

Christian looked at the picture for a long time. He wondered what it was like, being part of a big family that kept growing. His just stayed him and his mother. He looked at Midnight and her daughter in the picture. Midnight and Rick's daughter was a good mixture of both parents, with Midnight's copper-blond hair and petite body and Rick's deep blue eyes and finely boned face. She was a beauty, and it was clear she was going to be a handful for her parents in the very near future. Then he looked at Susan and her sister. It was obvious that Susan had gotten her father's stoic gene, but her sister hadn't. Elizabeth, at the age of eighteen, was a looker. She looked like her mother too, but she actually made herself up. Her hair was done, she wore makeup, she dressed fairly nicely. Where the hell's that one? Christian thought wryly as he turned over, trying to shut out all the thoughts whirling in his head. Eventually he succeeded and fell asleep.

He was awakened by movement in the room. Turning over, he opened his eyes. Susan turned from her dresser and saw that he was awake.

"I'm sorry, I didn't mean to wake you," she said.

"It's alright," he said tiredly. "It is your room." He rubbed his eyes. "What time is it, anyway?"

"About noon."

"Randy take Joe yet?"

"Yes, two hours ago."

Christian nodded. "I guess I could head for my own room then."

"Don't worry about it. If you're comfortable you can stay in here."

Christian grinned. "Always tryin' to get me in your bed, aren't you?" He was joking, but Susan's eyes instantly flashed angrily.

"You always have to do that, don't you?" she said, hands on her hips.

"And you have to learn to lighten up." Christian glanced behind her, to the pictures on her dresser. "So how come you didn't tell me you're marrying your father?"

"What?"

"Your father," he said, gesturing to the pictures. "He looks just like ol' Warren." He said her fiancé's name as if it in itself were an insult.

"He does not!"

Christian looked at her for a long moment, a lopsided grin on his face. "Describe Warren. You know, the regular character traits, hair, eyes, all that."

Susan looked back at him for a long moment. "Brown hair, brown eyes…" she began, but trailed off as she realized his description did fit her father's. "It's not the same thing."

"What's your father do for a livin'?" Christian asked mildly.

"He's a banker."

He raised a black eyebrow. "And what's Warren studyin' at school?"

Susan smiled triumphantly. "Economics."

Christian laughed. "Same fuckin' thing! It's all about money."

"What's wrong with that?"

"Nothin', except it's really boring. And what about your mum?"

"What about her?"

"Well, she's one hell of a looker. Why'd she marry a guy like your father?"

"Well, I'd imagine that she loved him—that is why people get married, you know," she said condescendingly.

"Yeah, but didn't I hear that they were gettin' a divorce?" Christian said, knowing he would shock her this time.

"How do you know that?" she snapped. She had only found out herself the day before, when her mother called to tell her she was coming to town to talk to her about it.

"I have my ways." He'd heard about it the day before in the office, when Rick and Midnight had been talking about it. "Point is, she made a mistake, and you're making one too."

"You don't know that," she said haughtily.

"Let me ask you this." The change in his tone should have warned her, but she stood fast. He moved to stand directly in front of her, bringing his lips to a fraction of an inch from her ear. "Do you react to him like you reacted to me?"

"That's none of your business!" Susan stepped back to get away from him, coming up against her dresser.

Christian stepped forward, closing the slight distance between their bodies, pressing against her ever so slightly. Susan's breath caught in her throat as her entire body started to tingle, as if in response to the question.

"In other words," he said, his lips extremely close to hers, "no."

He then stunned her by turning and walking out of the room.

Susan was surprised to feel disappointed that he'd left without doing anything more, much like a couple of nights before. She didn't like the direction of her thoughts lately.

That night Christian went up to the main part of the house again to check on Joe and make sure Randy didn't need anything. He knocked on their door and heard Randy tell him to come in. He opened the door and was surprised to see that Joe was awake. Randy had just come out of their bathroom with a glass of water and pills in her hand.

"Hey, man, how ya doin'?" Christian said, looking down at his cousin.

"Better," Joe said hoarsely as he moved to sit up, groaning.

"Glad to hear it."

"Takes a lot more than a little bug to knock me down for long," Joe said as he lay back down.

Randy quirked her eyebrow at him. "Little bug? Joe, it's pneumonia—it rates higher than little on the bug scale." But she was smiling, and it was obvious to Christian that she was extremely relieved that Joe was doing better.

"Well, look," Christian said, "I'm stayin' in tonight, so if you need anything, I'll be about."

Joe nodded. "Yeah, I heard you've been helpful about all this. I appreciate it, man. It's nice to know that I have backup in the house now." He sounded very earnest, and Christian once again felt warmed. It was nice to have some family. He'd talked to his mother often since he'd been in the States, checking on her progress, and she'd told him what Joe had done in terms of getting her a job with benefits and providing everything else she could possibly need.

Christian couldn't even begin to express his gratitude for this new generosity. So he planned to make it up to him by being as helpful as possible when it came to Joe or what was important to him, including his family.

When Christian left a little while later, Randy walked out with him.

"Christian," she said confidentially. "I wanted to talk to you when Joe wasn't around, or awake. I need to ask you a favor."

"Okay," Christian said, leaning against the hallway wall.

"I think part of why Joe got sick is that he's been overdoing it lately. He's been trying to take Susan to school two days a week and get up with me before I go to school two more days a week. Most nights he doesn't get to bed till after midnight, so it doesn't really give him enough sleep. Well, what I was hoping is that you could take over taking Susan to school and picking her up in the afternoons after you get off. Do you think you could?"

Christian nodded. "Yeah, no problem."

Randy smiled. "Great, thanks. You know, I really appreciate everything you're doing too. I know adjusting to all of us hasn't exactly been easy for you. I know that you're used to a kind of solitary life, and all of this is pretty hectic. But I am glad you're here, and I know Joe is too, and my children adore you." The last was said with a grin.

"Well, they are kind of easy to get attached to," Christian said, trying to sound casual, but it was obvious to Randy that he really did care about all of them. She said nothing, allowing him to think he was coming across the way he wanted to.

"Well, anyway, thanks," Randy said. She surprised him by moving forward and hugging him. His arms went around her, even as his face indicated his surprise. He hugged her close, thinking it felt nice to be part of something for a change.

He knew for all intents and purposes he was becoming part of a family, even if he hadn't wanted any of this.

You can find more information about the author and series here:

www.sherrylhancock.com

www.facebook.com/SherrylDHancock

www.vulpine-press.com/midknight-blue-series

Also by Sherryl D. Hancock:

The *WeHo* series follows a group of women from Los Angeles as they navigate the ups and downs of love, life, work, and everything in between.

www.vulpine-press.com/we-ho

The *Wild Irish Silence* series. Escape into the world of BJ Sparks and discover how he went from the small-town boy to the world-famous rock star.

www.vulpine-press.com/wild-irish-silence-series